2⁰ᵒ/Ten

9

THE LOST
HUNTERS

BOOKS BY JOSEPH A. ALTSHELER

THE FRENCH AND INDIAN WAR SERIES

The Hunters of the Hills
The Rulers of the Lakes
The Lords of the Wild

The Shadow of the North
The Masters of the Peaks
The Sun of Quebec

THE YOUNG TRAILERS SERIES

The Young Trailers
The Forest Runners
The Keepers of the Trail
The Eyes of the Woods

The Free Rangers
The Riflemen of the Ohio
The Scouts of the Valley
The Border Watch

THE TEXAN SERIES

The Texan Scouts   The Texan Star   The Texan Triumph

THE CIVIL WAR SERIES

The Guns of Bull Run
The Guns of Shiloh
The Scouts of Stonewall
The Sword of Antietam

The Star of Gettysburg
The Rock of Chickamauga
The Shades of the Wilderness
The Tree of Appomattox

THE GREAT WEST SERIES

The Lost Hunters   The Great Sioux Trail

THE WORLD WAR SERIES

The Forest of Swords   The Guns of Europe   The Hosts of the Air

BOOKS NOT IN SERIES

Apache Gold
The Quest of the Four
The Last of the Chiefs
In Circling Camps
The Last Rebel

A Soldier of Manhattan
The Sun of Saratoga
A Herald of the West
The Wilderness Road
My Captive
The Candidate

He pulled the trigger and sent his bullet directly at the target he had chosen

THE LOST HUNTERS

A STORY OF WILD MAN AND GREAT BEASTS

BY

JOSEPH A. ALTSHELER

AUTHOR OF
"THE GREAT SIOUX TRAIL," "THE MASTERS OF THE PEAKS," ETC.

D. APPLETON-CENTURY COMPANY
INCORPORATED
NEW YORK   LONDON
1939

Printed in the United States of America

FOREWORD

"The Lost Hunters" is the second volume of the Great West Series of which "The Great Sioux Trail" was the first. In this story young Will Clarke, who has long been a captive among the Sioux, and who has risen to high favor, has become a Sioux himself, not only in manners and customs, but in thought. The world is clothed for him in a new atmosphere and he believes with the Indians that good and evil spirits fill air, earth and water—in truth, all things. Hence, his eye and mind in this story are the eye and mind of a Sioux.

It is well known that bear, deer and wolf grow much larger in the great valleys of far Northwestern America than anywhere else in the world, and it may be possible that still more gigantic specimens will yet be found in remote regions. The struggle of primeval man with wild beasts carried on for ages is here reproduced in the advent of the Sioux warriors among them, armed only with bow and arrow.

The names applied to animals and inanimate objects in this book are not the coinage of the author but are those used by the Sioux.

CONTENTS

THE LOST HUNTERS

CHAPTER I

THE HIDDEN VILLAGE

THE snows of the great winter were melting and streams of water were rushing down the steep sides of the mountains, but the air in the valley where the little Indian village lay was yet raw and cold. The wind out of the far north had a sharp edge from the fields of ice over which it blew, and the four who stood by the stream drew closely about their bodies the heavy cloaks of buffalo fur that draped them from shoulder to heel. They wore also high moccasins of the tanned hide of the moose, leggings and hunting shirts of deer-skin, and round beaver caps with flaps for the ears. They needed warm clothing and plenty of it in the long period of fierce cold, through which they had passed.

The setting for the human figures was wild and primitive to the uttermost. Here time had turned back, and the world in its present aspect was like the last days of the glacial age. The narrow river was filled with huge cakes of floating ice, which now and then, banking up against some jutting point of earth, groaned and slithered and fought together, until they broke away, and were carried off by the rushing current. The peaks and ridges, rising to tremendous heights, were still clothed in snow, which gleamed so brilliantly under the great sun that the eye, after a few moments, turned away for rest.

"When you look up," said Will Clarke, "you see no signs of spring, but when you look down the broken ice in the river tells you it's at hand."

"It is so, Waditaka," said old Inmutanka. "The wind is cold, but it is not as cold as it has been for many months. You can hear, too, the fall of the melting snow on the mountains. It plunges down in great masses. Listen!"

Will removed the flaps from his ears, and then a distant crash like the roar of a remote battle came to him. He knew it was the sound of an avalanche, and, by its token, all the slopes and crests would be bare in time, save for the evergreens. He was glad. He wished to see the tender grass and young flowers peeping up anew, and he was eager to roam with the warriors over wide spaces. The tremendous winter had bound him in chains of iron, but now he felt that the links were about to be broken and soon he would be free.

The singular circumstances of his captivity, its remoteness, the primeval character of the village, and the high place of honor won by him with his captors, had made an extraordinary change in young Will Clarke. His nature was plastic and adaptable far beyond the common. He was essentially a creation of atmosphere, taking the color and texture of his mind from the things around him, as the waters of a lake are dyed by the skies that bend above them.

His own white world had moved far away. The figures of Boyd and Brady and the Little Giant had become dimmed. The object of his search, the great expedition that had brought him into the west, was only a vague thought now and then. He still carried the map left by his father, but the subject of gold was seldom in his mind. He was engrossed in the struggle for existence with people who at first had seemed strange and savage but who, in the battle against terrific winter and mighty beasts, had grown into the truest of comrades. He had a genuine affection for his foster father, Inmutanka, and Pehansan and Roka were, in every sense of the word, brothers of his in arms and the chase.

It was another singular fact that his appearance had altered, so powerful are the effects of propinquity and thought. He was tanned almost as dark as the Indians about him. He had grown taller and thinner, though more powerful. His cheek bones seemed higher and his eyes more oblique. He habitually spoke the Sioux tongue with an accent as perfect as that of Pehansan or Roka, and even to the skilled observer he would have passed as a native of the little tribe with which he lived. But the greatest proof of his transformation was that he not only looked, talked and acted as the Sioux, but thought as they did.

"How long will it be, Inmutanka," he asked, "before

3

the barriers are broken down enough for us to leave the valley?"

"Two weeks more and we may go if we wish," replied the Indian. "Old as I am, I feel the sap already rising in my veins, and as for you three who are young, you will be like the great bears breaking from their winter dens."

"I suppose we'll go back to the south and the warriors of the village will join the forces of Mahpeyalute?"

Inmutanka shrugged his shoulders.

"I cannot tell," he replied. "Xingudan has not talked with me about it, and, as you know, there are not many among us who are fit to take the great war trail. It may be that Heraka will speak ill of us when he hears we have disobeyed his wishes about you, and then it would be wiser for us to stay in the north. As we stand now we are a lost village, separated by vast distances from the Sioux tribes and we may go where we please."

"But I think it likely though that it will please Xingudan to return and join the main tribe to which we belong," said Will.

Inmutanka and Roka exchanged glances, a fact that did not escape the notice of Will, as he had learned from his Sioux comrades to be watchful always and to observe everything. But he had also learned to ask few questions, to keep his own counsel and to be silent. He seemed not to see.

"It may be that we will not retrace our trail," said

4

Inmutanka. "The spirit of look and see, old though he be, fills the soul of Xingudan."

"Look and see?"

"Yes, Waditaka, my son, to find new countries and to behold the wonders that are in them. The white men have roamed about the world seeking new rivers, lakes and mountains, but the Sioux also have ridden over the plains and amongst the great ranges, always with their eyes open to fresh wonders."

"I know it, Inmutanka. Before I came among you I saw only with the eyes of my own people, but now I see as well or better with yours."

A pleased smile passed over the face of the old Indian.

"We will go back to the village," he said, "and we will wait until Xingudan, in his own good time, tells us which way to take. We are not many and most of us are very old or very young, but we are strong and well. Though the great winter shut us in we have not suffered."

They walked slowly down the stream. Will's breath made a light smoke before him, but he had become so thoroughly inured to cold that the sharp wind merely whipped his blood, and the signs of spring that he had seen filled him with an exhilaration both physical and mental. He was warm, there was abundant food in the village, life was varied and what more could be asked by a youth who had returned to the primitive time?

They entered one of the deeper recesses of the valley, where the overhanging cliffs with their thick array of spruce and pine formed much shelter, and many joyous neighs and whinnies welcomed Will, the foremost ranks of the ponies crowding forward to nuzzle his hands and to show their affection. The three Sioux glanced at one another. Waditaka's power with horses was always a source of wonder and admiration with them, and it was due mainly to his advice and control that these invaluable animals had gone so well through such a fierce winter. They had stored much forage for them, and often they had been compelled to fight the great bears and panthers and the terrible mountain wolves, when, driven by hunger, they had come to attack the herd. More than one night they had kept fires burning and warriors on watch all about the little lateral valley that they had converted into a stockade.

"The young grass will be appearing soon," said Will, "and then we'll lead them out where they can graze. They'll enjoy it after being so long a period in what must have been prison to them."

"The sap rises in them as it rises in us," said old Inmutanka gravely, "and they will be glad to gallop away on the work for which they are fitted. As you know, Waditaka, many of these are buffalo ponies, trained splendidly and always eager for the pursuit of the vast herds."

Young Clarke's eyes glistened.

"Since we can't turn south into the mountains," he said, "and I begin to believe our elders think it unwise to choose that way, it will, perhaps, be better to go east into the great plains and hunt the buffalo.

6

They're plentiful, even in the extreme north, are they not, Inmutanka?"

"Aye, Waditaka," replied the old Sioux. "They roam far up in the land that you call Canada, even to the vast lakes in the uttermost north, beyond any point to which we have gone, and wherever the herds go the Sioux can live."

Will's face was illumined and he caught his breath. He shut his eyes for a moment or two and he beheld a wonderful prospect of vast green plains, illimitable forests, huge lakes, and miles of shaggy buffalo trailing on forever and disappearing continually under the dim horizon in the north. On their flank rode the Indian horsemen and one could go on that way for a whole life, finding new scenes and never tiring.

Old Inmutanka, who was watching him, saw his ecstatic state and he was satisfied. He had lived long, he was extremely shrewd, and he was very fond of this adopted son of his. He knew Will better than Will knew himself, and he played steadily to the wild instincts in the lad, instincts which were likely to keep him with the village, and which, if allowed to arrive at full bloom, would make him as much of a nomad as any of the Sioux themselves.

"The melting of the snow is not likely to be continuous," said Roka. "There will be pauses, checks, and other freezes. Spring will not come at once, though it is on the way, and perhaps before the village moves Xingudan will send out an expedition which will both hunt and explore."

"If so," exclaimed Will, eagerly, "I hope I shall be

7

one of the party! I think it's my right to go forth with those chosen!"

"Fear not, O Waditaka," laughed Inmutanka. "For such a duty our wise chief would select strong and enduring youth, and you are such."

They left the horses and continued toward the village, the smoke of which rose sharp and clear against the frosty blue sky. It consisted of only a few lodges, containing mostly the very old and the very young, and yet it was to Will the center of a world, offering all the variety of primitive life and holding the sum of his present interests.

Xingudan met them and all of them greeted him with respect. Will reflected what a wonderful man the old chief was. He was clothed in furs, he was wrinkled and withered, his age the lad did not know, though he was sure it was near eighty, but he was erect, his muscles were still tough and elastic, his mind had the calm and judgment of age, with the receptivity of youth, and there was not a brighter eye in all the village.

"We have been watching the signs of spring, Xingudan," said Inmutanka. "Roka, Pehansan and Waditaka, who have young bones, feel that we will be moving soon."

"But they do not know which way we will go, though they would like to find out," said the old chief, an enigmatic smile twinkling a moment in his eye. "Wait, my children, until the ice breaks up a little more and the snow melts down a little farther, and then all will be known. Patience is what our people always need most, and I am sure you have it."

"Your words are wise as always, O, Xingudan," said Inmutanka, "but my son, Waditaka, has one request to make."

"What is it? He is a good lad, and if it be within reason, it is granted, of course."

"If any expedition to hunt and explore be sent forth he wishes to be a member of it."

Old Xingudan smiled again.

"It would not be a good band unless it had Waditaka with it," he said.

Young Clarke felt a glow. It was the highest praise he had yet had from the venerable leader, whom he had begun by regarding as an enemy, and whom he now respected and liked.

"Thank you, Xingudan," he said. "It's an honor and I take it as such."

"And when you are out of the valley," said the chief, "you will not leave the other young men and begin a flight on your snow shoes to the people who were once your own? The temptation perhaps will be great. You will have but a thousand miles or two to go. You will have only about a hundred mountain ranges that pierce the sky to cross. You will have snow and ice upon which to travel for but a year, perhaps, and you will not have to pass the cordon of more than twenty tribes who are hostile to you and who would kill you at once or give you to a lingering death."

Xingudan's tone was dry and there was no twinkle

in his eye. Will accepted his words as fact and replied in like vein.

"No, Xingudan, I will not leave the band. Since I'm to go with it I'll betray no trust. Some day it's likely I shall escape, but not now. I know too well the vast distances and dangers lying between me and my own people, and for the present I'll make no effort to disturb my good situation."

"The longer Waditaka lives with us the wiser he grows," said the old chief. "Inmutanka has taught him the beginnings of wisdom, and some day he may learn enough to become a great warrior."

Will saluted respectfully and with his comrades went into the village, where a scene of primitive but none the less happy life was in progress. All the snow within the circle of the lodges had been melted by the fires, many of which were burning brightly, and the earth there was dry. Some of the women were scraping hides pegged to the ground, and others were jerking the flesh of bears or the wood bison. The children, too small to work or to join in the fishing or trapping, were playing their own forest games. Food of many kinds was broiling or frying over the coals, and pleasant odors permeated the air. Old men were bending new bows or making arrows.

It was a successful and happy village of ten thousand years ago, with an abundance of warmth and food, nearly everything for which the primeval man fought. There were rifles and some ammunition in the village, but they were not used now, being held in reserve, and even the blankets bought from the white man were laid away, their places taken by buffalo robes. Nothing modern was visible. In Will's mind, impressionable and filled with the dim visions of the past, the transformation was complete. They had really gone back ten thousand years, and he was one with those for whom the wheel of time had been reversed.

Thus it was that the sight of the village with its peace and plenty gave him great pleasure. He knew every man, woman and child in it, and understood all their variations of character and temperament. He had done some helpful deed for nearly every one of them, and he had been particularly kind to the old and almost helpless, who, in savage lands, usually fare so ill. So, his heart grew warm at the reception they gave him. In an Indian village when it was well supplied and safe from attack, as he had learned long before, life was light and careless. There was invariably much talk and chatter, and the young roamed about from lodge to lodge, playing games.

A favored place by one of the fires was made for Will, Pehansan and Roka. They were brave warriors and mighty hunters. They had won especial glory in the fight with the great carnivora that had come down from the north, and the people of the hidden village never forgot it. An old woman brought Will a tender piece of venison she had just broiled, his comrades were treated as well, and warmed by the bed of glowing coals, he ate and was satisfied. Meanwhile the life of the little community passed about him. The old went on with the household tasks now allotted to them, a warrior came in with the body of a deer that he had just slain, another brought the skin of a lynx taken in a trap, two boys proudly bore a burden of fish they had caught in the little river, and Will, with keen, roving eyes that quested continually like those of an Indian, noted everything.

As a warrior and hunter he was not bound to do anything except in the two pursuits to which he devoted his energies, yet enough of his white nature still clung to him to make him the champion and helper of the weak. He brought wood for a bent old man who was tending one of the fires, gave a woman aid in setting up a tepee, and an hour later was in the lodge that had been occupied throughout the winter by Inmutanka and himself.

The Doctor, as Will often called him, had advanced ideas and their home was easily the finest and most comfortable in the village. The two had lavished much work upon it. Several layers of bark made a floor impervious to damp, and heavy buffalo robes, soft and warm, were spread over the bark like a carpet. Will's rifle, never used by him now, rested on hooks, and the few remaining cartridges were hidden carefully away for some great emergency. He relied wholly upon primitive weapons. His splendid bow of horn hung near the rifle and he had three others of wood that he had made for himself, while at least a dozen quivers were filled with arrows. He also had lance and war club, and he had learned to handle them with skill.

Weapons were not the only furniture of the lodge. There were spare garments of buckskin, heavy overcoats of buffalo hide, caps of fur and long snow shoes. In the center, where they had made a hearth of stone, a low fire burned and threw out a grateful heat. It is doubtful whether in all the vast northwest there was a lodge better equipped for the use and comfort of those who fitted into the wild.

Will regarded it all a few moments with a pleased eye, and then lay down upon his own particular couch of furs, a bed that would have been too costly in civilization for many a rich man to buy. His thoughts moved aimlessly over a wide region but they never once turned upon the lost treasure that had brought him into the west. Instead, they wandered most about the problems that lay before the village. If the people moved farther into the north and then went down into the plains what fate lay before them? He knew that Indians were perpetually at war with one another. It was not true that the white man had introduced battle into the New World. Tribes had been exterminated by tribes long before Columbus set foot on San Salvador.

It was likely that the little band of Xingudan would be attacked as interlopers by the warriors of the north, and Will set his teeth firmly. They were his people now, and he would fight for them to the uttermost. He wished that he had a great supply of cartridges, and perhaps he might obtain them in time from some wandering trader, but there was the mighty war bow of horn, and with it in his hands, he was now one of the best marksmen in the village.

Although he expected war with hostile tribes when

the village moved, he did not feel fear. War was the natural state of the primeval man. It arose over disputed hunting grounds, rivalry or the suspicion with which one group of people in an earlier world always regarded another. Strangers as a matter of course were considered enemies. It would have surprised Will had he known how much of this feeling he had absorbed.

While he lay on his bed of costly furs and permitted his thoughts to ramble without sequence, the twilight came, and the wind from the high mountains grew colder. The work outside by the fires ceased, and old and young went to their lodges. Inmutanka entered and carefully closed the flap of buffalo robe over the narrow doorway. The light from the little fire on the hearth was sufficient for his eyes and Will's which had become inured to dusk.

"I have talked with Xingudan," the old man said, "and it is settled. In two days ten hunters, all young and strong, go forth on their snow shoes to explore. As you know, you, Pehansan and Roka are to be among them. You will go north and east until you reach the vast plains, and then, coming back, you will report to us what hunting grounds we may enter. It is a great trust and like most great deeds it must be done through hardship and danger."

"I am eager to go," said Will, "and I thank you and Xingudan for sending me. I've no doubt we'll find the finest hunting grounds in the world for the village, and that all of us will come back safely."

"I think so too, Waditaka. The hunting grounds

we must have. Ours are not really mountain people. When the warm weather comes all of us will grow very restless and will crave the plains. Our warriors are happiest when they ride to the thunder of the buffalo herd. That is why we have kept the ponies. Nothing could hold us in the mountains when the spring is here."

The flicker from the low fire among the coals was reflected in Will's eyes. His spirit lifted up at the thought of the vast herd and the swift horsemen on its flanks.

"I've never been a real buffalo hunter yet, Inmutanka," he said, "but I'd like to try it. I know I've a lot to learn, but I believe that in time I could ride with the best."

The old Doctor looked into the coals. He was a shrewd man. He had not lived seventy years in the wild for nothing. He was a consummate judge of character, and he did not wish this adopted son of his to leave the people who had taken him unto themselves.

"Life offers no greater thrill," he said, in the expressive Sioux tongue. "It is the first of all exploits to ride your horse up by the side of the mighty and charging buffalo bull and send your arrows into the game. It needs a steady hand, a true eye, and courage, always courage. Some are never able to achieve it, but one is not truly a warrior until he has done so. Moreover, it is in accord with the wishes of Manitou, who has sent the buffalo to the Sioux that by him we may live."

15

The flicker in the eyes of the lad became a flame, and old Inmutanka, from under his lowered lids, observed it.

"We are never tied to one place," he resumed. "As the buffalo travels far, so travel we. Our home is thousands of miles east and west and north and south. We grow tired of nothing, because change is always before us. If, for a while, we do not wish to follow the buffalo, we turn into the high mountains and trap the beaver. We risk our lives against the mightiest of beasts, the grizzly bear, and we slay the panther. Then, when the mountains weary us, we go back to the plains, and the buffalo is always there."

"I must surely take part some day in a great buffalo hunt with Pehansan, Roka and the others."

"You will have your chance, and you can choose the best of the ponies as your own. They all like Waditaka, who has the great gift with horses, and any one of them will obey his hand and voice."

Long the wise old Doctor talked of the chase and wild life, deepening the colors, softening the hardships, and painting a picture that glowed with fire and life for Will.

The lad presently closed his eyes and listened to the soft, musical tones of Inmutanka, as he talked on and on, describing the freest and most glorious life that human beings had ever lived. Soon he slept and the old Sioux, laying a buffalo robe over him, sat long by the remains of the fire. The tie of adoption among the Indians was as strong as that of blood, and Inmutanka did not wish to lose the son, who had been such a good son to him. He was satisfied with the evening's work, but he did not care to sleep. Instead, he listened to the rising wind as it whistled among the lodges, and he resolved that he, too, when the spring came again, should feel once more the thrill of the buffalo hunt. He had been speaking the truth, as he saw it, when he said it was the greatest of all thrills, and there was yet much vigor in his old frame. It was nearly dawn when he lay down on his own couch and drew the furs over his body.

The thaw was not resumed the next day, and the snow in the valley was firm enough to sustain snowshoes. They revised their calculations and decided that spring would be weeks in coming, but it was evident to the elders that the zenith of winter had passed and now was the time for the strongest and most daring to go forth and see what lay before them. So, the preparations for the journey of the ten were hastened. Will looked with sedulous care to his snow shoes, the use of which he had learned with pain and weariness, took down several times the rifle that Xingudan had returned to him, but at last put it back permanently, because one must not take too great a burden on his travels, though he did thrust into his belt his fine revolver and a small supply of cartridges for it. His chief weapon was to be his great bow of horn, and the large quiver of arrows. The others were armed in a somewhat similar manner, although he was the only one to carry any kind of fire-arm. Besides their arms they carried bags of pemmican, food in a light and sustaining form, which they expected to use only when their hunting failed.

Roka, the oldest, was to command by virtue of experience, and the ten men were to stand by one another through every form of hardship and danger, an injunction, however, that was scarcely needed, as among people situated in such fashion the principle that in union is strength had been learned long since. Yet Xingudan, as became a wise old chief, spoke briefly to them when they were ready for departure. He told them in terse Sioux that doubtless they carried with them the fate of all the village. They must be quick of eye and ready of hand, but neither eye nor hand would avail, if not directed by mind. Ten warriors must also be ten thinkers, else having seen much they might return and be able to tell nothing.

The ten listened gravely, taking his words much to heart, and the entire population of the village standing by uttered a deep murmur of approval. Then with brief farewells they sped away, the eyes of the two old men, Xingudan and Inmutanka, following them until they disappeared down the gorge.

Will felt some sadness at leaving his foster father and his friends, but it was soon blown away by the wind which their own speed made. The young blood rose in a tide in his veins. He was going to see the world and to share in great adventure. Roka led, Pehansan followed, Will came next and the rest followed, all in single file.

When they emerged from the valley they turned toward the north, seeking an outlet between the great ridges and peaks, passing nearly all the time through narrow defiles which the sun entered only in dim fashion. In these deep passes the snow was hard, not having melted at all, and they were able to maintain good speed, but after a while Roka began to lead more slowly. The first great burst of physical enthusiasm was over, and he was wise enough to nurse the spirit of his men and let it come back again.

At noon he halted in a small valley, and, since time had no particular value for them, they took off their snowshoes, scraped away the snow, built a fire and luxuriated. The mountains were full of running streams and little lakes, and Will and Pehansan, breaking the ice in one of the latter less than a quarter of a mile away, and letting down their lines, caught several large fish resembling pickerel.

The fish were delicate in flavor and the ten made their dinner of them, saving the pemmican, as they had intended. While they shared the food and refreshed themselves, the wind roared far above their heads, sweeping from peak to peak and from ridge to ridge, but the valley in which they lay was so deep that the air there scarcely stirred. The valley itself was sown with evergreens of tremendous size and height, but there were few bushes and vines.

Will noted the gigantic growth of the trees with great interest, and he surmised from the fact that the moisture from the Pacific Ocean reached all these slopes and gorges. A great fall of rain made for immensity, and he believed that the wild animals would be on a scale corresponding with the trees. The gigantic carnivora that had attacked the village in the winter were a proof of it, and his heart beat a little faster when he foresaw that they might meet again the great bears of the north. The huge timber wolves, too, beyond a doubt, would be abroad, and while one, alone, might fall a victim to them he felt no fear with this skillful and valiant band about him.

It was a full two hours before they put on the snow shoes and resumed a northward journey in the pass, the ground now rising but the mountains on either side seeming as high above them as ever. The trees were of undiminished size and their domed crests coming together protected them from the wind, the effect being that of continuous travel under a roof of great height. When the first gray of twilight came Roka stopped, the others stopping automatically with him, and the wise warrior surveyed the country.

"In the last mile," he said, "the ground has been rising much faster. If we pressed on, night perhaps would find us at a much greater elevation, with the cold very severe. Doubtless it would be better to make our camp soon. What say you, Pehansan?"

"If we can find a good place," replied the tall warrior. "The night is going to be very cold, and if our hearts are to remain happy within us we will need a big fire."

"Pehansan speaks the truth," said Roka. "It is likely that a lofty pass is before us, and, if we ascended too much, no forest might be there to shelter us. We will not go on more than a half hour."

Will listened to them, but said nothing. He was

20

all for the camp. His ankles were beginning to feel again the strain of the snowshoes, and they had no need of haste. Within the appointed time they found a recess in the side of the pass, clothed about so closely with great trees that it was sheltered from the wind. There by a pool, covered with thick ice, they built their second fire, and built it high.

Will believed that human beings had never been in the recess before, but Roka posted a guard as a sure watch against wild animals and wilder men. There were to be relays of two sentinels each, and Will, not being in the first relay, wrapped himself in his buffalo robe and lay down before their noble fire. His eyes were drooping and the flames were a red blur before him, but he heard the crackling of the wood, the roaring of the wind in the lofty tree tops, and a faint lonesome note which he took to be the howl of wolves. Then he fell asleep.

His own watch came about midnight and his comrade in it was a young warrior named Inmu, which in the Sioux tongue meant the Lynx. The fire had died down and it was hard to come out of the warm buffalo robe, but he never hesitated, and he and Inmu, a brave and good friend of his, walked back and forth with their bows in their hands and their quivers over their shoulders. Will heard gain the distant note which he had taken to be the howling of wolves, but it seemed to be a little nearer now.

"Think you they will attack us?" he asked of Inmu.

"We are too many," replied the young Dakota, as they called themselves in their own language. "There are ten of us, and it may be that the wolves, who are the wisest of all animals, can count as far as ten. Do you believe, Waditaka, that a great mountain wolf can count?"

"I don't know, Inmu. Before I was adopted into your tribe I certainly did not think so, but now I'm not so sure. Mountains and the wilderness change one's opinions."

"I asked you to hear what you would say, Waditaka. As for myself, I know that king wolves can count. You can hear the howls of four or five now, and the one louder than the rest is the voice of the king wolf. When he comes and sees between the trees he will know exactly how many of us are here, and you can believe what I tell you."

Will believed him, at least at the time. The wolves were approaching, and the single voice that rose over the others was a wail at once mournful and full of ferocity. Will shuddered. The howl of a wolf on a cold, dark night always gave him a feeling of loneliness and desolation. He glanced at the eight sleeping figures by the low fire, and he was glad that such brave comrades were so near. He looked at Inmu and he was glad that such a fine young spirit stood beside him, one with whom he could talk, one who would assist to banish the feeling t' at oppressed him.

"You are sure they won't attack?" he said to Inmu. "It would be a pity if we had to waste our arrows on wolves the first night we're out from the village."

"No, Waditaka," replied Inmu. "They will not attack our camp, though they may hang around it, hoping to pull down some incautious straggler. As I told you, the great wolves can count, and they know that ten warriors, every one of whom can pull a strong bow, are too many for them. Listen to their howling now! There is more grief than ferocity in it."

It was a curious fact—psychological and atmospheric perhaps,—but it seemed to Will, as it seemed also to Inmu, that a distinct change had occurred in the voice of the wolves. The note of ferocity surcharged with threat was going, and that of melancholy and grief was pervading all the chords, and octaves. King wolves and minor wolves alike were crying their woes to the chilly heavens. As a band they moaned and mourned.

"What does it mean?" asked Will.

Inmu laughed low, but with intense satisfaction.

"I understand them," he replied. "I can almost talk with them. I know what they are saying now. They are very sad, they are telling one another that we are too numerous to become their prey, and in telling it they are lamenting the loss of so much good food. They know that we are fat, that we have fed well, and prospered through the winter, that we would be juicy to their teeth if they could only sink them in us, and their hearts are torn with agony because such a precious repast is so near and yet they cannot partake of it. That is why they mourn so hard."

"Almost I believe you're a humorist, Inmu."

"No, Waditaka. It might seem so if I did not know the wolves, but speaking, or at least understanding, their language as I do, I only tell facts. Now we can

23

hear again the voice of their leader above all the others and I will put it into our Sioux tongue for you. He is chanting in his mournful wail: 'They are there, O, my comrades, the creatures that stand upright and walk on two legs, and that are better to our taste than any other living things, the beings that, larger than we are, are nevertheless helpless against us with their own bare paws! But they carry with them the strange shapes that send through the air the long twigs with sharp ends that burn like fire, when they strike us! These creatures are men, and I have counted the men, O, my comrades! They are ten, and they are strong and skillful! I have counted them, not because I have seen them, but because I have smelled them out one by one, because it is given to us wolves, the wisest of all beasts, to smell from afar and to know! If we rushed at them they would pierce our sides from a distance with the sharp sticks that would burn and burn and at last kill us! That is why, O, my comrades, I cry my grief to the heavens, and you cry your grief with me! The savory odor of them fills our nostrils, but our teeth must remain clean, at least tonight!' "

"I believe, Inmu, that you are translating exactly what the great leader says."

"Word for word, Waditaka. Did I not tell you that I understood him perfectly? He still howls. The strain of grief is yet in his voice, but another note is there too. It is one of advice, of instruction about the future. He is saying to the members of his band: 'Not tonight, O, my comrades, can we attack them!

And it is because of their burning sticks that they can throw from afar deep into our sides! Now why is our tribe the wolf the wisest of all living creatures? Why is he so much superior in wisdom to the huge lumbering bear, and the great, thoughtless moose? Because he does not live in the moment alone! Because he thinks of the next hour and the next day and the next week! Because he plans for the future. Because he thinks! That is why the wolf is the lord of all creation, superior to all other beasts, even to the one that walks on two legs who ranks next to him!'"

"Now that you translate it for me, Inmu, it sounds convincing."

"Truth is truth always, Waditaka. The cunning leader goes on: 'If we cannot eat them tonight, yet a time may come when we can eat them, O, my comrades! We are thoughtful and patient! That is another reason why we are wolves, the lords of creation, and all other living things are mere foolish beasts. The creatures that walk on two legs who call themselves men will watch through the night, and they will have their sharp sticks to use against us! As long as the dark lasts they will be wise, and they will be ready for us, but when the dawn comes they will grow foolish! Only a wolf, O, my comrades, can be wise both day and night! In the sunshine they will put the sharp sticks on their backs, and they will walk on, very careless, making much noise with their feet and talking! Then we will be in the bushes on either side of them, keeping pace with them, but as silent as still

25

water, O, my comrades! Their dull nostrils will not scent us even though we be so near! Fear will depart from the foolish brain of man, because light is all about him, but the wise wolf knows better, and he will watch be it dark or bright! The time will come when some one of them will stray from the others into the bushes, and his sharp sticks will not be ready! Then our spring will be swift and sure, and our teeth will sink deep into him!' "

Will shuddered.

"I'm glad you've told me the plans of the big scoundrel, Inmu," he said. "I'm going to stay close with the band tomorrow, and the next day, too, and if any chance should send me alone into the bushes, I'll have my arrow on the string. He may be a wise old wolf, as you say, but he was foolish to talk when a man here could understand him."

"It is true, Waditaka. There is no one so wise that he knows everything, and no one is so cautious that he can provide against every chance. The great wolf did not dream that I could speak his language. But he begins to believe now that he and his comrades have talked enough. Hear him! He is saying: 'O, my comrades, we are near to the camp of foolish man! We can see through the bushes the light of his fire! Our sharp eyes can pick out the shadows of the two who watch, and of the eight who lie on the ground asleep. We will now be as silent as the death that we have in store for them, and we will be as patient as the mountains that never move!' "

A shiver ran down Will's spine and he cast shuddering looks into the bushes. He believed implicitly every word that Inmu had said, and he expected to see there in dim outline the figures of the wolves, huge, gaunt and famished. He saw instead, or at least he believed that he saw, two coals of fire, and he knew they were the burning eyes of the great wolf who led his fellows. He watched them as they wavered and moved to different sides of the camp, and now he had the feeling that it was not so much the numbers of the warriors as the fire that protected him. He did not know it, but he was reverting then to the impulses and emotions of ancestors who had lived twenty thousand years ago, when flames in the night formed their sole but sufficient protection in the open against the huge carnivorous beasts.

"They're all about us now," he said to Inmu.

"So they are," said the Lynx, "a pack of perhaps thirty. They circle around and around our camp, like scouts, studying us and using all their wisdom and cunning to see what kind of men we are."

"And what do you think the master wolf is saying to his pack?"

"He speaks well of us," replied Inmu, with pride. "His words are not in his throat, because as you know he gives no voice now, but they are in his eyes. He says: 'O, comrades, I know when I look at them that they are ten chosen men of their tribe. There are no greater marksmen or stouter hearts among men. If we hunt them we will need all our courage and wisdom and patience. But to pull them down will be the greatest deed ever achieved by the lords of creation, the wolves, and so we will follow for days and days, until our chance comes.' "

"I see that you are troubled by no false pride, Inmu. You think well of the band to which you belong."

"Why not speak the truth?" said the Indian simply. "I but say what is also in your own heart, Waditaka. Now the wolves have gone farther away. They know there will be no chance for them tonight, and they deem it foolish to remain so close and risk an arrow. When the dawn comes they will follow our trail."

"We'll try to be ready for them, but our watch is over now, and when we wake the relief we'd better tell 'em what's lurking in the bushes."

The two Indians who succeeded them were warned, and Will was soon fast asleep again.

CHAPTER II

THE RED CIRCLE

WILL awoke after dawn and found the fire, dispenser of warmth and life, burning anew, fresh and vivid, and Roka ordered them all to eat a plentiful breakfast. Indians on the war path are usually very sparing of food, but this little band had not gone forth for war, unless war should be brought to it, and there was no reason why they should not take their comfort as they traveled, in particular as they had every reason to expect plenty of game. So, the morning, which was bright and cold, was full of cheer, and the tide of vitality in the white lad's veins rose very high. It seemed to him that he had the finest comrades a primeval world could afford, and life, with the new wonders about to be unfolded before him, was intensely interesting.

But his sanguine state of mind did not make him forget the wolves, to the ominous conversation of which Inmu had listened the night before. In the sunshine, his sense of their presence was as heavy as it had been in the dark. They could not be far away, slinking among the dense bushes and watching those whom they expected to devour. With a little, subdued laugh at his own caution, he resolved to keep well in the line when they started again on their snowshoes. It was evident, too, that Inmu had told all to Roka and that the leader believed fully, as he directed the men not to wander, and warned them that a pack of huge and hungry mountain wolves, full of cunning and tenacity, were the greatest of all foes to be dreaded.

Pehansan and two others, side by side, and with bows strung, scouted a little, reporting soon that traces of wolves were abundant on the snow on both sides of them, and that the tracks were of enormous size. Roka looked very grave.

"They are beasts that have come out of the far north," he said, "where all bears and wolves grow much larger than they do anywhere else, and as Inmu has predicted, they are sure to follow us. They will be a check upon our hunting."

But the others, with all the courage and pride of youth, cried out that they were not afraid. What were all the wolves in the world to them, no matter how large, when they could send their arrows straight and true? By day, at least, they rather courted the combat, and while the sage Roka was still resolved to be cautious, his eye gleamed with pleasure at the bold front of his young men.

After the abundant breakfast, they fastened on their snowshoes with care, and resumed their journey up the gorge, which led north slightly by east, and was here about a mile wide, with very high mountains on both sides, and dense fringes of bushes at the foot of either cliff, although the valley at first had been bare of undergrowth. Nor were the trees so large as they had been farther down, and Will surmised that they were approaching a high pass.

They bore toward the cliff on the right, and the white youth more than once thought he saw the snowy bushes there shaking. About the fourth or fifth time he called the attention of Inmu to it, and the young Dakota, keen of eye, confirmed his observation.

"You know what it is, Waditaka?" he said.

"The great wolves following on our flank."

"Beyond a doubt. I know it as truly as if I saw them. They will keep their place all day and tonight they will wait their chance to cut out some incautious one among us."

"I'm sure I won't be the incautious one."

Inmu laughed.

"Nor will any other of us," he said. "We will be very careful until we grow used to them, and then, when familiarity makes us forget the danger or despise it, a warrior may wander from the band, and lo! the wolves are upon him. That is why the lords of creation, as they think themselves, follow and wait. They are quite sure their patience is greater than ours and that their time must come."

A shiver once more ran down Will's spine. There was something awful in the patient ferocity that could follow for days and days and yes, for weeks and weeks! A single unguarded minute in a month might be fatal, and a month contained a multitude of minutes. It was almost impossible to keep at unbroken tension so long. He recognized anew the formidable character of the danger assailing them.

It grew warmer toward noon, and they heard the sound of sliding snow on the slopes. Roka thought deer might be found in the undergrowth and they wanted game, but, owing to the threat of wolves, he did not send out any hunters. In the afternoon the ascent became greater, as Will had foreseen, and when the second night came they built their fire at a narrow point in the pass where the cliff rose at a vast and almost perpendicular height. Shortly after dark, the wolves gave tongue a few times but then were silent.

"They are merely telling us," said Inmu, "that they are still following. They do not expect to catch any of us tonight, or they would have kept still."

Will was in the first watch, and, when his time to sleep came, he protected himself thoroughly in his heavy buffalo robe. But he did not sleep long, a sound like a groan and a grind awakening him. He sprang to his feet and found all his comrades also standing. It was very dark save where the fire smouldered, and the mountain far above them was moaning. It was thence that the sounds had come.

In a few instances the grind and groan changed to a roar and then, snatching up their baggage, they leaped for their lives. Will saw a white wall rushing down upon them, and he knew now that the mountain had given forth a cry of pain, because an avalanche was rent from its side. He ran instinctively toward the center of the pass and waves of snow poured over him. It was not the snow that he feared, but the trees and stones brought down with it. Luckily none struck him and as he ran he collided with Inmu who shouted that he was unhurt.

"Back down the pass!" cried Roka, and ten struggling figures obeyed him as best they could. One was bleeding in the shoulder where he had been struck by a stone but his hurt was not bad, and Roka, able and experienced, had all his wits about him. The avalanche was of narrow front, and their rush soon carried them to its edge, where the depth of snow was not so great. Nevertheless Will had been thrown down twice, but on each occasion he regained his feet without harm.

They had just emerged from the white shower, when Roka uttered a fierce shout of warning. The warrior with the bleeding shoulder was in advance and he was staggering a little when a long, sinister shadow emerged from the bushes and leaped straight for the man's throat. Will, for caution's sake, had left his great horn bow strung, and he never understood exactly how he did it, but an arrow fairly jumped from his quiver and then to the string. The next instant it sang through the air and was buried to the feathers in the throat of the leaping wolf. The huge figure was still carried by its impetus through the air, but it stopped short of its destined prey and, yet open of mouth and slavering, fell with a crash on the snow.

Behind them the avalanche roared for a minute or two longer, and then was still. The wound in the side of the mountain ceased to bleed, but Roka and his warriors, in the dim light, looked down at the figure of the slain wolf.

"It was a deed well done, Waditaka," said Roka with emphasis. "If your arrow had not been so ready and true, Tatokadan (the Antelope) would have been killed instantly by the monster's terrible bite. Teeth like those would have torn through his neck as mine go through a corn cake. I say again, it was a great deed, greatly done."

Will flushed in the darkness with pride and pleasure.

"It was no will of mine, O, Roka," he said. "It was Manitou that made me do it."

"All our good deeds are done by Manitou," said Roka devoutly, "but your arrow, nevertheless, was well sped, Waditaka. The wolves were waiting their chance, and thought they saw it, when we were struggling from the avalanche, but with true caution they sent forth only one to make the leap. You do not see the shadows of any more, do you, men?"

"No," they replied with one voice.

"Pull out your arrow, Waditaka," said Roka. "We must not waste a single shaft."

It required the combined strength of Will and Inmu to withdraw the arrow from the neck of the wolf, and then the white youth, wiping it carefully on the snow, replaced it in his quiver. The wolf, even in death, was a most formidable beast, belonging to the largest of all the wolf tribe, those found in the northwestern mountains of North America, a full seven feet in length, fanged and powerful.

"If we were not traveling far we would take his

skin," said Roka, "but we must leave him to the others of the pack."

"It's a pity we help to feed wild beasts that want to feed on us," said Will.

"It cannot be prevented," said Roka. "We will go back down the pass, beyond the reach of avalanches, and make a new camp."

As they withdrew they heard the patter of feet, and saw the rush of shadowy forms, wolves coming forward to devour their dead comrade. A half mile back, and they built their fire anew, but early the next day they resumed the ascent, passed by the clean skeleton of the monster Will had slain, and then advanced over the new snow brought down by the avalanche. As the pass became very narrow they were in constant fear of other falls, but they reached the summit without mishap, and looked into a vast valley, timbered heavily and extending toward the east, a bare surface in its center evidently the frozen and snow-covered surface of a lake. Beyond it high mountains showed dimly. Will reckoned that the valley was at least twenty miles long and that it might have an exit toward the northeast through a narrow gorge, in which direction they must travel in order to reach the great plains.

"What is the plan, Roka?" he asked.

"We will descend into the valley," replied the leader, "seek game there, delay two or three days and then go on."

A few moments later, he gave the word and the flying column on snowshoes went forward, the slope now becoming so precipitous that the men were compelled to use great care. Will's ankles grew weary and he hoped that when they reached the floor of the valley they might be able to dispense with the snowshoes. It was certainly far more comfortable to walk on the soles of one's own feet.

"Maybe the deep snow and the height of the pass will keep back the wolves," he confided to Inmu. "I'm willing to suffer tired ankles if the same fate overtakes those fierce prowlers."

"Not a chance of it," replied the Lynx, with emphasis. "The leader of the wolves said to his pack that they would follow us, no matter how far we went. You will take note, Waditaka, that we have yet seen no game, and it is likely the wolves have seen none either. So they follow us, as their only hope. We must be on guard against them all the time."

"I'm afraid you're right," said Will. Such a deadly pursuit shook his nerves a little, but he steadied himself, and grasped with confidence his splendid bow of horn. The last part of the slope was very steep, and they were all thoroughly weary when they reached the valley, where the snow was not so deep, as it had been in the pass and the upper valley. They also saw tracks of game, and knew they had come into a land of plenty, but it being nearly dark they built the usual fire and passed a peaceful night.

A warm wind was blowing in the morning, and there were signs of a thaw. A little brook near them was running free of ice, but Will's hopes that they might dispense with the snowshoes could not yet come true.

"When we pass out of this valley into the next one perhaps we may walk on solid earth," said Roka, "but for a while we will have to travel on runners."

"Since we've seen enough to know that game is abundant about us," said Will, "why not let Inmu and me seek a deer? We ought to find one down by the brook, and you know that sooner or later we'll have to shoot game."

"That is true. Take your bows and go. But be sure you keep together."

They promised strict heed to his advice, and, bows in hand, departed joyfully among the trees. The heavy traveling had grown monotonous and any diversion was welcome. Good marksmen with arrows, they had no fear, and they sped along on their snowshoes, looking here and there among the bushes bordering the brook. It was a fine little stream flowing rather swiftly, and they were sure game would soon be found on its banks. Inmu announced several times that he had seen elk signs and in their eagerness they left the camp far behind them.

Elk was noble game. The gigantic deer of the far northwestern mountains might weigh fifteen hundred pounds, and Will's heart throbbed with anticipation. He had become a hunter with all a hunter's instincts, and he believed, as his ancestors thousands of years before him had believed, that the elk was given to man that man might live on the elk. He looked at the tracks in the snow and saw that they were fresh. The big fellow could not be far away, and the pulses in his temples began to beat hard.

"We'll get him," he whispered to Inmu, "and he'll furnish food enough for many days."

"We will overtake him in less than half an hour," said the young Dakota, "and our arrows will find his heart."

He, too, had all the ardor of the chase, and, fitting their arrows to the string, they hurried forward, presently catching a glimpse of the great body among the bushes. He was all they had hoped, vast beyond the average of his fellows, like all the animals of this region, and picking at a shrub he seemed totally unaware that hunters were near. Will and Inmu cautiously edged a little nearer. The great animal, still unconscious that creatures so much smaller but so much more dangerous than himself were close by, continued his gastronomic business with the shrub.

"Suppose you take his throat, and I will aim at his heart," said Inmu.

"Agreed," said Will. "You give the word."

"Up bow!" whispered Inmu.

Up went the bows.

"Fit arrow!"

The arrows were on the string.

"Bend bow!"

The two great bows curved deep.

"Take aim!"

Will looked at the throat and Inmu looked at the heart of the elk.

"Let go!"

38

The two arrows whistled through the air, and each went straight and true to its mark. But the elk was a mighty animal. An enormous amount of vitality was stored in his huge frame, and, although smitten deep at both points, he made gigantic leaps across the snow, the two young hunters following as swiftly as they could.

"Hold your second arrow!" cried Inmu excitedly. "He has been struck mortally! It is merely a convulsion that is carrying him on!"

Will put back in his quiver the arrow that he had snatched from it, but he ran at full speed in pursuit of the elk. The bounds of the great deer were becoming shorter, and the life blood was pouring from him. It was evident that he would soon fall, but as he began to stagger a long, dark form stole from the bushes and seized him by the throat. He went down with a crash as the teeth of the wolf gave him the finishing stroke.

Both the white youth and the red were seized with rage when they saw the monster leap upon their prize and take it for his own. Such impudence was beyond endurance, and their hands flew again to their arrows.

"Hold your shot!" cried Inmu. "One of his comrades may be near and you will need it for him! Let me kill this wolf!"

The arrow of the young Sioux whistled through the air. The range was short, and it pierced the wolf to the heart, but the teeth of the killer remained clenched in the throat of the deer, and the two fell dead together on the snow. Will was about to rush

forward, but Inmu's hand on his shoulder held him
back. A second figure gliding from the bushes made
a leap for the elk. Will instantly shot an arrow, but
as the beast was in the air it struck him in the flank
and did not inflict a mortal wound. Growling and
trying to snap at the barb it ran back among dwarf
pines.

"We'll dispose of our elk," said Inmu, and drawing
their knives they went forward to cut up the body,
being compelled first to drag away the body of the
huge wolf, the teeth of which were still deep in the
flesh of the great deer. It required all their strength
for the effort, and they looked curiously at the savage
animal, a dark, dirty gray, long, muscled powerfully,
and formidable even in death.

"He is bigger even than the mountain wolf of
Montana and Idaho," said Inmu. "Now I know he
belongs to some fierce tribe of wolves that has come
down from the lands of eternal snow and ice. I
think, Waditaka, that the great animals we drove off
in the winter have told their brethren of us, and that
they are resolved to pull us down and eat us."

"And then we'll be waylaid on our journey not only
by the wolves, but by the bears, and maybe by other
ferocious beasts, of which we haven't yet heard?"

"It seems to me, Waditaka, I can hear the wolves
moving among the dwarf pines now not far away.
Perhaps the arrow has fallen out of the shoulder of
the one you shot, and he was not badly hurt, otherwise his comrades would have eaten him. I think
they must be watching us now. Suppose you be ready

with your finest arrows while I finish cutting up the elk."

Will felt that the caution was fully justified. He heard many rustlings among the pines, and, once or twice, he saw long, sinister shadows pass. He was back in the primordial age, when man was in incessant danger from fierce wild beasts. It occurred to him that the pack now expected to secure an uncommon prey, a magnificent elk and two human beings together. Inmu, to facilitate his task, had taken off his snowshoes, and, as the area around the elk was now well trampled, Will, always glad to get rid of these cumbrous aids to walking, did likewise. The pressure of his moccasined feet upon the snow gave him more confidence, but the feel of the great bow in his hands was the strongest assurance of all. The revolver, the only firearm in the little expedition, was in his belt, but he did not think of it at the time. His trust was wholly in the bow and in the sharp arrows that filled his quiver.

Inmu stopped now and then in his task to listen. It was evident to Will that he was apprehensive, and he had great faith in the wilderness lore of the young Dakota.

"I think more wolves have come," he said at last.

"It seems so to me, too," said Will. "There's a constant brushing of the pine boughs and the light pad of feet."

"We may be attacked. The wolves now know what arrows are, but, like chiefs who lead their warriors into battle, they may be willing to endure a loss

41

for the sake of a great gain. A vast elk and two human beings, well fed like ourselves, would make food enough for a great pack of the hungriest wolves that ever lived."

"Stop, Inmu! Don't talk of such horrible things!"

"But we must think of them, Waditaka, and so it is well to talk of them, too. I will call to Roka. He may hear us, and, then, if the whole band comes, we and our elk will be safe."

He uttered a long, wailing cry of the Dakota, a note which would carry a vast distance in the clear, mountain air, and both waited eagerly for a reply, but none came. A minute or two later Inmu sent forth a second call. As before, no answer came from Roka, but a rustling in the pine thickets told them that not they alone were listening.

"Did you hear the master wolf laugh?" asked Inmu, gravely.

"Laugh, Inmu? What do you mean? Why, a wolf can't laugh! And I heard nothing but the brushing of their bodies against the pine boughs!"

"You are foolish, Waditaka. You have a vain conceit because you are a man, and so you think that only men can laugh. The master wolf who considers himself superior to a man can laugh, too, but he laughs in his own way, and I, who listened not only with my ears, but with all my other senses, heard him. There was meaning also in his laugh, and I understood it. He said to his comrades and to the new followers that have come to him that we had foolishly wandered away from the other eight of our band, that we had

42

slain an elk of immense size, but that we had slain it for the wolves, not for ourselves. He said that tonight we would fall a prey to them. Do you think he spoke the truth, Waditaka?"

"No, I don't! Nor do you, Inmu!"

"Hark! I hear him laughing again, although you do not, and these are the words that run through his laugh: 'They cannot escape us a second time, because we know how to be patient, O, my comrades! So, the skies work for us! See how the clouds come! The air grows dark! By-and-by the snow will pour down, and it will make a thick, white curtain between these two and their friends! Then we will steal upon them! They will not see us until it is too late! They cannot loose their arrows before we spring, and then we can devour them and their elk!' "

Will looked up instinctively. The trailing clouds covered nearly all the heavens, and it had grown much darker. He knew it was going to snow soon, and the new danger was fast closing in upon them.

"We've many sharp arrows," he said, "and both can shoot them fast and true."

"But if the snow comes so thick that we can see through it only a yard or two?"

"Then we'll build a fire. There's an abundance of dead wood under the snow."

"Well spoken, Waditaka."

"You're better at that work than I am. While I watch the bushes suppose you stop your task with the elk and build the fire."

Inmu began at once to drag up dead brush, work-

ing with a speed and energy at which Will marveled,
and throwing it into heaps all about the elk and themselves. Well the young Dakota knew the need of the
hasty bonfire. It had turned so dark now that the
pine bushes were growing dim, but the wolves there
were stirring and creeping a little closer. Inmu prayed
to his Manitou and to all his lesser gods that the snow
would hold off yet a while longer. It was the white
deluge with its covering for attack that he dreaded
most. And the pack, seeing what he and Waditaka
planned, might not wait for the snow. So cunning
a wolf as the huge leader would know that fire was
intended, and he might try to forestall it with a rush.

Inmu never worked with more desperate speed, and
Manitou helped him. He flew straight to the wood,
he never made a false step, and when at last his leaps
were finished and he drew out his flint and steel the
sparks flew forth at once in a more copious shower
than he had ever seen before. Throughout all his
labors he had never ceased to send forth at frequent
intervals his clear call to Roka, nor did he stop now,
as the wood ignited with speed and flames ran all
around the circle.

"You have been beaten, O, *Xunktokeca* (Wolf)!
The snow will come too late!" he chanted. "You
thought you could creep upon us through the white
veil! You know many things, but you did not know
that we could build a fire so quickly! There is now
red fire between us and you and you do not dare to
cross it! Wolf is not the master of man in all things,
because we can create the fire which protects us, and

44

you cannot! You are mad with anger, O, King of the Wolves, because we have cheated you so! Ah! you do not laugh now! You snarl! But we do not care for your snarling! We are safe within our red circle!"

The soul of the young Dakota was filled with fierce exultation. He and his comrade had not only saved their lives but they had snatched from the wolves a prey they had deemed sure, and, for the moment, at least, he was near enough to them in type to rejoice at the chagrin of their enemies.

"You're sure our wood will last long enough, Inmu?" asked Will.

"It will last until Roka finds us."

"And the pouring snow won't smother the flames?"

"No, Waditaka. When a fire is strong enough, snow and rain only feed it. Look, the snow comes at last and behold our flames leap higher!"

There was a rush of great flakes, and the fire sputtered beneath them, but it burned more brightly. A circling white bank moved up closer and closer, but through the blaze Will thought he saw dark shadows outlined against it, shadows that, transmitted through red, assumed gigantic size.

"I see the wolves," he said, "and I think they look at least ten feet tall. I think, Inmu, I must send an arrow at the shadow nearest us."

"It will not help us to slay one of them," said the Lynx, "save that it will be a relief to our minds."

"And that I call an important aid. A calm mind at such a time is worth at least twenty arrows."

"Waditaka speaks a great truth. To have peace

doubles our strength, so let fly, but first be sure that
your aim is good."

Will bent his bow, looked well, and his shaft rushed
to the target. The stricken wolf uttered a howl, and
then was dragged back to be devoured by his comrades. When they were engaged in their cannibal-
istic repast Inmu sent an arrow among them and slew
another. While he also was feeding his comrades
the two youths sat in the center of the fiery ring, and
ate strips of the elk, which they fried on the coals
in front of them. The snow, all the while, was increasing in volume, the circling white bank came very
near, but they knew the wolves would never dare
the fiery ring. The imminent presence of a danger
which yet could not reach them, gave them, inured as
they were to wilderness life, an extraordinary sense
of comfort, and of actual mental luxury. Inmu could
not keep from taunting the disappointed leader.

"Come on, O, wolf!" he cried through flame and
snow. "We are here, not more than fifteen or twenty
feet from you! We are waiting! We grow impatient! There are so many of you, too! Why don't
you spring! Ah! you are afraid! And man, not wolf,
is really the king!"

The Indian leaped back and forth within the fiery
ring, and continually shouted defiance, his spirits growing wilder and wilder. It was evident to Will that he
felt to the full a sort of fantastic enjoyment, as he
shouted to the wolves to come on and attack, and
prove which was the superior, wolf or man. The
snow poured more heavily, but, as Inmu had truly

46

predicted, it merely fed the flames, which ate voraciously into the dead wood, their crackle and roar rising above the steady swish of the snow.

Will could never account for it, but either a kind of mesmeric influence passed from the young Dakota to himself, or the power of a scene so wild and primitive filled him with extravagant spirits. He began to shout with Inmu, shout for shout, and he flung spoken taunts at the wolves, as if they understood every word they said. In truth, he believed at the time that they did understand. Once a darting shadow came near, and quick as a flash Inmu sent an arrow into the heart of a wolf, which made a convulsive spring back into the bushes, to be devoured there by his comrades.

But Inmu did not forget, as he shouted, to vary his taunts with his call to Roka. His piercing cries cut through the driving snow and distance, and the forest rang with them. Will, who perhaps was listening the more intently of the two, suddenly held up his hand.

"What is it?" asked Inmu.

"I thought I heard an answer to your call. Listen!"

Inmu ceased to bound and stood perfectly still a moment or two. Then he sent forth a shout containing the utmost power of his voice, and, when he had waited an instant, he exclaimed joyfully:

"I hear it. Roka is speaking to us! He tells us to be of good heart, that he and Pehansan, and the others are at hand! Now come, you wolves! It is your last chance to attack us before our comrades are here!

Come and take our elk, a fine, fat elk, food for a hundred of you!"

But the wolves did not attack. The relieving shout of Roka now rose clearly, and the master wolf, hearing it, was too intelligent to press the attack. He and the pack melted away in the forest and the snow, and, ten minutes later, Roka and his men arrived, fairly flying on their snowshoes. Will and Inmu welcomed them with joyous shouts and then sank exhausted upon the ground. Roka stood an instant or two on the snow outside the fiery ring and regarded them with gravity and approval.

"You have done well, Inmu and Waditaka," he said. "You have found a good elk which will furnish food for us for a long time, and you have known how to defend yourselves against the giant wolves of the north. Now roll yourselves in your buffalo robes and sleep. We will do what remains to be done."

They spread their robes on brush and wood inside the ring and then, wrapped in them, shut their eyes. Only the hardiest could have slept on such rough beds, but both the white lad and the red were asleep in an amazingly short time. Meanwhile, eight pairs of strong and cunning hands worked with wonderful dexterity. Their great blades flashed as they finished cutting up the elk, and they disposed of the pieces so they would freeze and keep. Now and then, one of them would stop work to brush the snow from the sleeping figures.

"They are brave and wise youths," said Roka to Pehansan. "It is well that we brought them with us.

It was reserved for the youngest to find the elk, and they mean luck to us."

Pehansan nodded assent. The ten were already knitted firmly together by the needs and dangers of the wilderness. Necessity often forced union upon primitive men and they recognized its great advantage. Besides, everyone felt esteem for every other one, as a hunter and warrior of approved mettle. But the eight who worked were far from gloomy or apprehensive now. They knew their numbers protected them from attack by fierce carnivora. They had that for which primordial man struggled all through his life, food abundant and good, and they interrupted their toils now and then to eat great broiled steaks of the elk. When the congenial task was finished Roka bade all except Pehansan and himself to sleep, and those two watched until dawn.

When Will awoke the snow had ceased, but its depth had increased by at least a foot and a half in the night. Nevertheless the space within the ring of fire had been kept clear, and the fire itself had never been permitted to die down. He rose in a buoyant mood and looked around at his red comrades.

"It was a bad night," he said, "but it's a good morning."

"So it is," said Roka, "and we are well provided here. We can live."

"What do you mean to do? Are we to go on at once through the valley and then over the mountains?"

"It will be wiser to wait. More snow may come, and we might get lost in it. There is wood in great quantity and we can have fires all the time, though we remain for many days."

They spent the morning in throwing back snow and widening the bare area, keeping the cheerful flames burning at a good height, and in the afternoon they broke a path to a brook. In the evening they did nothing but sit within the circle of the fire, wrapped in their warm robes, and listen to a warrior called Hoton (Crow) tell tales. The teller of tales was a recognized and respected institution in nearly all Indian tribes, and Hoton, though young, had a distinct gift. Much of the legendary lore handed down through generations of Sioux was stored in him, and his accounts of the great animals that once walked the earth gave them all many pleasant shudders.

"It is true," he said, "that ages and ages ago the wolves were three or four times as large as they are now, and it may be that those attacking us are survivals of that old, old time. The bears and panthers also were then great monsters, before which man always fled. Man lived only by hiding from the great brutes, which were the undisputed lords of the earth. He was a poor, stooping creature, cowering in holes in the ground and in hollow trees."

Will had read something like this in books, but in his new state of primitiveness he merely accepted the books as cumulative evidence that Hoton's statement was true. He had learned to have wonderful faith in Indian legends, which, for all he knew, may have been passed on for several thousand years.

"A man threw a stone, and he rose a step higher

among the beasts," said Hoton. "He made a club, and he went up two steps at a bound. He invented the lance and he jumped three more. Then he invented the bow and arrow and he went up five at a leap, and, when the white man across the sea found out how to use powder and bullets, he stood on top of the stair."

"But as we haven't powder and bullets with us, save those in the cartridges for my revolver," said Will, "we've gone back down the stairway a few steps."

"But we are still more than a match for the beasts," said Roka, "though I think the greatest in our world will be sent against us. Perhaps the evil spirits that are always in the air wish our destruction."

"But the good spirits favor us," said Pehansan, "and they will fight and conquer the evil."

A long, faint cry, like a moan, came on the wind.

"That is one of the wolves which Inmu and Waditaka defeated," said Roka. "He and his comrades hoped still to pull them down while we were away, but since we have come and are ten strong, they know they will have to wait a long time for another chance."

"But they will wait," said Will. "I know it."

The flakes poured down again that night, and the next morning the snow was another foot deeper. They could have made some progress on their snowshoes, but, still bearing in mind that haste was not needed, they remained quietly in camp. Will, having acquired the tremendous patience of the Indian, was not unhappy. His world for the time being passed in an orbit of about fifty feet, but it was full of variety and interest. He watched the warriors cook steaks of the elk, and he helped them. He studied the skies and tried to foretell from them whether it would rain or snow, or turn colder, or warmer. He listened to the wind in the trees and tried to detect in it another howl of the disappointed wolf. Then the stories of Hoton were numerous, picturesque and well worth hearing. The fires were very high, very ruddy, very warm and one could read all kinds of fortunes in the magnificent beds of coals that had formed. When there was nothing else to do one could fold his buffalo robe about him and sleep beautifully. Life was not so bad, surrounded by friends, safety and plenty.

Yet danger was always hovering about them. At twilight Tarinca (the Deer) went down the runway they had made to the brook for a drink and just as he stooped a huge beast leaped for him. Doubtless the deep snow made an unsteady base for the spring, as the wolf missed the fatal hold and merely ripped Tarinca's shoulder, striking in the deep snow beyond the runway, where he floundered for a moment or two. But the precious instants saved Tarinca's life. Uncommonly agile and alert, and with the fear of death pressing on him, he leaped back, fired an arrow that wounded the brute, and then, lest the wolves be at hand, ran with all his might down the runway toward the camp.

Tarinca reached the fiery circle and the wounded wolf disappeared, but Roka was alarmed. He gave orders that no one was to leave the camp alone, nor

even in twos or threes should they go except in full
daylight. Tarinca's wounded shoulder was bathed
very carefully with melted snow to remove the poison
from the wolf's teeth, and then bound up. His iron
health and hardiness would do the rest. In view of
the warning, the fires were built a little higher the
next night, but the following day it turned so cold
that the surface of the snow froze, and they decided
to leave, carrying with them their fresh supplies.
Every man bore, including his equipment, a weight
of more than a hundred pounds, but the coating of ice
sustained their snowshoes, and traveling slowly they
reached the lake which they had seen from the slopes.
Here in a very dense grove which gave them partial
protection, they made a new camp, and, with the aid
of their tomahawks, built two wickiups, each large
enough for three, which supplied the balance of the
protection.

They halted there, because a warm wind was blowing, and Roka foresaw an immense thaw accompanied
by driving rain. His forecast was right in both re-
spects, as the clouds, coming out of the Pacific Ocean,
surmounted the lofty ridges, and poured upon them
a deluge that lasted two days and two nights. Hundreds of streams ran down from the mountains, and
every brook and creek was flooded past the brim. The
water would have taken all the life out of them had it
not been for the dryness afforded by the wickiups,
but the waiting in such close quarters, even with
patience like theirs, was painful. Will was glad that
Hoton was in their wickiup, as the Crow, who had

invincible spirits, whiled away much of the time with tales, most of which had to do with great wild beasts.

Twice in their stay Will heard the howling of the wolves above the swish and pour of the rain, and he knew that the terrible man-eaters were hanging to their trail, waiting and hoping. There was something horrible in such ferocity and tenacity, and, as well as he could in the narrow space, he sharpened anew the arrows in his quiver.

On the third day the rain ceased, but the valley looked like a vast swamp. The ice had broken up on the lake and nearly all the ground was covered with water. The slopes of the mountains fairly smoked in the thaw and their peaks were lost in the mists and vapors.

"It will be best to stay here two or three days longer," said Roka. "The snow is melting so fast that soon it will all be gone in the valley, at least."

But they did not have to remain inside the close and narrow wickiups, and they spent the whole time outside now, managing to build another fire under the trees. Here Will, with a tincture of the white man's habit still in his veins, took vigorous exercise, stretching and tensing his muscles and expanding his chest. But the Indians, true to the customs of centuries, made no exertion that was not necessary. Their lives had always required so much physical effort that when there was no work to be done their idleness was complete and utter. But they sat by and watched Will with lazy interest.

"Why do you swing your arms so hard, Waditaka?" asked Hoton, the teller of tales.

"That the blood in them may circulate freely and that their muscles may grow."

"Manitou has made you what you are, Waditaka. Do you think you can improve upon his work?"

"Manitou merely gave me a start, Hoton, and then he told me to do the rest. In the sacred Book of the white people to whom I once belonged there is a story of men to whom various numbers of talents were given by Manitou, and when Manitou, some time later, asked what they had done with them those who had increased their store were praised and rewarded, but the one who guarded his and kept it just as it was, neither more nor less, was punished. It is what my former people called a parable. What you have you must improve. You must turn your five talents into ten."

"What are 'talents,' Waditaka?"

"An old name for money. It occurs often in the sacred Book of the white people, called the Bible, but in the parable of which I tell you it may mean anything, your strength, your spirit, or whatever you may do best."

"Then if I should kill two of the terrible wolves that follow us it would not be enough; if I had the arrows and the strength I should go on and kill four."

"I think that states it well enough, Hoton."

"But the wolves, which consider themselves lords of the forest, would think me very wicked if I killed two of them, and doubly wicked if I killed four.

55

Manitou made the wolves as well as ourselves. Why should he reward me for killing his creatures?"

"I think you're trying to get me into arguing in a circle, Hoton. I'll go back where I started, and merely say that what you have you must make better. Now, I'm trying to keep myself strong and flexible. I feel much stronger already."

"I am glad of it, Waditaka, because now you may cease waving your arms like a bough in a strong wind and may stop hopping about like a dog with a thorn in its foot. All that you say may be true, but it pleases me better to see a man rest, when there is nothing to be done."

Will failed to convert any of them to his theory of exercises, but he kept it up alone, usually accompanied by the whimsical comment of Hoton, who was in his way a humorist, and who loved to chaff Waditaka, because the youth took it in good spirit, and often paid him back in his own coin. Meantime the warm wind blew steadily, and the surface of the valley began to dry somewhat.

CHAPTER III

THE LORDS OF CREATION

WHEN the ice in it was gone, the little lake, about a mile long, and one fourth that distance in width, disclosed itself in attractive fashion. Will surmised that if so much muddy water from the melting snows on the mountains were not pouring into it its color would be a bright blue. Doubtless when it was breaking into rippling waves in the spring, under the influence of the gentle wind, it was the very embodiment of lonely beauty. Three times he strolled along its shores, and the third time he resolved to take a short swim.

It would be a cold plunge and he felt the need of a bath. Indians in winter troubled themselves little about such things, but cleanliness was a necessity to Will. Besides, he was extremely hardy, and could stand icy water, for a little while, at least. Selecting a shelving cove, he decided to swim out to a tiny forested island about thirty yards away, the place chosen being about a quarter of a mile from the camp, as he did not wish to be observed by Hoton and the others, who would certainly tell him he was mad.

But as he put down his bow and arrows, and rapidly took off his clothing he was very glad he had decided upon the swim. Surely the waters were already turning to that gorgeous blue he imagined they would be in the spring, and certainly the wavelets looked warm. Casting aside his last garment he sprang far out, and went under, head and all, in order to temper the first shock. He came up beating the water, spluttering and feeling a glorious thrill, and then, not forgetting wisdom in pleasure, he swam straight to the little forested island, where he leaped upon the land, and exercised a minute or two with great vigor. Then he made ready for another leap and the return swim to the mainland, but his muscles seemed suddenly to stiffen and his whole frame was affected by a sort of chill paralysis.

A huge mountain wolf was sitting upon his bow and quiver, and, with his jaws open and slavering, was looking straight at him, his cruel red eyes expressing the certainty of triumph. Will stared at the wolf and the wolf stared at him. The monster uttered neither yelp nor whine and did not stir an inch. His whole attitude and manner expressed the very quintessence of victory. As Will gazed at him, horrified, his size doubled and by-and-by his teeth and claws lengthened threefold. At least, it looked that way to his stunned spirit. Beyond the least doubt it was the father and king of the wolf world.

Will came out of his paralysis and drew back. Then all his pulses began to beat with mad vigor. In his excitement he forgot whether wolves could swim or not, and he retreated yet farther toward one of the trees. The wolf did not stir, but continued to gaze

at him intently. One paw rested on the splendid bow and the other on the quiver. That fact in itself was proof that he had Will where he wanted him. The besieged lad shivered. Then a cold wind blew across his chest, and he shivered again. He climbed hastily into the tree and shouted for help as he had never shouted before. No answer came. His very desire to get away from the Indians now put them beyond the sound of his voice.

His mortification was equal to his alarm. He had trapped himself, and instantly the aspect of everything was tinged with the hue of his mind. There was no blue about the lake. Its waters were muddy, cold and repellent. The wind was rising and its breath was icy. He had his choice of going over to the mainland and being devoured by the wolf, or of staying where he was and freezing to death. Sitting in the fork of the tree he began to wave his legs and beat his chest to keep warm. But the wolf only laughed. Will's assertion, that he always maintained against all doubters, was proof that he laughed, because he was there to see and hear and the doubters were not. Moreover, he could read the monster's eye and understand what it was saying through its various shades of expression. And its shade of expression at this particular time certainly indicated a laugh.

"O, man," said the wolf, as Will read his look, "I have you at last. You have tricked all my comrades and slain some of them, but you cannot escape me now. I wait patiently for the feast that I know is sure."

Will distinctly saw the wolf lick his slavering jaws,

and once more he shivered violently. The chill struck directly to his marrow. Then the animal cocked his head a little to one side and the besieged youth was sure that he saw a cruel twinkle in his eye, a twinkle that said just as plainly as if it had been put into words:

"You are nice and fat. You have been feeding well here in the valley and you have not exercised enough to reduce your flesh. You will make a most tender and juicy banquet."

Will looked down at his bare body. There was an alarming number of curves and rounded outlines, showing that the wolf's unspoken words were true. In this crisis of his life, when it was desirable to be lean, he was undeniably plump, just the sort of lad that a hungry wolf would wish to find up a tree. He grew furiously angry. He broke off a bit of a bough and threw it as far as he could in the direction of his besieger. It fell in the water and made no turmoil there, but the eyes of the wolf gleamed again and said very plainly:

"You need not grow angry and struggle, O man! You cannot avoid your fate! I am waiting here, as sure as death and as patient."

The silence and certainty of the wolf made Will's wrath rise higher than ever. He began to shout at him and reproach him. He wanted to make him growl back. He wanted to draw from him some sign of wolfish emotion. Anything but that implacable gaze and unending patience! The wolf rolled over his bow with one paw and his quiver with another, and then pushed his clothing disdainfully. That was the only sign he made. He was not to be disturbed by the squealing of his rat in the trap.

Will stopped shouting and gazed at him in a kind of fascinated horror. Then, after a minute or two, he came to himself with a shudder. The wind was rising and he would surely freeze to death if he stayed there. He began to scramble up and down the tree from the low boughs to the high and back again, over and over, but it was precarious exercise and it brought little warmth. The wolf merely sneered. His eyes said clearly to Will:

"Jump, man, jump! Jump like the grasshopper! For like the grasshopper you think but little, and your life is to be even shorter! It amuses me to see you bound here and there, before I eat you!"

He stopped abruptly and sank to rest in the fork of the tree. He would not spend his last minutes entertaining the wolf that was going to devour him. But when he had rested a little he began to send forth a piercing call, imitating as nearly as he could that of Inmu, the night when they were in the fiery ring. No doubt this very wolf had been in that besieging circle, and was enjoying now the triumph that he had won alone, when the united pack had failed.

He had not known before that he had such splendid vocal organs, and he sent forth a stream of shouting that cut the air like the lash of a great wind. The wolf showed amusement. His eyes said:

"O, man, you tire yourself for nothing! Why not prepare in peace for your last moments?"

But he continued to shout and he noticed suddenly that the wolf's eyes were beginning to speak a different language. His head was cocked again on one side, and he was saying to himself:

"I hear a new sound! It is in the forest behind me! Something comes!"

Will saw from the wolf's look that a fresh current was about to be injected into the stream of events. He did not know what it was, but whatever it might be it could not make his situation worse. So he not only shouted, he fairly howled, just as a primordial man chased up a tree by a cave tiger or a cave bear may have roared for help. Nor did he shout in vain. The wolf suddenly rose to his four paws, stood a few instants in a dignified manner and then trotted into the forest. But before he was hidden by the shrubbery he turned upon Will one look. It was still sneering and the shivering youth understood very clearly that he said:

"O, man, you have been saved by chance, but I shall come again."

Then the deep woods swallowed him up, and just as he disappeared Roka, Pehanson and Hoton came into view, their emergence from the trees occurring at the very point where Will's weapons and clothing lay. It was these articles that they saw first, and they gazed at them in astonishment. Will's first feeling had been relief at his escape, but his second was of overpowering mortification. However, there was nothing for it but to climb down in every sense of the word, and reveal himself, as one who had been trapped, and who stood bare to all the winds of adversity.

The three warriors, after looking at the weapons and clothing, glanced at the lake and caught sight of Will swinging himself from the tree. They uttered a shout of astonishment, but the lad, resolved to save a bad situation as much as he could, made a tremendous leap into the water, swam with a few strokes to the mainland and then, shaking himself violently until the drops flew in every direction, began to dress in haste and resolute silence.

"Did Waditaka turn himself for a while into a fish?" asked Hoton.

No answer.

"I see here the tracks of a wolf," said Pehansan. "It may be that Waditaka was besieged on the little island. Is it so, O, my young brother?"

Will still refused to reply and slipped on his deerskin tunic.

"Waditaka would swim in the lake when it is yet winter," said the irrepressible Hoton, "and while he has lost his tongue, we know that he has paid the price. We can swim in water, but only Waditaka can swim up into the boughs of a tree, where we first saw him. Did you go up there, Waditaka, that you might pray better to Manitou?"

Will flashed him a glance, and then compressed his lips. No word could come between them.

"Waditaka has a great soul," continued Hoton. "Only he could sit up in a tree on a winter day, without any clothes and not feel cold. We who are born

Dakota are proud of our endurance, but we yield to Waditaka. In all the annals of our race there has been no such hero as he. Generations from now the young maidens will sing of Waditaka, the great Waditaka, the unconquerable Waditaka, the mighty warrior, who defied all the icy winds out of the north."

Will flashed him another savage look, but was yet silent.

"Perhaps Waditaka will swim to the island every day to pray," continued the merciless Crow. "If so, it would be well for one of us to stand here while he is on the island and guard his weapons and clothes from the wolves."

Will made a great struggle with himself and conquered. Then he began to laugh, realizing that many an annoyance sure to grow if you fought with it could be easily laughed away.

"Make all the jests you please, Hoton," he said. "I admit that I'm open to 'em. The truth is I went into the lake for a quick swim, and the wolf surprising me held me on the island. I should probably have frozen to death in the tree if you three hadn't come. I was never before so glad to see you."

"Let it be a lesson to you, Waditaka," said Roka gravely. "Never separate yourself from your bow and arrows. Situated as we are a man who does it almost makes a present of his life to the wolves that are always following us."

"I've certainly had a splendid illustration of what you tell me," said Will, resuming his weapons. "Do

64

you think we could trail that hideous brute and kill him?"

"We might, but we would have to follow him two or three days and that would take us too far away from our errand. Tomorrow we will start on it again."

They made Will warm himself a long time before the big fire, letting the heat fairly soak through every muscle and fiber of his body, and Hoton staying by him saw that the task was done thoroughly. It was not a time to risk deep colds and illness, but, the precaution taken, Will escaped all harm. That night, however, the wolves howled often, though at a safe distance.

"You were right about the wolves talking," the lad said to Inmu. "I saw beyond question when I was in the tree that a wolf could talk. And he could talk, too, without moving his lips. He talked with his eyes and I understood him well. Do you know that when he went away he told me he would come back, and that he was sure yet of making a dinner off me?"

"It is a threat to be remembered," said the young Dakota. "You must be on your guard against him."

A warm sun shone the next day and the ground dried rapidly. For the sake of the increasing firmness they postponed their departure yet another day, and they also hid their snowshoes, of which Will was devoutly glad to be rid, concealing them under a mass of leaves and brush, weighted by stones.

"We must bury 'em good," said Will. "It would be just like those wolves if we didn't put 'em down too deep to come here and tear 'em to pieces out of sheer malice with their teeth and claws. It's lucky for man that animals can't think about one thing a long time. If they could, and the great meat-eaters made up their minds to have us, even though they followed us to the crack o' doom, we'd be living pretty precarious lives."

"It's not a sure thing that the wolves, at least, can't think of one thing for days and days," said Inmu. "Haven't those following us shown that they can? And now spring is approaching the great bears of the far north will come out of their dens and attack us again. I foresee that our journey will be one long battle with huge beasts."

They slept once more by the good campfire, and, at dawn, departed, leaving the wickiups to remain as they were, if chance so willed it, to serve them again when they returned that way. Then they coasted northward along the shore of the lake, which was now really the beautiful blue that Will had once fancied it to be, its little waves breaking upon one another and crumbling into millions of bright bubbles. Passing it they entered a mighty forest, which stretched away to the neck of the valley. They carried heavy packs again, but as they walked on their own feet now, the walking was easy and the spirits of the young warriors were uplifted.

Curiosity, too, was alive. They were on the march once more and they wondered what they were going to see. What lay beyond the narrow neck through which they would pass when they went out of the valley? But that which they did see almost at once was a large number of great tracks.

"The wolves have passed ahead of us," said Roka, examining them minutely. "In some manner unknown to us they have divined which way we would go and intend to lie in wait for us. But they are not alone. Some of the great bears have come out of their caves. See!"

He pointed to footprints far larger than those of the wolves. Obviously they had been made by the huge bears of the far north, double or triple the size of ordinary grizzlies, and Will shuddered a little as he looked at them. He felt that the wolves now had allies that the hardiest hunters would fear to face.

"How many bears were there, Roka?" he asked.

"The tracks show three," replied the leader. "But they were not with the wolves. They passed afterward. The traces are fresher."

"Can the wolf talk with the bear?"

"That I know not, but it is likely he can. They will form a union against us."

When they camped that night in the neck of the valley they worked until late, making new arrows, tipping them with the horn of the elk that Inmu had killed. Then Roka posted two sentinels, and the rest of them slept between two big fires. It was evident to Will that the leader was nervous, and he shared the older man's apprehensions. The tenacity of the wolves had been proved already, and the advent of the great bears made the danger much more formidable. But no attack was made nor was there sound in the darkness from any animal, and the next morning they did not find track of either wolf or bear ahead of them. Will thought it possible that they might be free now from this terrible pursuit, but, when he expressed his hopes to Inmu, the young Dakota shook his head.

"The wolves will never quit us until they are dead," he said.

"Then why not kill them?"

"What do you mean, Waditaka?"

"Instead of letting the wolves always hunt us, suppose we turn aside for a while and hunt them."

The idea seemed to impress Inmu.

"We should have thought of that before," he said. "We might speak of it to Roka."

Will himself made the suggestion to the chief, who took it seriously.

"We will lay a track for the great pack," he said, "and we will fight the wolves with the advantage on our side. I think we can find such a place ahead, where the neck leads out of the valley.

Will did not ask about the details, but he felt pride that his plan was to be adopted, and he marched on steadily just before his friend, Inmu. They passed presently into the neck, a long, narrow pass leading out of the valley. The cliffs of jagged stone rose on either side to a height of several hundred feet and were crested with dark masses of pine. The pass itself was curved, and for that reason they could not tell its length. When they were well within its shadows Roka, who was leading the file, stopped.

68

"How long would you say it is until night, Waditaka?" he asked.

Will looked up astonished, but he gazed then at the sun, which was just visible over the western cliff, and replied:

"About two hours."

"I asked you the question, Waditaka, to see whether you have learned to read the skies as we do who are born Dakota. Your answer is right, but there is more also behind my question. I will explain it by asking another. Can you climb the cliffs that hem us in?"

Will surveyed the stony walls with a measuring eye.

"If you attack a wall you find it's seldom as steep as it looks," he replied. "Besides, there are so many jutting crags that I could go up the cliff without much difficulty if I were pushed to do so."

"It is well, Waditaka. All of us can climb it bearing our burdens and the reason will appear later. We will make our camp a little farther on, and await the wolves who are ahead of us. Since they are eager for our lives we will show them that they seek us at the price of theirs. Great will be the battle!"

Roka spoke with authority and pride, and although his tones were not loud his words were like a trumpet call. Will glanced at the dark faces and he saw the dilation of every eye. His own pulses leaped. They were tired of fleeing before an ambushed terror. They would turn and show that they were those to be dreaded most. The martial souls of the young warriors thrilled.

"In these lone regions," said Roka, "the wolves dispute with man the mastery of earth. They claim to be superior to us. Then we will let the battle prove which is lord of creation here, man or wolf."

Every warrior uttered a deep murmur of approval.

"You always choose wisely, O Roka," said Tarinca. "Show us the way in which to fight."

"Not with our bows and arrows alone," said the leader. "We must use our heads also, because the wolves are cunning and wise. I think, though, that Manitou inclines to our side, because he has given us a battle ground that is to our advantage. See carefully to your weapons. Is your bow in perfect order, Waditaka?"

"Yes, Roka."

"It is needless to ask you, Pehansan?"

"It is ready, O chief."

"And yours, Inmu?"

"Yes, my chief."

"And yours, Hoton?"

"For the greatest battle of our lives, O chief."

"And yours, Tarinca?"

"Ready for instant use, Roka."

"And yours, Hinyankaga?" (Owl).

"Fit to draw arrow at once, great chief."

"And yours, Wanmdi?" (Eagle)

"The string craves the arrow, Roka."

"And yours, Tatokadan?" (Antelope)

"My bow calls to my arrows so strongly that they are about to leap from the quiver, wise chief."

"And yours, Capa?" (Beaver).

"My arrow is eager to sing through the air, brave leader."

Roka looked upon his young men with just pride. No weaklings there. Valiant warriors with the souls of real kings, they turned gladly for battle with a cunning and powerful foe.

"If it were given to me to wave you aside and choose nine in your place then I would choose you nine over again," he said.

Every man uttered a deep murmur of thanks, and Roka went to work. He chose for the camp a comparatively level space where the valley was very narrow, and then found enough dead wood fallen from the cliffs above to build a fire. They also builded it high and they cooked much food and ate much and talked much. The whole camp bore an aspect of carelessness and gayety. It would have seemed to the eye of an outsider that the ten no longer feared anything and like those who are without fear took no precaution. Nor was their gayety merely assumed. The thrill of coming conflict, battle at time and place of their own choosing made their pulses leap and their hearts beat high. Yet, by order of Roka, they kept close to the fire.

Will saw the sky darken and heavy clouds of dusk creep up the pass, and he had an overpowering sense of the strange and uncanny. Once more he was rapt back through immeasurable time into the primordial world, in which man fought incessantly for life with the great wild beasts.

When they had eaten their fill, dispensing with water on this occasion, they permitted the fire to die, but they drew up logs before them in the attitude of sleeping men and spread over them as many of their garments as they could spare. Fortunately the air was not cold and the hardy warriors could spare much. These preparations were brief, but the night came on fast, and the darkness quickly grew very heavy in the pass. The fire was almost out and the figures of the warriors were but shadows. There was no sound. No breeze, even, was drawn through the pass, and the cedars far above their heads were motionless. It was so still that they could have heard the pattering of light feet at a distance, if the wolves had been approaching.

"Pehansan," said Roka, "climb upon the crags, fifteen feet will be high enough, and see that every man is in a good position, where he can wait and use his bow well when the time comes. Inmu and I will remain here. We will be the bait."

"You are our chief, O, Roka," said the tall warrior, "and I am not one to question your orders, but I claim the place here with you. I am, next to you, the oldest in the band, and the honor is mine."

"It would be, Pehansan, but the men on the crags will need a leader and none other is so fit as you. Your place there will be one of great glory."

"I accept, but I ask you, Roka, that you and Inmu do not wait too long. Death under the teeth of the wolves would not be pleasant."

"I know that full well, Pehansan. It is not in my mind to die. I find life very sweet. Go now, the full darkness has come, and if we wait it will be too late. Any wolf is cunning and wise, but these of the great north are the wisest and most cunning of all."

Pehansan leading his seven men climbed up the east side of the pass, being careful to make no noise, finding, after some search, easy positions in which they crouched. Will's bow was strung and he laid his quiver between his body and the wall, but where he could draw the arrow with a single motion. Then he looked down at two dark figures, those of Roka and Inmu, who had lain down by the side of the logs before the dying fire. At the distance, it was impossible to tell them from the inanimate wood, upon which the spare garments had been laid. All looked alike, the two men and the eight logs. They had purposely made the figures, ten in all, because Roka like Inmu believed that wolves, or at least the master wolf, could count, and, if their suspicions were to be lulled, the numbers must be the same as they had always been.

Will was filled with admiration for the two daring men who lay there, and who would be practically beneath the spring of the great wolves. Courage and self-sacrifice were not confined to his own race. He was learning to the full the variety and power of primitive virtues. He felt an immense pride in belonging to such a band.

A full hour passed and the eight watchers on the crags never stirred, nor did the figures around the fire, which had now gone out. No air yet moved. Not one of the dead leaves was shaken. Will listened intently for those soft foot falls that would tell of the enemy's advance, but they did not come. His sense of something strange and uncanny, something that was happening in the dawn of the world, grew and obsessed him. He had been stalked by the Indian, but now he was being stalked by great beasts, and, in that savage world to which he had reverted, man was put on an equality with the fierce carnivora only by the bow which he carried. He stroked the horn of his own splendid weapon, and felt that it stood between him and death.

He could not see his seven comrades on the cliff, because they were hidden by crags and projections, and the two, lying before the fire, were so still they must certainly have ceased to breathe. He was alone in a desolate world, and his nerves quivered a little. One could wait with more patience, if the touch of a comrade was on either side of him. Then he steadied his muscles. Why should he be shaken when Roka and Inmu were lying there directly in the path of the pack? Once more he admired their extraordinary courage and resolution, because the wolves that were coming against them were not ordinary wolves, but the great wolves of the north, surcharged with ferocity and tenacity, and believing themselves lords of creation, superior to the men whom they were now hunting.

Will looked steadily toward the exit of the pass. The tracks had shown that the wolves had gone ahead of them and had probably been waiting somewhere in ambush at a narrow point. Smelling the fire and the presence of man they would come back, although they might wait patiently until the night was far gone. Then it was for man to be as patient as the wolf and not to fail in the first test.

It grew a little colder and he drew his buffalo robe closely about his body, lest his muscles become stiff. Once or twice he bent his bow to see that it retained all its flexibility and power, but mainly he watched the northern end of the pass, although at intervals he cast brief glances at the dim figures of Roka and Inmu, recumbent before the dead fire. It was wonderful how much they were like the logs with the spare garments upon them. It was only by remembering their numbers that he could tell which were animate and which inanimate.

He never knew how much time had gone, but, while he was gazing intently into the northern end of the pass, he saw a darker figure appear against the dark. At first it was just a great blur, but gradually it took the shape of an animal, and then he knew it definitely to be a wolf, a wolf monstrous beyond all human imagination. It looked like the evil creature of a dream, though Will knew that the distorting dusk and his fancy had enlarged it. But it was a monster, nevertheless, and then he saw the figures of other wolves behind it.

The wolves unquestionably had seen the ten shadows lying before the fire and from a long distance they had detected the man odor that came from two of them. Will believed as truly now as Roka and Inmu that they could count and that Roka's cleverness in presenting ten recumbent figures, the same as the number of men on the march, had deceived them.

"Be ready, Waditaka, but wait until I give the word," came a sharp whisper, and then he saw Pehansan near him, leaning forward from the shelter of his jutting spur.

The wolves, figure after figure, detached themselves from the dusk and came forward. Will saw then that the master wolf was not the first that had appeared, instead he was near the middle of the line, and he rose a half foot in height above any of the others, huge as they were. They were stalking the camp as if they were human beings, guided by a captain skilled in war, and, at sight of so much cunning, mingled with so much ferocity Will's hair rose on his head. He looked at the ten figures, expecting that two of them would now rise and spring for the shelter of the crags, but they did not stir. Truly, the nerves of Roka and Inmu were superhuman.

The wolves broke their line now, and spread out exactly like flankers and skirmishers, advancing slowly and absolutely without noise. Theirs was a formidable attack made with so much secrecy. Only trained eyes, looking for them, could have seen them. The nearest was now within distant arrow-shot, and Will glanced again at Pehansan, but, though the face of the tall warrior was tense and eager, no word came from his lips. Will understood and admired. Pehansan, like Roka, when the strain upon the nerves was almost beyond endurance, had nevertheless the power to wait until the right moment in the face of appalling danger.

He had been staring into the darkness so long that he could see with fair distinctness. The wolves, about forty in number, were spread out in a creeping half circle, and the master wolf, towering above his fellows, was at the center of the curve. All of them were within bow-shot, but Will divined now that the word would come from Roka and not from Pehansan, and surely it would come soon, because another minute or two and the wolves would be able to spring. Before he drew many more breaths the question whether man or wolf was lord of creation here must be decided.

Every minute became an age. The figures of the creeping wolves again became distorted and gigantic in the dusk, looming like great primeval monsters. Would Roka and Inmu never stir? Had he been in the place of either of them, no matter how high his courage, his heart would have beat so hard that it would have come near to bursting. His hands shifted nervously along his bow.

Then he saw Roka and Inmu leap suddenly to their feet as if they had been propelled by mighty springs, and it seemed that with the same motion their arms flew back, drawing their arrows to the head. The next instant the shafts, deadly and winged, flew through the air and were buried deep in the bodies of two wolves. Twice and thrice the shafts flew and both warriors, throwing back their heads, uttered tremendous war cries of challenge and defiance that rang and rang again through the narrow pass. But the reply came in a growl so fierce, so full of ferocity that every nerve in Will's body quivered. Then the wolves leaped.

"Now! Now! O, my children!" cried Roka. "Fill the air with your arrows!"

Will saw Roka and Inmu leap for the crags and pull themselves up out of reach as the wolves snapped at their heels. Then he saw nothing but the pack, the red eyes, the tremendous fangs, and claws, the great, lean figures, and he heard nothing but the continuous snarling and twanging of the vengeful bow-strings. The target was near, the need was imminent and never before had ten warriors, strong and true, shot so fast and with so much force.

Will was tremendously excited but he never forgot to take aim. He sent arrow after arrow into throat or heart, and always he was urged on by the shouts of Roka.

"More arrows! More arrows, O, my children!" cried the leader. "They would have battle, now give them their fill of it! Who is the lord of creation, O, you wolves, man or wolf? You bite and you snarl in vain! The stone of the cliff does not feel either your teeth or your claws! But you feel our arrows! Now, five of you are dead! Now ten and more! You shoot well! You shoot gloriously, O, my children!"

The voice of Roka rang continuously through the pass, and now and then his men also burst into thrilling shouts. Will shouted with them. He was as much a wild man in the dawn of the world as they. A fierce excitement burned through every vein, yet his head remained cool for battle, and he obeyed the command of Roka to all his warriors to send no arrow wild. His great elk horn bow sang and sang, and his arrows were buried deep in the bodies of the fierce beasts that strove with such rage to reach them.

The combat was all on one side. The generalship of Roka had proved triumphant. Strong and cunning as they were, the wolves could not scale the crags from which came a stream of arrows. Several leaped almost to the feet of the warriors, hung there desperately a few moments, and then fell to the ground. Will saw a hideous, snarling mouth scarcely a foot below him, and he pressed back against the cliff. But before the wolf could fall he sent an arrow to its very head in its throat.

"The victory is ours, my children!" cried Roka. "Not one of us is harmed, but half of them have fallen! Man, not wolf, is the lord of creation! Faster! Send in the arrows faster, and we will destroy the whole pack!"

Will wondered why the wolves persisted so long in a fruitless attack, but he believed afterward that it was due to a consuming rage. Surely if they had not lost their cunning and wisdom for the time they would not have fought on against such terrible losses. Nevertheless the end came. All the survivors turned suddenly and fled like shadows for the upper end of the pass, but Roka was in no mood to spare any that

79

could be reached; nor was it the part of wisdom to let them escape.

"Shoot! Shoot!" he cried. "Send your arrows as long as you can reach a wolf!"

The ten shot so closely together that the arrows in groups followed the wolves as they fled, but, when the last left alive were gone, Will sank back exhausted against the face of the cliff. The scene had been so savage and his emotion had been so great that he felt faint, and the world reeled before him.

"The battle is won. The victory is greater than we had hoped," said Roka, dropping lightly to the floor of the pass, where Inmu and Pehansan quickly followed him. Nothing could shake their iron nerves. Will recovered completely in a minute or so and let himself down from the niche that had been such a coign of vantage. The ten warriors stood in a close group, bows and arrows ready lest the wolves return to the attack, and looked upon the field of the slain.

Three or four badly wounded beasts, seeing man come down from his victorious heights, rose and tried to limp away, but they were swiftly dispatched with arrows, and then the warriors counted the fallen. Twenty-eight were stretched upon the earth, all larger than the greatest mountain wolves that any of them had seen, before the village was pitched in the lone valley. But the master wolf, the one that towered a full half foot above all the others, was not among them. Evidently his cunning and wisdom had been sufficient to save him, and they would have to reckon with him at another time.

The results, however, were so great that every man felt immense gratification. They built the fire anew and they built it bright and high. Then they cooked and ate slices of the elk, which they had made secure on the crags before the wolves came, and, wrapped in their buffalo robes, lay down before the flames. But none of them could sleep yet and Hoton, the teller of tales, in particular, was filled with the glory of victory.

"There has never been such another encounter with wolves in all the history of the Dakota nation," he said. "Twenty-eight of them have we slain, every one a giant. I shall sing of it when we return to the village, I shall sing of it many times."

"And when you are old," said Pehansan, "you will make it forty-eight wolves, and then sixty-eight, and then eighty-eight."

"Aye, Pehansan, so I will, and those who come after me will make it two hundred and those who come after them will make it four hundred. Our deed will grow and grow as long as the Dakota nation lasts, for such is the way of man."

They would have removed some of the huge wolf skins, the hair of them being thick and long to endure the intense cold, but the weight of their packs was already great, and they were compelled to let them go. After a long rest by the fire they completed an important task, which at first they had thought of leaving for the morning. They recovered nearly all their arrows, and, as some of them had to be cut from the bodies of the wolves, the task was unpleasant and tedious. But they persisted and when the last arrow had been wiped clean and returned to its quiver, they took their places again by the fire which now burned so splendidly in the pass.

Then sleep soon overcame all except the two who watched, and the relaxation was so complete that they were buried in deepest oblivion. But the sentinels, never more wide awake, constantly replenished the fire and toward morning listened to low sounds in the dusk, where surviving wolves had crept back, other animals with them, and were devouring the dead bodies of their comrades.

CHAPTER IV

THE DANGEROUS FORD

ROKA and Pehansan arose at dawn, but they did not awaken the others, and they bade the sentinels lie down beside them. Then, arrow on the string and muscles alert, they inspected their field of battle, and looked for traces of great bears. But the ground was too hard to show tracks.

"It may be," said Roka, "that we will not have to deal with them until we finished with the wolves."

"And as many of the wolves with their leader are left alive," said Pehansan, "they may yet give us much trouble."

"It is true, Pehansan, but the victory we have won must not make us careless. We shall meet many more dangers, but with the young warriors we have we can conquer them all. Never did anybody have more splendid young men!"

"Truly spoken, Roka. They are brave and skillful and they are at the age when one dares anything."

The start was not made until about noon. When there was nothing urging the Indian he always took an abundance of rest, being able to lie in a completely relaxed state much longer than the white man. Will now had this power, and, when he opened his eyes about the middle of the morning, and saw there were no preparations to start he closed them again, falling into a pleasant dream in which the whole terrific scene of the dark hours passed before his eyes again.

When the sun was at the zenith they took up the march, packs on backs, and passed through the neck of the pass, emerging by the side of giant cliffs where the wind struck them with tremendous force. But all the warriors, stoical as they were, uttered murmurs of admiration. Before them lay a steep descent then a wilderness of faint green, vast forests already touched by spring, and far beyond, around the whole three quarters of the circle, lofty mountains tipped with snow. Silver gleams of water, rivers and little lakes, appeared through the foliage.

"It is a good land," said Roka, "but we must pass through it and reach the wide northern buffalo plains which we know lie to the east."

Will and the young warriors were not averse to the great journey. They were anxious to go and see.

"In a country such as this we may find tribes that will attack us," said Pehansan. "It is the misfortune of the Indians that they should be so much at war with one another."

"Perhaps," replied the astute Roka, "but there are not many people in the far north, where the cold lasts so long. It is possible that man has never been in the region that we see before us."

"And if so, my chief, the great animals will be all the more numerous because there has been none to slay them or to fight them."

"Likely enough, Pehansan, but we have the bows that have served us so well, and if we should use all our arrows we can make new ones."

They began the descent, Roka, in his right as leader, going first, the others, as usual, following in single file. The going was not difficult for warriors as sure of foot as they, the way taking them through alder, pine, birch and aspen which grew larger the farther down they went. Half way to the bottom and Will glanced back.

"Look!" he cried to his comrades.

Upon a jutting rock, far above them, stood a gigantic wolf, colored tawny gold in the blazing sunlight and enlarged in the glowing beams to a size beyond that of any wolf that ever existed in any age. It was the master wolf himself, and Will knew that his gaze was a threat, full of ferocity and vengeance.

"He is telling us that he will still follow us," he said.

"Since we have destroyed most of his pack," said Inmu, "he is resolved more than ever to pull us down and devour us."

"Truly spoken," said Roka. "The king of the wolves now has revenge added to the other reasons why he wishes to sink his teeth in us. He has not given up the fight. He does not yet concede that man and not wolf is the lord of the wilderness."

The great wolf did not move. In the glowing sunlight his figure grew larger and larger, and his attitude was full of menace. Once more Will felt the hair lift on his head. They had been victorious the night before, but he realized now that they had won a battle and not a campaign. He felt a certain admiration for the giant leader.

"He does not yield easily the leadership of the forest," he said to Roka.

"No," replied the Dakota. "He will not give up. I do not think they will attack us again in the open, but we must guard now against ambush."

"And, as we're going to enter dense forest, ambush will be easy there."

"It looks like it, Waditaka. Once more I say to all of you that we must remain close together."

When they looked back again the great wolf was gone from the jutting crag, but Will still felt the weight of his threat, and he resolved, when they reached the dense forest below, to take no incautious step. Another hour and they reached a region of magnificent timber, the trees rising in vast cones to a height of two hundred and fifty or three hundred feet. Will knew that the whole region must be watered by the plenteous rains of the Pacific brought by the high clouds over the mountains. He renewed his old belief that they were far north of the American line in a land as yet untrodden by white men, a land in which everything was on a great scale.

The ten were delighted by the splendor of nature visible all about them, the size of the trees, the great mountains with their white crests towering on the circle of the horizon, the obvious richness of the soil with the young grass already showing under the dead leaves of winter, and the inevitable conclusion that the forest

86

swarmed with all kinds of game great and small.

"Ours are a people who love to hunt the buffalo. We could find a home here, but we would not be happy in summer unless we were on the plains," said Roka.

They penetrated some distance into the forest before night came, and camped by the side of a cold stream that rushed down from the mountains. Tarinca and Hoton, dropping their lines into the current, caught a species of large trout which they found very savory and delicate, and they were light of heart when they ate supper, despite the dangers that still clustered about them.

Inmu, Pehansan and Will, scouting about the camp, found many tracks of game, particularly of the ordinary deer, the mule deer, the elk, and of the great Alaskan moose, then unknown to white men, save to a few wandering prospectors. The three looked with intense interest at the huge imprints and Will, building up the body from the hoof, concluded that the animal making them must have weighed more than a ton.

"We shall have noble game to follow," he said.

"So great that I am almost tempted to leave the plains forever for a life in the forest," said Pehansan.

They did not find any tracks of wolf, and, because of the lack, their hearts grew lighter. They would not admit it to themselves, but the ferocious pursuit had weighed heavily upon their nerves, and their spirits were frayed somewhat by it. But they found instead tracks belonging to the cat tribe, and Pehansan pronounced them those of the puma or panther. enlarged far beyond the ordinary size, as all animals seemed to be in these remote and highly vitalized valleys.

"The puma, cougar or panther, whichever name you call it, is usually a cowardly beast," said Will, "but I don't fancy the looks of these tracks. Maybe, like the wolves and bears, the panther takes on uncommon ferocity in this region."

"He is rarely found so far north," said Pehansan, "and maybe only a few lone animals of the kind are wandering here."

They followed the great tracks, large like those of a lion, until they were lost at the edge of a small water-course, and then returned to the camp. Will was apprehensive. While the panther was cowardly most of the time, the lion often ran away too, and here in the north these isolated, gigantic specimens might not be afraid of man. He knew from his reading that in the far interior of South America the jaguar, while lacking in the height, often attained the body and weight of a great tiger, and he suspected an attack.

That night when he was on guard with Inmu by the fire, he heard a crying in the wilderness, a sound much like the wailing of a woman, but the two knew better. It was made by the great panther, which no doubt, from some place of vantage, was watching their fire with yellow, angry eyes. The panther's cry was the most weird and lonesome of all the sounds Will had ever heard. It was a combined note of ferocity and despair, and it made the lad's blood grow chill in his veins.

"If that brute would quit weeping and wailing," he

said to Inmu, "I'd like it better. It sounds to me like mock grief over the fate he intends for us. He's shedding what we white people call crocodile tears."

"I know nothing of the crocodile," said Inmu, "but I do not like the presence of the panther. The wolves could trail us on the ground only, but the panther can hunt us from the trees also."

"And do you think this panther or a lot of 'em, if he has friends, will follow us as the wolves have done?"

"I do not know, Waditaka, but we seem to have come into a country that belongs to the animals only. Maybe they will join together and destroy us before we grow too strong, and before we have a chance to take their country from them, as the white man treats the red man."

"You can't tell me, Inmu, that wolves, bears and panthers will form an alliance for the annihilation of man! Why, such a thing was never heard of in the history of the world!"

"Waditaka, who has read many books where the wisdom of the wise is stored, has never before claimed that he knew everything. Does he say that a thing has never happened because he has never heard of it?"

"No, I don't, Inmu, but it appears incredible."

"Our legends and tales, passed on from father to son through countless generations, tell of many strange things not in the books of the white man. You do not believe all of them, and I say to you in reply that I do not believe many of the tales in your books. Listen, the giant panther is crying again!"

"You understood what the master wolf said that night when he howled outside our camp, now why is it that you can't interpret any of the panther's talk?"

"I have not said, Waditaka, that I could not, but even Waditaka himself could not learn a language in a few minutes. Be patient and perhaps I will understand."

Will and Inmu walked a little distance from the fire. The long, whining cry, full of ferocity and complaint, rose again and again. It was a curious note. It seemed to spread and fill the air. It was impossible to tell whether it came from a point on the ground or high up among the trees. Inmu listened with extraordinary concentration.

"Now I know his language," he said at last. "His words run so: 'You have fought with the wolves, O, man, and so far you have been the victor, but you have not yet fought with me! The wolves run upon the ground and they may lie in ambush there, but you know where to seek them! I find my way in the trees! I lie upon the bough where you do not see me, and when you think I am far away I spring upon you! I, the giant panther, am the real monarch of the woods!'"

Will, despite himself, looked up and scanned every bough within forty or fifty feet of them. He was relieved to find no huge and tawny form crouching there. Inmu's eyes had followed his, and, noting his change of countenance he laughed low, but with great amusement.

"You believed my words, O Waditaka," he said.

"You believed the threat of the panther, as I told it to you, and you looked in the trees for him."

"I don't know whether I did or not, Inmu, but, at least, you created an illusion in my mind, you were so much in earnest. For the time, I suppose, I had faith."

"You had faith, then, and you will have it again. The panther is still talking, Waditaka. You can hear him yourself. He is saying: 'You are in the deep forest now, O man, and that is where I hunt best. You cannot look at the ground and the sky at the same time. When you are thinking least of me I shall come. I am more dangerous than the wolf because I am larger and stronger than he, and I have my choice of two paths while he has only one. I am more dangerous than the great bear because I am more cunning and I hate more.' "

"I don't believe he's telling the truth wholly, Inmu. I doubt whether he's more cunning than the great bear, although he's right when he says he hates more. Taking it by and large, I've a pretty good opinion of bears, and I don't believe they hate much. I fight 'em in self-defense only."

"Truly spoken, Waditaka. The bear is the noblest of animals, though not the wisest, perhaps. He is not so cunning and tenacious as the wolf, and he does not steal upon you like the panther, but he has paws and teeth more terrible than either. And we do not really know that the great bears of the north, the monstrous ones, do not remember and follow even as the wolf does."

"But we've had no encounter with 'em yet, at least, not since that fight in the winter when we went out from the village."

"But we have seen their tracks. We will yet meet them."

"Let's wait until then. We've now to deal with the wolves and the panther. There goes the tawny brute again! What's he telling us, Inmu?"

"He is saying: 'I have warned you now, O man, that I will come when you are least expecting me. I am not the panther of the south. I am far larger and far more fierce than he and you cannot escape me. This is my last warning to you. Now I go.'"

The ferocious crying in the wilderness ceased and they heard only the light crackle of the fire behind them. Will felt cold.

"Inmu," he said, "I almost believe you've been telling me the truth."

"You believe it wholly, Waditaka. When I gave you the words of the king wolf did they not come true? And what I take from the lips of the panther will come true also. You know it."

Will said nothing, but again he examined very carefully the boughs of all the adjacent trees, and, when his watch was over and he lay down, he chose a place that no animal could possibly reach by a single leap from an overhanging bough. The sharp eyes of Inmu noted the fact, but he kept silent, merely smiling to himself. Will awoke an hour later, and once more he uneasily inspected the trees. But they were free from crawling animals and the voice of the panther did not come out of the forest again that night.

Dawn disclosed a wilderness magnificent, untroubled and apparently free from danger. The young warriors rose, expanded their chests, and were eager to be led forward. Like the great animals, they seemed to have acquired new size and strength in the fertile valleys of the far north. There was something in the soil and climate that made for growth.

"Let us go on," said Hoton, the teller of tales, "I wish to see all the mountains and rivers and lakes and what they contain, and when I return to the village I will tell of them as none of you can."

"As none of us will," said Wanmdi, whose name meant the Eagle. "O Crow, you know that whatever we may achieve it will not be the half of what you will tell."

"Then you should rejoice because of it, O Eagle, because though you may do little I shall make it appear to the village that you have done much. Thus, without running the risks you will seem to the people a slayer of great beasts, and a mighty warrior."

"You are well named the Crow, because you can chatter forever. If the wolves attack us again I will ask Roka to send you forth to talk to them, and your tongue will run so fast and so long that they will fall dead from sheer weariness. Thus we will save our arrows."

"And if I can do it, Wanmdi, will I not deserve to be created a great chief?"

Will listened to them with amusement, knowing

there was no animosity in the controversy of the Crow and the Eagle. He had long since learned that among themselves the Indians were talkative and had an abundant fund of jest and irony. They loved to chaff one another in their own peculiar way.

"Hoton," he said, "both you and Wanmdi should fly through the air if your names mean anything. Now, tell me, since the animals grew so great up here why shouldn't the birds do the same? Won't we find eagles, for instance, mighty of beak and talon, and twice as large as those we've known in our own lands farther south?"

"It is a wise question that you ask, Waditaka," interrupted Roka. "I have never known eagles to attack man, save a little child now and then, but, since we are threatened by wolves and bears on the ground and panthers in the trees, it may be also that great birds in the air will try to molest us."

All the young warriors, driven by the same impulse, looked up, but the blue heavens were unflecked by any dark objects that could be turned into fierce carnivorous eagles. Nothing floated there against the emerald sea save the little white clouds, and they signified only peace.

"I don't think we are to expect any attacks from the air," said Hoton.

"Learn, O Hoton," said Roka gravely but in a spirit of instruction rather than reproof, "that a clear sky is no proof we will never have a storm. Because no enemy is in sight now we must not conclude that none will ever appear."

"It is true, wise chief," said Hoton, "and gladly I admit it. I have learned in this wilderness of marvels to expect everything."

"And to be ready for anything, my Hoton. A mighty talker are you, but a brave warrior also. None did better than you in the great fight with the terrible wolf pack."

The blood of gratified pride came into the bronze of Hoton's face at the words of praise that Roka so rarely spoke.

"I thank you, Roka," he said briefly, but speaking from a full heart.

"And keep on talking," said the leader, smiling. "It is well, that a band should always have one with a light and gay tongue. When a river is happy its waters sing to themselves, and when the tongue of the Crow goes on and on we know that we are doing well."

"In truth, Hoton is our minstrel," said Will. "Like the knights of old, we are cheered up by him when the day's work and fighting are over, though he has neither lute nor song."

"Minstrel! what is that, Waditaka?" asked Roka.

Will explained as well as he could to a group that listened with great attention and interest, and the leader nodded sagely.

"I think I understand, Waditaka," he said.

They talked in the same vein as they walked, because they anticipated no attack from any source as long as the daylight lasted. The forest did not lend itself readily to ambush. As in the smaller valley it was almost free from undergrowth, and they walked

between ordered rows of magnificent trunks. Despite
the great canopy of leaves that would appear later on,
turf grew there, and already enough of it had appeared
to make a springy carpet for their feet. Their packs
grew lighter and the spirits of the young warriors,
already high, ascended into empyrean heights.

"The air blowing upon us is life itself," said Hoton.
"If it grows any stronger Wanmdi and I, true to our
names, will rise high in the air and fly ahead of the
band."

"Behold the great moose," said Will, pointing to the
right, where a huge animal stood between two trees,
regarding them, a moose probably doubling in weight
his brother of the farther south.

"Maybe he, too, claims to be the lord of the forest,"
said the irrepressible Hoton, "but, unlike the wolf, he
does not yet know man, nor is he so cunning and wise
as *Xunktokeca* (Wolf)."

"The moose, no matter how great his size, will attack us only at certain times," said Pehansan, a mighty
hunter who knew the ways of all animals, "and we are
glad he and his brethren are here. Food for a great
Dakota war band marches on those four hoofs."

The moose regarded them with a stately air of disdain, and then walked away among the trees. A half
hour later, they came to a deep, swift stream, cutting
straight across their right of way, the water an intense blue and free from ice.

"We shall have to swim it," said Roka, "unless
we find a ford."

They searched several hundred yards both up and

down the stream, but they did not care to look long for a ford. They were too hardy to fear either the current or the cold, and selecting a comparatively narrow place, with easy slopes for the departure and the landing, they prepared, baring their bodies and making their clothing, weapons, ammunition and food into packs that they could carry on their heads, thus keeping them dry. Roka, as became his leadership, swam first and arrived safely on the other side. He was followed by Hoton, Wanmdi, Tarinca and others until only Will and Inmu were left on the first shore.

Will was preparing to take the stream when a fierce shout of warning came from Roka and an arrow whistled over his head. He turned and was paralyzed for an instant as he saw a great wolf leap straight for his throat. It would have been his last minute, but another arrow fired by Hoton, great talker and great warrior, sang close to his face, and pierced the neck of the leaping brute through and through. The momentum of the wolf was so great that his dead body knocked Will down, and, although he quickly sprang to his feet again, he was dazed.

A mighty yellow shape launched itself from the over-hanging bough of a tree, but it was met in mid air by four arrows, which did not slay, but which broke its flight. The huge panther dropped almost at Will's feet, and the snap of its terrible fangs missed him but little. He sprang back, and the shout rang in his ear:

"Swim, Waditaka! Swim, Inmu! Swim for your lives!"

The great panther had risen to its feet for another spring and the wolves also were closing in anew. It was the impulse of both Will and Inmu to stretch out their arms, bend their bows and fight then and there, but those on the other bank knew better. Conscious of the desperate need and with muscles of steel eight men shot their arrows close together and so fast that before one struck its target another had left the bow. Never were arms and eyes more true. The whistling shafts were a bristling wall between Inmu and Will and their enemies. They stood out all over the body of the great panther, and wolves died almost at the feet of the two. And always above the deadly rustle of the arrows and the terrible growling of the beasts, rose the commanding shout:

"Swim, Waditaka! Swim, Inmu, for your lives!"

Will and the young Dakota collected their senses at last, and, still carrying their packs on their heads, leaped into the stream, then swam desperately for the other bank, where their comrades, great marksmen, stood covering their struggle for life with flight after flight of arrows. Will reached the bank, struggled up, and sank down almost unconscious. But he recovered himself quickly, and began to dress with all speed, Inmu, close at hand, being engaged in a similar task.

"It was a narrow escape, Waditaka," said the grave voice of Roka. "We underrated the cunning of the wolves and of the great panther, and you two came near being trapped at the ford. But the panther, monster though he is, has paid the price. Look!"

Will turned his eyes toward the other shore. The panther, tawny and vast, was outstretched there, the shafts of more than a dozen arrows protruding from his body. By the side of him lay eight dead wolves, and he knew that others must have limped away wounded. Truly, the eight warriors on the other shore had shot magnificently, and Will's heart swelled with gratitude and pride.

"Roka," he said, "Inmu and I owe our lives to you. Never were arrows sharper, and never did they fly faster."

"We shot so well because we were not willing to lose our youngest two, but not our least valuable warriors," said Roka, as he unstrung his bow. "But you will notice, Waditaka, that the king wolf is not among the slain. He laid well his plan to trap our rear guard at the ford, and, though he has been defeated with a large loss, he himself is yet alive, and, madder with rage than ever, will continue to follow us."

"Do you think, Roka, that the panther was in alliance with the wolves? That the great animals, though of different kinds, could really form a league to attack us?"

"That I know not, Waditaka. It is a secret of Manitou, and he will not tell it to us, but whether by chance or intent, the panther came at the same time the wolves did."

"He looks from here about three times the size of the ordinary cougar or panther, and the feathers of a lot of good arrows are standing out of him. Shall we cross and cut 'em out? We'll need 'em."

Roka shook his head.

"No, Waditaka," he replied. "We will not dare the ford again. We might be attacked a second time when we were separated, and not fare so well as we have now. Perhaps the great bears themselves would come. The arrows in the panther and in the wolves are precious to us, but we must do without them and make new ones."

"But ours is a great victory, a magnificent victory," said Hoton, teller of tales, who had been fairly bursting with unspoken speech. "I shall be the first to tell it to the village, when we return. I claim it as my right."

"It is yours, Hoton," said the leader, smiling. "Man of many words though you are, yet valiant warrior you be too. And none other is so fit as you to sing of it, when we return. We know, too, that the tale will not suffer in the telling, and that when it is spun our valor will grow."

Hoton, whom words alone could not now content, lifted up his voice, a full, Dakota bass, and sang in blank verse:

"To the deep river we came
The wild waters we swam;
From the woods rushed the wolves
Fierce, on our flank, they hung.

Inmu and Waditaka were alone,
Out of the tree the panther sprang;
Mighty was his long, yellow body,
Terrible were his teeth and claws.

The arms of Roka and Hoton tired not;
But our arrows flew in deadly showers,
Lo their comrades shot swiftly, too,
Into the heart the sharp points bit.

Fast fell to death the raging wolves,
The great panther is pierced through;
The bank is strewn with their slain,
Bright victory comes to Roka's men!"

The air rang with his triumphant song, and the others joined in the last verse, when he sang it over again.

"I think, Hoton," said Will, "that with your judicious compound of self praise and flattery you deserve to become some day a great medicine man, and adviser of the war chiefs."

"Why so?" asked the teller of tales.

"Because in the shooting of the arrows and slaying of the great beasts, you put two men first, just a little ahead of the rest, yourself, whom you value highly, and Roka, our chief, to whom you must concede a merit at least equal to your own."

"Did you not say, Waditaka, that I was fit to become a medicine man, and is not that what a medicine man would do?"

Roka himself smiled. He liked Hoton, who was in very truth what Will had called him, the minstrel of the band.

Roka decided that they had remained long enough on the bank, and, as they were now refreshed and warm again, they cast one glance upon the opposite bank, where the proofs of their prowess were so numerous and departed through the forests. But before they had gone far they heard snarling and snapping behind them on the other shore. Will shuddered. It was the wolves coming once more to devour their own dead.

Roka did not make the march long. He knew that his men, little though they showed it, had been shaken somewhat by the terrible battle at the ford, and they went into camp long before sundown, still among the huge trees which were free from undergrowth, thus disclosing at a great distance any enemy who might possibly approach. He also had a double supply of elk steaks served and they drew upon a precious little store of corn meal for thin cakes, at the cooking of which Tarinca and Wanmdi excelled.

"We will stay here a while," said the leader, as they sat before the fire, and ate with keen pleasure their meat and unusual bread. "In a day or two we will hunt more game, though four warriors will go on the search while six remain here. Game should not be hard to find, as we have seen its traces everywhere. Then we will make arrows to take the place of those we left in the bodies of the beasts on the other side of the river. A band such as ours, which is to explore, hunt and fight, travels on its arrows. Unless we make new ones we shall soon be helpless against any foes that may come."

The hunt was begun the next day by four warriors, headed by Tarinca, and they brought in a fine deer. They saw no sign of any enemy, and Roka knew it was because he had sent out four men instead of two. The master wolf was somewhere in the forest, watching them, but, cunning and wise, he would not attack four who had proved themselves to be of such mettle. The young men, born hunters, wanted to seek more game, but he would not allow it, saying they already had as much as they could carry, and now all of them could work at making arrows.

They spent a happy week there in the great forest, replenishing their supply of shafts, which they made with such speed and skill, filling every quiver to overflowing. They would have built wickiups had they needed them, but there were only flurries of rain, although a warm wind blew almost continually from the south, and the skies were soft and cloudy. Under such stimulating influences spring began to unfold rapidly in the mighty wilderness. Far above them in that high canopy of trees myriads of buds were bursting into bloom. Young grass was springing up from the earth, wherever the sun could reach it, and, in sheltered places, wild flowers bearing the most delicate shades of pink and purple and blue were coming into bloom. The majesty and sublimity of the great northern forest were now tempered by gentleness and beauty.

The young warriors, despite their hard work with the arrows, luxuriated. They varied their diet with excellent fish from several of the innumerable streams, and, at night, all save those who watched had many and untroubled hours of sleep. Roka, looking at his men, felt in very truth and not in fancy that they were acquiring a new stature and a new strength, like the great animals of the region, and, wise leader that he was, he rejoiced.

CHAPTER V

THE ATTACK BY AIR

THE peace about them was so deep and long that the youngest warriors began to think their dangers had passed. The absence of tracks, disclosing the proximity of great animals, was convincing to them. Surely the king wolf himself, having seen so many of his pack slaughtered, had given up the pursuit of such formidable game, and had gone in pursuit of easier victims. The great panther had been slain. They had seen his dead body fairly sprouting with arrows, and perhaps he had no brethren to avenge him. But Roka, and Pehansan who stood next to him in the command, refused to relax caution. They continued to insist that if any hunting was done the hunters should always be four and that the other six must remain together at the camp.

Elk and moose, of enormous size, were abundant, but they did not shoot at any of these large animals, preferring for the present the smaller game, and not willing to let the huge bodies rot in the forest or be devoured by wolves. While they enjoyed hunting keenly when hunting was necessary, they did not desire to kill game merely for the sake of killing. Their sport was always compounded with need, and, if the need did not exist, there was no sport.

"If we do not wish the meat of deer and buffalo," said Roka, "then let deer and buffalo live. The white people kill them too fast already."

"It will be a long time before white people come into this great northern sea of mountains," said Will.

"May they never come!" said Roka devoutly. "It may be that Manitou has reserved this region for the red man and that when the white man comes to its edges he will say, 'Stop, or perish beneath my thunderbolts!' "

"I hope you're right," said Will earnestly. "Some place should be set aside forever for hunters and forest rovers. There ought always to be a wilderness filled with mystery and the unknown."

He felt during this week in the giant forest that he was growing wilder than ever. Once or twice he took the revolver out of his belt and looked at it curiously. He had never fired it since they left the village. It seemed to be a sort of inverted anachronism. What had a man of ten thousand years ago to do with cartridges and pistols? The bow and the arrow were the weapons meet to his hand. But he kept the revolver, nevertheless. His reason told him a time would come when it would fill a need that bow and arrow could not.

They found fine quail in open places, and, although it took superlative skill to kill them with arrows, it was done, and they were a welcome addition to their larder. Fat wild ducks and wild geese were found on the numerous streams and they shot a number of them, very juicy and tender. So far as flesh was concerned they had feasts beyond those of any epicure in any capital of the world.

They still spared the moose and elk, and these colossal specimens of the deer tribe, feeling their immunity, hunted food near them, paying no attention to man, save to gratify a natural curiosity now and then. One evening just before twilight the ten were around the fire, preparing supper, when Will noticed a vast, heavy shouldered, hook-nosed figure, outlined against the setting sun, in truth almost in the center of the red beams. It was the largest moose that he had ever seen, the largest, he believed, that anybody had ever seen. By its side the ordinary deer would have been a dwarf.

Ungainly, but majestic and still, it gazed fearlessly at the ten warriors. The longer Will looked at it the bigger it seemed to grow, expanding steadily in the vivid beams.

"I think it must be the father, or at least the king of all the moose nation," he said. "I wonder if it means its fixed stare at us to be a warning that this is the land of the beasts, and man must not come."

"I do not know," said Hoton very gravely. "It is Inmu who reads the language of the animals, but the moose does not raise his voice, and so he cannot tell what is in the heart of the great deer."

"But Inmu does not always have to listen to voice. Sometimes he can read through its eyes what an animal thinks."

The face of Inmu was rapt. He had been gazing fixedly and a long time into the eyes of the moose.

"He is telling us," he said, "that though we have had days of peace and no foe has appeared, great changes will soon be upon us. Waditaka was right when he thought this the land of the animals only, in which man is forbidden. The moose himself tells us so. He bids us go!"

There was not one among them, not Will himself, who did not believe every word spoken by Inmu. Of course, he could read the heart of the moose through his eyes. Now that he told them the words of the animal they themselves understood.

"The horns of the moose can be terrible," said Roka, "but his hoofs can be far more so. The hoofs of the great bull elk before us would cut through our bodies, bone and flesh, like battle axes."

"Since we wage no war on the moose," said Hoton, "why should he wage war on us?"

"Because we have come into the country that belongs to him and the other great beasts," replied Roka. "It is true also that the moose cannot trust man. At any time, if we are pressed for food, we may turn upon him and slay him with our arrows. Can any wild animal trust man? He may know that the present is only a brief peace between him and man. No, my warriors, none of the beasts can ever feel safe for a long time in the presence of our kind."

"You tell the truth, Roka," said Will, regretfully, "and yet in the legends of the white people, to whom I have belonged, there is a story that man and the animals once dwelled together in peace on the earth."

"It is only a story, Waditaka. Once the great beasts pursued us and now we pursue them. Perhaps Manitou has ordained that this should be our day."

"The big moose is leaving us," said Will. "I feel that our period of ease and safety is over."

"We will start again tomorrow," said Roka. "Our quivers are now filled to overflowing with new arrows and we must be on the way."

The young warriors were willing enough to go. It was a wonderful region in which they had been staying, but they knew that others just as wonderful or more so lay beyond, and they were eager to penetrate new mysteries. They had been used to hardship and danger all their lives and fear did not enter the strong heart of youth. Although they did not know the meaning of the word, they had entered upon a great period of romance, and they intended to realize it to the full.

"We press on toward the east, do we not, Roka?" asked Will.

"Always, Waditaka, because we mean to reach the great plains there, where the northern buffalo herds range. It will take us several days, though, to pass out of this valley, and before we leave it we may have other deep streams to swim across."

"And if so, Roka, I suggest that all of us take the water side by side. That attack by wolves when Inmu and I stayed behind shook me up a lot."

Roka smiled.

"We shot well then," he said, "and covered your

retreat, but we might not do so well next time. It shall be as you say, Waditaka. We will all cross together."

The nights had become so temperate that after their cooking was over they allowed only a small fire to burn, but Roka never neglected the watch. Always two men were on guard, usually for periods of four hours, and on their last night there Will with Hoton kept the second watch.

Hoton was good company. He and Will could talk in low voices without disturbing the sleepers, and Hoton's imagination, always vivid, was very much alive then. His mind was upon their journey, and he predicted that they would come to great rivers, mountains higher than any they had seen before, and multitudes of huge wild animals.

"But we shall conquer all, rivers, mountains and beasts," he said.

"Among the white people they have an expression, 'a bad start, a good ending,' " said Will, "and, as tonight looks far from propitious, perhaps we can expect a brilliant march later on. Look, Hoton, how the clouds are hiding the stars from us!"

In the vast canopy of branches over their heads the buds had now burst into bloom, making a kind of bright veil between them and the sky, but the two young sentinels, gazing through it and upward, saw heavy clouds drifting up with slow certainty from the southwest. The warm wind though that blew steadily had no touch of damp in it, and the darkening vault did not seem to betoken rain. The wind presently increased and it sang through the lofty tree tops in an extraordinary manner. It seemed to the listening youths as if solemn music were being played far, far over their heads.

"The great trees always fill one with wonder and admiration," said Will. "It is said that there are vast trees in California five or six thousand years old, trees that so far as one knows never die a natural death, and perish only through fire or stroke of lightning. Trunks thrown down by lightning will lie on the ground half a thousand years before they begin to decay. The trees here may not be as enduring, but they must be as high. Their tops seem to touch the sky."

"Maybe Manitou makes them so tall because he wishes to reach down and touch their new green leaves with his hands."

"Or they stretch themselves to reach his feet. Whatever it may be, Hoton, I hope that neither the ax nor fire nor lightning will ever take down the noble forest about us. It grows much darker."

"So it does, Waditaka, and the wind playing among the buds three hundred feet or so above our heads has strange, new songs."

"It is true, Hoton, and there is a decided change in the note. It has to me a threatening, or at least a sinister sound. Either the state of the air affects the spirit or the spirit affects the state of the air. I cannot tell which."

"No one can ever tell. Look how the high treetops move and hark to the song of warning among them! It says:

"Warriors who watch,
Your rest is over.
Easy days are gone,
Earth and air threaten."

The slow darkness now became swift. It poured up from the southwest in a vast bank, black and almost solid, and always the sinister whistling and shrieking went on over their heads. The stars were blotted out. The last coals of the fire died, and it was with difficulty that the two sentinels, sharp and trained though their eyes were, could see the figures of their sleeping comrades. Will and Hoton stood close together, for the sake of company and because there was strength in union. Will knew that the young Dakota, believing thoroughly in the spirits of good and evil, was sure that the evil were abroad in the somber darkness, and that the good were in hiding. He felt that way himself, because, for the time at least, he was as much of a Dakota as the Dakotas themselves, and shared fully in all their beliefs.

"It's not a song far up there now, it's a crying," he said. "What does it portend?"

"I do not know, Waditaka, but I think that before long we shall see."

Will felt an extraordinary quiver in his blood, and his hair was cold at its roots. The sense of an immense desolation and of an uncanny air about them oppressed him. It was hard to keep a watch in such intense gloom, and one must rely on ear. Yet the angry and complaining cry of the wind was so full that he could scarcely hear anything else. He drew still closer to Hoton, and the two did not speak for a while. Then Will was sure that he detected a new note in the sound. It was like the whirr of vast wings, and he was quite sure, that for a few moments his heart ceased absolutely to beat. Then Hoton grasped him by the shoulder suddenly and with convulsive power dragged him down.

Will, as he fell, still grasped his bow and held it aloft. He saw a dark body and a great stretch of wings shoot through the air where his head had been. He saw great red eyes, a long, terrible beak, and the outstretched wrist that held the bow was scored across by a long talon, as if it had been burned with a red hot iron.

"Shoot, Waditaka, shoot!" cried Hoton, who was also lying on the ground.

As well as he could in his position Will sent arrow after arrow at the dark, flying figures, and Hoton shot even faster. The reply was a harsh and angry screaming, the beating of great wings, and the gleam of beak and talon. Then the darkness swallowed up the invaders and the wind whistled alone. Roka and the others had sprung to their feet, and were asking insistently what was the matter.

"An attack from the air," replied Hoton. "Great birds, of what kind I know not!"

"Down again!" cried Will. "They're coming back!"

He intended to drop to his knees, but as he went

a heavy wing struck his head and threw him flat.
For a few moments he was dazed, but he was conscious that the air was filled with the beating of wings,
the rush of bodies and the flashing of beaks and talons.
All the Dakotas were shooting arrows as fast as they
could, and were shouting to one another. Will struggled back into a sitting position and loosed a shaft
at a dark, heavily-feathered body just overhead. A
harsh scream of pain and ferocity was the reply and
he knew that he had hit, but probably had inflicted
no mortal wound, as the shadow disappeared, and with
it all the others. The second assault had been re-
pulsed and the assailants were gone in the thick night.

"Build up the fire!" cried Roka. "There is nothing
that prowlers, whether of earth or air, dread more
than fire and light!"

He was the first to kick away the ashes from a few
coals yet alive. Two of the men quickly blew them
into a flame, two more piled on dead wood at all
speed, while the others stood ready, arrow on the
string. The fire blazed up rapidly. Never had it
been more welcome to them and they built it higher
and higher, until it was a roaring pyramid, luminous
and brilliant, piercing the heavy, vaporous darkness
that had enfolded them, and casting ruddy gleams in
a wide circle. Then the ten stood, arms in hand,
trying to look beyond the light into the darkness and
then gazing at one another.

They were shaken, shaken as they had not been at
any other time on their great march. The face of
the stern and dauntless Roka was an ashy gray, and

Pehansan stared into the gloom with uneasy eyes. Beyond all question the ten feared whatever it was that flew beyond the circle of light, and they stood very close to the fire, which for tens of thousands of years had been man's greatest protection against fierce carnivora of all kinds. Once or twice they thought they heard the flapping of invisible but mighty wings out there in the sinister darkness, and a quiver ran through the blood of every man. But they were as brave as ever Achilles or Hector, these sons of the wilderness, and, despite the high beating of their hearts, they stood ready with bow and arrow. A long time passed, though, and nothing came.

"I think," said Roka, "that fire will guard us even better than our bows and arrows until the dawn. As there is so much light here, and we have certainly wounded some of them, I do not believe they will come back again. Is that your opinion, too, Pehansan?"

"It is, Roka, but if I tell you what is in my heart I will have to say I do not wish to sleep any more this night. I do not fear what walks on the ground, because we walk there too, and we meet the wolf, the panther and the bear on equal terms, but I do fear that which comes in the dark and in the air, because I cannot follow."

"You speak the mind of us all, Pehansan. We will await the dawn together. I think none care to sleep."

For further protection they built another fire and then sat between the two, talking in low voices, still under the spell of the heavy, vaporous gloom, and of the uncanny attack by the winged creatures of the darkness. It was a slow dawn, but it came at last, gray and pale, though a dawn nevertheless. The great trees took definite outlines before them as if they were coming out of a fog, and over the far mountains the dusk lifted.

Roka would not let his men stir from the fire until they had eaten a sustaining breakfast. Then they made a careful search, and picked up several large grayish feathers which no warrior in the band was able to identify.

"What do you think they were, Roka?" asked Will.

The leader shook his head as he looked with a doubtful eye at a huge feather left in his hand.

"I do not know, Waditaka," he replied. "They may have been great owls of the north, vast beyond any of which we have dreamed, used to preying on small animals, ignorant of man and so ready to attack him, or else mighty eagles which, like the animals, may grow here much larger than those farther south. We do not know, and we may never know. But this I do know. I hope never to be attacked again in such manner."

After they had eaten and their nerves were fully attuned they searched the ground minutely for their arrows, going even beyond any possible limit to which an arrow could have been shot, and recovered all but five.

"The five have been carried away in the bodies of the birds," said Roka. "It was not such bad shooting in the darkness and against flitting figures in the air."

The slight wound across Will's wrist was bound up.

116

Beyond that he paid no attention to it, as it was certain he would take no poison from it, owing to his youth and iron health. Then they gladly left the camp, which had been so pleasant hitherto, and as the day had turned from gray to gold their usual high spirits returned.

"Wonderful will be the tale we will tell when we return to the village," sang the irrepressible Hoton. "We have not only fought with the beasts of the earth, and conquered them, but we have fought with the terrible winged creatures of the air, and conquered them, too. Lo, the attack came in the dark, and it was fierce and terrible but the young warriors, directed and encouraged by Roka and Hoton, beat them off! Mighty are Roka and Hoton, and promising are the young warriors with them!"

"Hoton," said Will, "our great journey will always be remembered among the tribes, but those who made it may be forgotten, save one."

"And who is he, Waditaka?"

"None other than yourself, Hoton. A voice sometimes speaks louder than a deed. You will be the teller of what we have done, and you will sing its greatness. All the while it will be Hoton more, and the rest of us less, and the time may come, when it will be Hoton wholly and the rest of us nothing."

"No, Waditaka, no! Who am I to cheat you of your credit? The rest of you helped me much last night in the great battle against the birds! I shall always admit that without you I might not have beaten them off. It is true, too, that the five arrows carried away in the bodies of the birds were shot by me, but you nine did the best you could. No, Waditaka, no! The warriors who are to come generations from now will always say that Hoton had help. Nor will the singers and medicine men forget the names of those who helped him."

"It is the spirits of the air, the good spirits, that help us," said Tarinca, who had a deeply religious nature. "Without them and the aid Manitou gives to them we could do nothing. Often when we have been at the verge of death they have sent us aid and have delivered us."

"I do not deny the aid of the good spirits," said Hoton, "but the spirits will not do all for a warrior. If he does not go forth to battle, be it with man or beast, with a willing heart, then the spirits leave him to himself."

But the talk soon shifted to lighter themes. Their spirits were uplifted too much for austerity to prevail long. Hoton chanted more songs of the Dakota and now and then other warriors joined with him. Roka did not seek to silence them. They were quite sure the great forest was not inhabited by human beings, and by day they had no fear of the animals. Noise, in truth, while the sun shone was likely to drive away the mighty flesh-eaters.

They came to a creek, deep and swift, which required swimming, but they made ready and entered it all in a line, arriving at the farther shore without attack or the sign of it.

"It is because we were prepared and left no one behind who could be attacked," said Wanmdi. "The wolves knew it. They must be lurking behind us somewhere in the forest, and their king has been watching us, as he always does."

"Wanmdi is right beyond a doubt," said Roka, gravely. "The great wolf not only has his own eyes, ears and nose to tell him what we are doing, but also the evil spirits who whisper to him. While the good spirits are for us, the evil spirits are on the side of the fierce beasts."

"It may be, O, Roka," said Pehansan, a thoughtful man, as well as a great hunter, "that the beasts take another view, and that they think the spirits fighting on their side are good, while those who help us are bad."

"It is likely, Pehansan, and yet we cannot tell the difference between good and bad save through our own minds. We cannot see things as the beasts see them, and, if man and beast come into battle then the spirits that are on the side of man are good spirits to us."

The next night, to the great joy of them all, was very clear and bright, with a full and gleaming moon and hosts of friendly stars quivering and dancing in a dome of brilliant blue. Nevertheless they built their fire high again, as they wished to take no vain risks, and they sat about it, with bows strung and arrows ready, the glances of most of them turning toward the air rather than the earth. But Roka was confident that another winged attack would not occur.

"I think," he said, "that the vapors and darkness

of last night inflamed the great birds of the north. When the brain is heated, be it the brain of man, animal or bird, objects are not seen as they are, and they may have come against us, when they would not do so at any other time."

"The five arrows they took away in their bodies are proofs to them we'd best be left alone," said Will.

The night seemed to grow in brightness. All the great stars of the north blazed in the sky and hung low. The forest was filled with a silver radiance. They saw almost as well as in the full day, and Roka, choosing Will, Inmu and Hoton, made with them a wide circuit about the fire. They found nothing until the circle was almost complete, and then it was Hoton who pointed to the earth.

"See," he said, "the father of all the bears came for a while to watch us."

It was a vast footprint they looked upon, the largest any of them had ever seen. Will had learned to reconstruct almost any animal from the size of its track, and he judged that the bear, making the one before him, was at least double the size of the big grizzly of Idaho and Montana and for all he knew it might have, too, double the ferocity of the grizzly, which in all truth was fierce enough. In his heart, he was more afraid of this monstrous beast than of wolf or panther.

"Shall we follow its trail a little?" he asked Roka.

The leader nodded. The huge footprints veered toward the north, and the four followed them, keeping very close together. The ground was still comparatively free from undergrowth and Will was glad of it, as the eye always had a clear range for several hundred yards, and there was no chance for a giant bear, ambushed, to launch himself upon him at a single spring. Roka was deeply interested.

"He marches in a straight line," he said, "and so he must have had a plan. A bear without a plan would have wandered about. He saw as much of us, perhaps, as he wished, and now he is going somewhere. Ah, we now behold part of his plan!"

The trail of the great bear had merged suddenly with that of another as great, the second beast coming from the west, and the two then going on together.

"It may have been just his mate," said Pehansan. Roka shook his head doubtfully.

"Had time and place been ordinary it would have been so," he said, "but the thoughts of the bears are on war. Let us follow the trail, and see if something else does not happen soon."

A mile, and a third bear joined the first two, another mile and a fourth was added, the trail leading straight ahead, as if the definite plan still prevailed. Roka was still very curious, but he decided that they had gone far enough. They were now four or five miles from the camp, and if the bears had a plan they must disclose it themselves. They walked back to the camp, watching closely every clump of bushes that might conceal an ambushed beast, and they were glad when they saw the cheerful flames again, shining across the moonlit spaces. The six who had been left behind listened eagerly to the story of the four who returned.

"I think the next attack upon us will come from the bears," said Pehansan. "The wolves have failed, and the panthers have failed, though they do not give up their purpose. But both wolf and panther will step aside for a while to give the bear a chance. What think you, Roka?"

"As you do, Pehansan. Wolf and panther are both cunning. They know now that our arrows are flying death, and they are willing for the bear to try our mettle. And remember, my warriors, that the bear is wise. Those that follow us may be even wiser than those we have known, and as the bear is the strongest animal in the world of the Dakota we must be watchful and keep our arrows sharp."

A strong watch was posted, but nothing occurred that night, although they crossed a bear trail the next morning, and Roka inferred that several groups of the monstrous beasts had been about them in the dark. But as usual their buoyancy grew great in the bright sunshine, and they courted attack. The country, however, became more suitable to ambush. Heavy and almost continuous undergrowth appeared, and it was cut by many little streams marshy at the edges. Night approaching, they looked, as usual, for a suitable place in which to light their fire, and it required some time to find it, as they wished high, dry ground. They finally chose a knoll near the banks of a narrow and deep creek, which, like all others in that region, flowed with a swift, cold current, fed by the snows on the high mountains. Dead wood was drawn up in abundance and they built a high fire, which they always felt to be their prime necessity, their greatest guard against the wild beasts, and, when this task was finished, Will started toward the creek for water.

There was no undergrowth on the knoll but it was plentiful beyond it on every side, and Will was compelled to push his way through twining bushes. Bearing in mind the continuous caution of Roka that everything was to be feared, where the country afforded hiding and ambush, he carried his strong bow in his hand, and his quiver, well filled with arrows, over his shoulder.

The twilight had just come and the forest was turning gray, but the fire was a great core of light, and it seemed to Will as the low boughs closed behind him that he still felt its warmth on his back. He also heard the pleasant talk of his comrades, and once more his heart thrilled to them. They were his companions in a great adventure. They had set forth into the mighty northern wilderness, as much explorers and as daring as Columbus and his men. The forest was as unknown to them and as mysterious as the waters had been to the Italian.

Will at that moment looked a Sioux as much as any of Roka's men. His face was tanned dark by long exposure to winter storms and all other kinds of weather, and his dress was like theirs. Through long association he had acquired their manners and even their intonation of voice. It is true, too, that while he looked like a Sioux, he also acted like one, and, what was a more telling proof of a plastic nature and the power of propinquity and habit, he almost always thought like a Sioux. He looked upon the great animals with the same eyes as theirs, and like them he filled the air with good and evil spirits.

True to his character now as a son of the wilderness, he advanced through the bushes with caution, peering here and there, lest one of the wolves so much to be dreaded might be lurking in ambush. He was continually looking down instead of up, and at a point where the growth was thin he was startled by a tearing sound almost over his head. A quick glance showed him four great legs and above them a huge, looming body.

Will sprang back by impulse, but a thick pine bush stopped him, and then, by the same impulse, he snatched an arrow from his quiver and fitted it to the bowstring. The bull moose, vast, lowering and formidable, was as much startled as he. But, interrupted at his feeding, by the insignificant creature that had come stealing on two legs through the bushes, he turned savagely and charged. Will, swift and skillful though he had become had time to let fly only a single arrow. It struck the great beast in the shoulder and was buried deep there, but it was only a fillip to the anger stored up in twenty-five hundred pounds of tremendous vitality.

The moose struck with the terrible sharp hoofs that would have cut the lad into shreds, but he leaped aside and the shoulder of the animal striking him on the head sent him whirling. He fell among the bushes, but had the courage and tenacity to cling to his bow. The bull, puffing fiercely and anxious to finish the foe that had stung him, turned and leaped again, bring-

ing his hoofs down like tremendous cutting knives.
It was only the unseeing rage of the great beast that
saved Will then. He was prone, but half hidden in
the low bushes. One hoof grazed his legging and cut
it away as if it had been shaved off by a razor, and
the moose drew himself back to spring again.

Aroused by his appalling peril, Will gathered his
strength, rolled over and over, and the next leap of
the moose landed his four hoofs where he had been,
but from which place he was now a half dozen feet
away. Then he sprang to his feet, fitted another arrow
to the string and shot it. But he was impeded so much
by haste and the bushes that it merely struck the side
of the bull, ran under the skin and came out again.
Then the huge beast went mad. The blood, pouring
from his side, and his eyes distended, he crashed
through the bushes in such fierce pursuit of Will that
the lad did not have time to discharge another arrow.
He knew that roaring and puffing death was hot on
his heels, and he doubled and dodged like a frightened
rabbit pursued by a lynx.

He ran behind a great tree, came to a small gully
and darted up it. The moose missed him and then
crashed away at a great pace toward the north. Will,
after running a couple of hundred yards, realized that
he was not followed any longer, and crouched panting
in the gully. He had not thought to call for help, but
the warriors, hearing the noise in the thicket, had
come at speed.

"Waditaka! Waditaka!" they called.

"Den!" (here) panted Will in Sioux, and then the

head of Pehansan appeared above the bushes, followed by those of Inmu, Hoton and Tarinca.

"What is it, Waditaka?" asked Pehansan. "The thicket is torn as if it had been threshed about by a whirlwind! You look as if you had been running for your life, and your legging hangs only by a string!"

"I have been running for my life, O, Pehansan," replied Will in a whimsical tone, yet one full of relief, "and as you see, I ran well and with success. Among the bushes, where I looked too low, I walked straight into the biggest moose that ever lived, the king of all his tribe. He was the king beyond all doubt, because he had his crown and diadem on his head, and carried his scepter in his hand."

" 'Crown!' 'diadem!' 'scepter!' I do not understand those words! Have the senses of Waditaka gone away for a little while?"

"I forgot. Maybe my senses did go wandering for a space. They had cause enough. I was attacked by a gigantic bull moose, Pehansan. I wasn't doing anything to him, and it was wholly unprovoked. He charged me all over the thicket. I fired two arrows into him. I filled him with pain and anger, but I don't think I did him any serious hurt. It was one of his hoofs that cut my legging loose, and I'm grateful to Manitou that he didn't cut any closer. When he missed me in this blessed little gully he charged away, raging, toward the north, and the faster and longer he goes the better I'll like it."

The mouth of Pehansan slowly widened into a broad smile.

"I cannot but believe that Waditaka speaks the truth," he said. "He and the moose are well parted."

"As I said, I was doing nothing to him."

"But often we attack the moose when it is doing nothing to us. Can we expect *Ta* (moose) to be more friendly than man?"

"I don't care whether he is friendly or not just now, Pehansan, but I want him to be distant."

"I should have been here," said Hoton loftily. "With my swift arrows I would have slain *Ta,* and, when the rest of you came running, I would have been standing with one foot on his body, singing the song of the great hunter."

"Perhaps," said Pehansan, "and perhaps also we would have found your body, cut into little pieces by the hoofs of the moose. We are glad that Waditaka has escaped. *Ta,* wounded and enraged, is a terrible animal to face."

"But I would have faced him and I would have sent the arrows into his body fast enough to make an unbroken stream in the air," said Hoton.

"It was lucky either for you or the moose, Hoton, that you were not here," said Pehansan, "but it is quite clear that another is now added to the list of our enemies among the great beasts. *Ta* belongs with *Xunktokeca* (wolf), *Warankxi* (bear), *Inmutanka* (panther) and the great birds, the kind of which we know not, but which may be *Wanmdi* (eagle) or *Hiyankaga* (owl). We have one more enemy to meet, and there are times when the hoofs of *Ta* are as bad as the teeth and claws of *Warankxi*."

They returned to the fire, and Roka, who had been anxious, shared to the full Pehansan's belief that they now had a new enemy in the moose.

"Waditaka is not to blame," he said, "because by his story—and Waditaka always tells the truth—the combat was forced upon him. It seems, Pehansan, that we shall have to meet all the animals in battle before our great journey is finished."

"But we have the young men with whom to meet them," said Pehansan, looking around at the gallant faces.

"That is true," said Roka. "Now, Hoton, tell us the story of that forefather of ours who saw the great buffalo herds coming for days and days out of the vast caves thousands of miles to the south."

And Hoton, with burning eyes and vivid gesture spun the tale, while the others sat and listened and the fire flamed and flickered.

CHAPTER VI

WARANKXI

WILL repaired his legging with needle and bone
and thread of sinew, before he went to sleep,
and he was devoutly glad of the quarter inch
of space that had saved his leg from the hoof of the
moose. He was an adept at the work, and Roka
watched him with an approving eye as he handled bone
and sinew with skill and speed.

"He is a true Dakota now," the leader said in an
aside to Pehansan.

"But the day will come when his own people will
call to him," said the tall warrior. "We are what we
are born. If you and I, Roka, were placed among
white men, no matter how well we might like them,
no matter how much they might like us, we would see
some time or other, though thousands of miles away,
the tall tepees of the Sioux, and we would hear the
thunder of the buffalo herds on the endless plains.
Then we would have to go."

"It is the truth, Pehansan. Yet Waditaka is ours
on the great journey, as much as Inmu, or Hoton, or
the others. Nor will the time ever come, when he will
be willing to raise a hand against any of the people of
Xingudan's village."

"It is as you say, Roka. Though the Dakota and the white men be at war, Waditaka would never let fly an arrow at you, or me, or any of his comrades."

Will completed his repairs, and Hoton, at the same time, finished his dramatic tale of the way in which the myriads of buffalos were continually renewed. Then Roka commanded them to build the fire higher, and, as usual, he posted guards of two in relays. He also gave orders the next day that no man was to leave the camp or the band on the march alone. It was evident that besides the dangers of which they knew, there were dangers yet unknown to be dreaded, and he would not risk the loss through carelessness of a single one of his warriors. Roka was not only proud of his young men, for every one of whom he entertained a strong affection, but he felt that it would be a great feat if they could make the mighty journey, and he could bring them all back alive and well to the village of Xingudan.

A peaceful night was granted to them, and they resumed the advance the next morning, coming to a limited stretch of open country, much like a prairie, free from all kinds of tree growth, except little clumps of bushes here and there. It was not more than three or four miles across, the great forest rising again at the far edge, and beyond that the line of mighty mountains, blue on the slopes, and white at the crests with eternal snow.

The prairie itself was rich in sylvan beauty. Under the warm airs that had been floating up many days from the south the grass had grown high and its first delicate green was turning to a deeper hue, but its grassy surface was thickly sown with vivid wild flowers of varied colors. Down the center flowed a creek of deep green fed, like all the streams of that region, by melting snows. On its edge were some low vines bearing early berries which the young warriors ate with great delight, the berries forming a pleasant variation from their perpetual diet of game. The whole prairie was filled with splendid golden sunshine, in which the ten reveled.

"I think," said Roka, "that this prairie opens out in the great forest as a breathing place."

"Or maybe," said Pehansan, "it was put here by Manitou that we might stop a while and see the sky without any boughs between. The mighty forest is magnificent and noble and we admire it, but there comes a time when we wish to gaze up at the unbroken blue."

They built their fire near the creek and Capa and Tatokadan shot a deer less than half a mile away, a task they found uncommonly easy, as the game was almost tame, showing conclusively that man had been a stranger there. In truth, the prairie fairly swarmed with the different kinds of the deer tribe, ordinary deer, mule deer, and several gigantic elk. They also saw a small herd of the plains buffalo, grazing quietly near the northern end of the open ground, and Roka and Pehansan had no doubt that on the slopes toward which they were advancing they would find the gigantic wood bison. Wolves of the smaller kind were hanging on the fringes of the buffalo herd, but they saw none of the great timber wolves, their tenacious foes.

"Nothing can happen to us here," said Will, as they sat by the fire and ate their deer, sauced with berries. "It is too peaceful and beautiful. Listen to the birds. They didn't sing in the great forest, but they have plenty of voice now."

Although it was twilight the birds darted in little flashes of blue or gray from one clump of bushes to another and from full throats poured forth their joy. Will found their music uncommonly soothing, and it confirmed him in his opinion that here, in truth, was a place of rest.

"Inmu," he said, "you've interpreted for me the talk of the wild animals, now can you also tell me what the birds are saying?"

"No, Waditaka," replied the Lynx, "I cannot; they merely chatter and trill and their chattering and trilling is without meaning."

"It's just chattering and trilling to you, Inmu, because, while you understand the animals, it is evident that you don't understand the birds. Now, while I don't understand the animals I do understand the birds. Each to his own gift!"

"I do not dispute it, Waditaka. What, then, are the birds saying?"

"The gray one in the bush to our right, who is trilling with such vigor and enthusiasm, says to his comrades: 'Look! Look, my friends! Behold the men who have come into our land! They build a great fire and sit beside it! They have sharp arrows, but the

arrows are not for us! The men are our friends!
They like us! They like to hear our songs! They
would not harm us! Their sharp arrows are for the
bears and wolves!"

"Very good, Waditaka," said the wise Roka. "That,
no doubt, is what the gray bird is saying."

"But the green one in the bush on the other side of
the fire is singing a different song," said Hoton.

"How do you know, O Crow?" asked Roka.

"Because I, too, can understand the words of the
birds," replied Hoton, "and I have been listening especially to the words of the green one, since they are
much more important than those of his gray comrade."

"Then what song of so much importance is the
green bird singing, my Hoton?"

"He is saying over again the same great truth that
he said just now. Listen! Here go the words: 'Who
is the tall young warrior sitting between Waditaka
and Inmu? Do you ask me that, O my comrades?
Behold how handsome and strong he is! Look at his
lofty head, his fearless gaze, his noble manner! If you
could gaze into his eyes you would see them filled with
truth and honesty and courage! Know you that he
would face twenty hostile warriors, alone and una-
fraid! There is none so wise, so brave and so just
as he, save, perhaps, the wise Roka! And then you
ask me, my comrades, who he is! Why do you ask
me? I am ashamed of you, my comrades, for asking
such a question! His fame has spread all over the
world! That is the matchless young warrior, the

pride of the whole Dakota nation, the flower of the Indian race, the famous warrior, the invincible Hoton! Listen to that renowned name, and never forget it again!' Now they all sing together, the gray ones, the blue ones, the brown ones and the green ones: 'Hoton! Hoton! Hoton! Hoton the Strong! Hoton the Wise! Hoton the Brave! Hoton the Swift! Hoton the Great Hunter! Hoton the Mighty Warrior! Hoton! Hoton! Hoton!' Ah, it is surely a grand, beautiful and true song!"

They listened to him with admiration, and, after the silence, save for the singing of the birds, that followed, the wise Roka said solemnly:

"Hoton, great are your gifts. The words that you take from the bird's mouth may be as you tell them to us, because none of us can say that they are not. But, Hoton, when you are an old man and you die, and you are buried in your grave with your pony, and you rise up a warrior again and go off to the great hunting grounds, Manitou will say to those about him: 'Here comes Hoton! Put him where the deer are largest and thickest, because if you do not he will talk to me so much that I shall have no time to receive the other warriors who are always coming in a stream.'"

"And it will be a just reward for me," said the indomitable Hoton.

"And now, my youths, to your blankets," said Roka, "for at dawn we start again on the great journey."

All of them awoke when the sky began to brighten in the east, and Hoton and Capa went down to the edge

of the creek to gather for their breakfast some of the
early berries which afforded such a grateful relief,
while Will and Inmu began to build the fire anew, the
others helping with different tasks. Will was bent
over the coals, blowing them into new flame, when
he was startled by a roar, so fierce and savage that
it made his blood quiver. The roar was followed
instantly by a cry, a cry wrenched from a human being
by mortal pain.

Will straightened up, instinctively seized his bow
and quiver, and turned toward the creek whence the
sounds had come. He saw one of the great bears of
the north, hideous and monstrous, reared up and
crushing Capa between his forelegs. The bow and
quiver of the young warrior had dropped to the
ground, and he seemed lifeless. But Hoton, the talker,
Hoton the boaster, Hoton the valiant and faithful,
stood a bare ten feet away, and he was sending arrow
after arrow like shafts of lightning straight into the
throat of the monster.

The grip of the bear was about to close, and he was
also reaching down his tremendous fangs for a bite
which would fairly take off the head of the young
Dakota, when Hoton, shouting fiercely, ran in and
smote him with all his might across the mouth with
his bow. The bear dropped Capa, who fell senseless
to the ground, and struck a mighty blow at Hoton
with one paw. Well it was for the valiant boaster
that he wore a thick and padded fur cap and that he
was so close in, as the heel of the paw struck him on

the head, but the claws, projecting like spikes of steel and as deadly, went beyond.

Hoton fell, as if he had been shot, squarely across Capa, and the bear, roaring with rage, struck blindly into the air with his terrible spiked paws. Then he turned to grope for his fallen foes, but the delay of a few moments had saved them from being torn to pieces.

The valiant Dakotas, Roka and Pehansan at their head, rushed forward and poured a stream of arrows into the bear, which was a terrible object, standing far higher than a man, shaft after shaft protruding from his body, striped now with red by his flowing blood. The warriors, shouting with all their might to divert his attention from their fallen comrades, attacked him in a half circle.

The bear whirled here and there to face his foes, who were stinging him in every part of his body with their fiery little darts. A crafty and cunning animal at most times, he was now quite mad with rage and pain. He also had been down among the vines at the creek's brink, eating the berries which were so delicious to his taste, when the two insignificant creatures, walking on two legs, came there in search of the same savor, and almost ran into him. He had never seen man before, and having grown up the unchallenged monarch of the wilderness, feeling prodigious strength in every ounce of his vast body, and knowing his tremendous teeth and claws to be weapons unrivaled by any other, he had expected to sweep away without trouble the impertinent intruders upon his berry ground.

He had struck down the first two who came, though he had been stung often while doing it, but now he was faced by a swarm of the little creatures who sent their sharp darts into him from every side. He forgot all about the first two, and with eyes blinded by blood, he struck random blows at the swarm. He did not notice that they steadily drove him away from the two who lay on the ground, the one across the other, the tactics of the wise Roka, who did not forget, even in those wild moments, to protect the unconscious Hoton and Capa from a chance blow of that terrible paw.

The bear, after the manner of his kind, kept up a continuous growling and snarling as he fought his elusive foes. He was losing much blood but he felt no decline in his strength. His body was so vast and his hide so thick that no arrow had been able to inflict a mortal wound, and his vitality was so immense, unexcelled by that of any other animal in the world, that he believed he could wage the battle until he wore out his enemies, light and agile though they might be.

The rage of the bear mounted steadily. He had known nothing else to stand before him. The great bull moose, even in his anger, did not care for an encounter with that prodigious, hulking figure, and the fierce timber wolves, numerous though their pack might be, turned aside. But the new creatures, two of whom he had struck down so easily, danced before him, kept beyond the reach of his claws and teeth, and

yet struck him from a distance. The pain from so
many sharp darts increased, until it grew unbearable.
Then, roaring his anger and dismay, he turned, and
for the first time in his life ran, crashing through
vines and bushes, leaving a red stream as his trail,
fear tugging at his heart until it grew into panic and
dismay.

He not only ran, but he ran as he had never run
before. The speed of the huge body was amazing.
It beat down bushes and vines, clove a way across
the prairie and then into the forest, always hurried
to new speed by the shouts behind, and the continuous
stinging of the fiery little darts. In the dense forest
the great bear disappeared, the pursuit ceased, and he
sought some remote covert where he could lie, lick
his bleeding wounds and think of revenge.

Roka had stopped his eager young warriors at the
edge of the dense thickets. He knew that the bear
might turn on them there, where they would be so
hampered that they could not use their bows.

"We will not follow the bear into his hiding," he
said, "but stay here on the open prairie where we have
the advantage. Like the big bull moose, he has carried away some of our arrows in his body, but it is
better to lose our arrows than our lives. We will now
return and see how much breath is left in the bodies
of Hoton and Capa."

The young warriors were eager to go into the forest
and slay the bear at any risk, but they knew that Roka
spoke words of wisdom. Moreover, they were anxious
to look after their fallen comrades. As they returned

to the scene of the battle's beginning they uttered a delighted shout when they saw Hoton and Capa on their feet, but leaning against each other, the valiant two staggering forward to meet them.

"How now, O teller of tales and singer of songs, O boastful Hoton!" said Roka. "How did it happen that when the bear struck you on the head you did not strike him back as hard?"

"O, wise Roka," replied the indomitable Hoton, "I did not strike him back because I did not wish to spoil sport. If I slew him then and there you and the others would have had no chance to take part in the hunt, and so, wise Roka, I held my hand."

"A good reply, O brave boaster. Sometimes it is almost as well to be ready with words as with deeds, and I say to you, Hoton, in the presence of all, that you are ever ready with both. It was a gallant act to rush under the claws and teeth of the demon bear and save the life of your comrade, Capa. I have seen many valiant deeds but I have never in my life seen one more valiant, Hoton, the brave."

For once Hoton, the boaster, was at a loss for words, and he merely said, from the depths of a grateful heart:

"I thank thee, Roka."

Both Hoton and Capa needed repairs. The brave boaster's head was still ringing from the glancing blow of the bear's paw, and although he tried to hold himself erect the world reeled before him, and there were myriads of black specks before his eyes. Capa's shoulder was torn and bleeding, and Roka and Pehansan set to work at once, bathing it carefully and binding it up. They also hunted among the bushes for herbs of which they knew, and made him a strong tea, a powerful decoction that soothed his nerves and induced sleep. Then they rolled him in his robe by the fire and bade him seek sleep, which he soon found.

"Now his wound will heal rapidly," said Roka, "because he is young and pure of life, but the brain within the head of Hoton will ache for a day or two. One cannot stand beneath the stroke of a bear's paw and go unharmed. It will be best for us to stay here until they are well."

He was right about Hoton, as the valiant boaster endured severe pains in his head for a day and night, though he would make no complaint. But at the beginning of the second day they died down and by the end of it were gone entirely. Capa's shoulder, as Roka predicted, healed rapidly, and he would have only the faint trace of a scar, which on occasion he could show proudly.

The others hunted a little on the prairie, and set snares at the edge of the creek for wild ducks, which they prized highly, but they were very cautious about the berry patches, never approaching them until they were quite sure that another one of those terrible lumbering forms was not hidden in the depths of the bushes. On the second morning after the battle they saw proof that a bear had been there again, as the bushes and vines were torn and trampled in a new place.

"I don't think the one we fought could have come

back," said Will, "at least, not yet. Too many arrows were sticking in his body to allow a return visit so soon."

"It must have been his mate," said Pehansan. "Of course, he had a mate, and he told her about the berries and the fight. She wanted the berries so much that she overlooked the danger from us, and in the night came after them. Often, Waditaka, the she-bear is bolder and fiercer than the male."

"She was truly bold, Pehansan, to come back here after the reception her mate got."

It happened that Will and Pehansan were the very two who soon had proofs of the female bear's savagery. They were hunting on the north side of the prairie, it being their fancy to secure a young doe, and jerk the tender flesh for their journey, when they chanced to come near the dense underbrush that grew here in the forest. The very doe they wanted was not more than a hundred yards away, and kneeling in the grass, which had now grown high, they were creeping forward for certain arrow range. But before they were within the required distance the she-bear, almost the equal of her mate in size, and doubt-less his superior in ferocity, charged from the thickets with a mighty roar, and had covered half the distance to them before they could spring to their feet.

Will and Pehansan did not pause to fight. Their experience with the first bear had shown them that arrows sent by the mightiest arm might be of no avail, and bow in hand they took to flight toward the camp, now a full three miles away. Pehansan's legs were very long, and they were as strong as if they were made of steel. Will was an uncommonly fleet runner, but never before had the two made such time as they now made across that little prairie, so green and spangled so beautifully with flowers of varied and vivid hues.

"Shall we turn and loose a few arrows at her?" gasped Will.

"Not now," replied Pehansan in the same strained tones. "They would but sting her into greater speed."

"But she gains on us!"

"Here is the creek before us, flowing in a narrow bed between high banks. We may dodge her there!"

They leaped into the stream and ran swiftly with its current. The she-bear came to the edge, having lost sight of them among the bushes that grew at the fringe, sniffed for their trail and then caught the pleasant perfume of rich, luscious berries hanging on vines not ten yards away. Perhaps her mind, despite her immense size and undoubted ferocity, had little continuity, as she instantly forgot all about the two bipeds she had been pursuing, and began a luxurious feast on the berries.

Pehansan was the first to notice they were no longer pursued, and drew Will to a halt.

"The she-bear has stopped and is eating berries," he said. "Much as she craved our flesh, Waditaka, she likes better what grows on a vine, and I am glad it is so, because I have run enough."

"And I, too," said Will. "Look at that beast! Look how she is clawing at those berries and sweeping them into her mouth by the pawful! Enjoying herself after making us run for our lives! Pehansan, what makes the bears in this part of the world grow so big?"

"I do not know, Waditaka. Manitou has willed that it should be so, and it is so. What need is there for us to inquire why?"

"Shall we go back a little and sting her with an arrow or two? She has no right to be feasting and enjoying herself, after making us run for our lives until we have no breath left."

"No, Waditaka, no! Do you not see that it is wise to leave alone the great bear of the north, when it is leaving you alone? Her mate carried away our arrows in his body and we lost them. Even if we should escape her second attack she would take our arrows with her in the same manner into the forest, and it is hard work making arrows."

"True, O, Pehansan, and maybe you're right when you say the female bear is more to be dreaded than the male. She certainly shows no fear of us or of anybody, but goes on tearing to pieces a whole berry patch that should be ours."

The two stood on a little swell watching the work of devastation go on, and their feeling was one of mortification. It hurt their spirit to be defied thus by an animal, but clearly she was queen of the realm, though in very truth a savage queen.

"If I had my rifle, now back in the village, and plenty of cartridges, I would go for her," said Will.

"But it is back in the village and you will not go for her," said Pehansan.

Tired of watching the huge brute devour the berries they went slowly back to camp, and related what they had seen, Roka confirming Pehansan's judgment in leaving the she-bear alone. The next day four bears of the same gigantic kind appeared among the berries, which were now plentiful along the banks of the creek. The she-bear of the day before was not among them, as the acquaintance of Will and Pehansan had been so full that they would have been able to recognize her. This was an entirely new group, and it became apparent to the Dakota that they had pitched their camp in a dangerous place. Berries were good to the palate of a young warrior and they were also good to the palate of a great bear. So, they were likely to bring bear and warrior together.

But Roka and Pehansan refused to move to a new site. Their pride was stirred. They would not go forth and attack the bears, but they would not let the fear of them drive them from camp. The younger warriors were eager to send a shower of arrows among the feeding brutes, but they dared not disobey the wise leader.

The bears, increased presently to six and afterward to eight, roamed along both sides of the creek, tearing at the vines, swallowing the berries by the mouthful, and having a truly merry bear time.

"They enjoy the berries all the more," said Roka, "because they are perhaps the first of the season."

"And that is doubtless why so many of 'em are here," said Will. "They have passed the word on to one another that the prairie is full of just what they want, and so they come. But the one we wounded isn't here. We'd know him by the arrows sticking out of his body."

The bears were having a glorious time, and it was quite evident that they had not met the wounded one, as he would have told them that the new creatures who hurled pain from a distance were to be dreaded. As it was, they showed the most utter indifference and a complete disrespect of Roka's band, feeding along the creek until they came to within a few hundred yards of the camp. Roka deemed it wise to build up the twin fires and keep the warriors between them.

"I know the great bears of our own mountains," he said, "but these are so much larger that they might attack us, when the others would let us alone, if we made no hostile movement against them."

"Behold," said Inmu, in tones of deep disgust. "They now play with one another! Having eaten their fill they shout their contempt for us by enjoying their sports almost within bow shot of our camp. It is a great insult to us, O Roka!"

"It is as you say, Inmu," replied the leader, his eyes darkening. "They act as if we were not on the face of the earth, and it is hard for a Dakota to endure an insult from Warankxi. But it must be done. Courage alone does not make a warrior great. He must be cunning and wise also. He must know when to hold his hand, and he must even know, too, when it is time to run away. To run away is one of the hardest of all things for a young warrior to do, but when he is older and wiser it grows easier."

"You speak words of wisdom, as you always do, O Roka," said Hoton, who now, free from his headache, had the buoyancy of mind that always follows recovery from ill, "but I will challenge the beasts. I will dare them to come here within the fires and attack us."

"Very well, Hoton, if you wish it," said Roka, indulgently. "The sound of your voice, whether you say anything or not, is always pleasant in my ear."

Hoton stood at his full height and turned a defiant face to the monstrous group.

"Come, O, bears!" he shouted in a voice like rolling thunder. "Here is man, a new foe of yours, man who has been disputing with the giant wolves the leadership of the forest, and who is ready to dispute it with you! You weigh as much as a man many times over, and his teeth and nails are puny compared with your mighty claws and fangs! Then come and see how he will meet you! Though his body is little by the side of yours his brain is great compared with yours! Why do you stay back, O, cowardly beasts!"

"Hoton would not make such a challenge," said Inmu, "if he did not have the fires about him. He knows that the bears, like all the other animals, dread the flame."

"And that," rejoined Hoton, "is why I am so much more a lord of the forest than the bear is. I know when to issue a challenge and where. The bear does not. Did I not say that my brain was bigger than that of the bears?"

"But the bears don't accept your challenge," said Will. "They pay no attention to it."

Much to Hoton's disgust he told the truth. The huge brown animals could not have failed to hear him, but apparently he and his comrades did not exist for them. They continued their gambol, pushing one another and running about, as if they never meant evil to any creature.

"Louder, Hoton," said the pious Tarinca. "These are deaf bears. If they heard a challenge from a mighty warrior like Hoton they would not stay back."

Hoton refused to answer. He merely glared in silent indignation.

"At least," said Will, "we shouldn't let 'em eat up all our berries. We ought to drive 'em off in some manner."

"I think I know a way," said Roka. "We will try burning arrows."

It took them a long while to shred down the inside of bark with their hunting knives until it formed a kind of tow which they could attach, flaming, to their arrows near the head, but the bears gave them plenty of time. After a period of athletic sport they returned to the demolition of the berries, and then they took a second turn at play. By this time the burning arrows were ready and the ten advanced very cautiously toward them. It was evident that they were not noticed at first, but, when they were about half way, Will saw the largest of the bears raise his head, sniff the air and then look at them.

"Fire now," said Roka, who knew that it would

be dangerous to go any nearer. "But be sure you hit."

He told off rapidly the bears at which each was to aim, and directed them, as soon as their shafts were sped, to run back at all speed to their place between the fires. The members of the monstrous group, growling ominously, were already advancing, and ten bowstrings twanged together. The flaming arrows sang through the air, and not one missed. They were buried deep in the great bodies and the bunch of fire attached to every one burned on.

All the bears roared together. The pain of the barb was not nearly equal to the pain from the fire that flamed against their bodies. They rushed forward in their swift, lumbering fashion against the impudent creatures that had stung them in a double way, but the warriors darted back with incredible speed to their fires, seized torches and swinging them aloft began to leap and shout.

The bears paused. They were scorched with pain and mad with rage, but the fire daunted them. It was something they could not fight. It hurt horribly, and if they struck it with their paws it hurt all the more. Smaller parts of it were alive and clinging to them, where it was devouring hair and hide and eating a way into their bodies. The agony was terrible and, monarchs of the wilderness though they had been, they turned and fled across the creek, and over the prairie and into the forest beyond.

"Ah!" said Hoton, throwing down his torch as the bears began their flight, "I have driven them away."

"And I suppose the rest of us had nothing to do with it!" said Will.

"You helped me. All of you helped me. I admit it, Waditaka. Ho, *Warankxi!* Why do you go so fast? We are here waiting for you! We are much smaller than you are! Why do you not come and eat us? I am Hoton, the famous Dakota warrior, of whom all of you have heard! Come and fight me! Stop, you cowards! Ah! Do the arrows sting? And do the little fires burn against your sides? Know now that man is king of all the world! That the red man is king of men! That the Dakota is king of the red men, and that I, Hoton, am king of the Dakota, the greatest warrior of them all! Now, they are gone! The forest has swallowed them up, and they may not come again, because they know I am here!"

"I think you speak the truth, when you tell us they will not come back," said Roka, thoughtfully. "The bunches of fire will soon drop from their sides, but they will not forget. We have conquered them on this day, but remember that we may be attacked on other days, when we have no fire to use against them. We will be safe from them though as long as we are here on the prairie."

The leader predicted aright. No more bears came to the berry patches, but Will and Inmu, who went to the edge of the forest seeking a species of large, fat, and exceedingly juicy quail abundant on the prairie, caught a glimpse of a long, lean, yellow body lying on the great bough of an oak.

"*Inmutanka!*" (Panther) said Will. "It seems

scarcely right that so treacherous an animal should bear the same name as my adopted father back in the village."

"Many of us bear the names of animals," said Inmu, "but it does not follow because your father is named Inmutanka that he is treacherous and blood-thirsty like *Inmutanka* there in the tree. I am Inmu, in your language the Lynx, but I cannot sit on a bough and snarl and spit and scream like the real *Inmu*."

"I hope not. Shall we send an arrow at *Inmutanka?*"

"It is a temptation, Waditaka, but perhaps it is better not to do so. He might run away, or in his excitement he might attack us. We do not know. Roka does not wish us to take any idle risk."

They withdrew a little and, bows and arrows ready in case they should be attacked, watched the panther, which presently raised its great head and glared at them from cruel, yellow eyes.

"It is as large as the one we killed," said Inmu. "Maybe it is his brother, and has come here for revenge, waiting until we enter the forest, when it can drop from a bough upon our heads."

"If I thought that, Inmu, I'd open upon it now with my arrows."

The young Dakota laughed.

"Do not be afraid, Waditaka," he said. "These be great warriors with whom we march, and Roka and Pehansan, who are older than the rest of us, see and hear everything in the forest. The panther will not leap upon us, at least, not upon the band, when we are not expecting him."

They left the panther and returned to the camp, where Roka, when he had heard their story, gave orders that nobody should enter the forest for the present.

"Spring is coming very fast," he said, "and soon all the trees will be clothed in leaves. Then it will be hard to see the giant panthers as they lie along the low boughs. Together we need not fear them, but if one of us should be alone a great beast might spring upon him."

The young warriors obeyed him, but it required much self restraint, as they were eager to go in the woods and prove to the panther that they were masters. They were born hunters and fighting men. The Dakota had been nothing else, through all the generations, and they liked a challenge from *Inmutanka* as little as they liked one from *Warankxi*. But Roka was a stern leader, and, fearing him, as well as respecting him, they obeyed him.

"What do you think has become of the great wolf king?" Will asked Pehansan. "We have not heard from him now for many days."

"And that, Waditaka, makes him all the more dangerous," replied the tall warrior. *"Xunktokeca* is the most cunning of all the wild beasts, which makes him most to be dreaded. He is more terrible even than the great bear. He thinks further and remembers longer than any other wild animal. I know that the king wolf with what is left of his band is in the forest, awaiting us. Perhaps he has gathered to himself new wolves, and now has a pack larger than before."

Will was not frightened. He had implicit confidence in himself, and in the courage and skill of these gallant comrades of his, but Pehansan was right. The very next day they saw the tracks of wolves at the north end of the prairie, where the group of buffalo fed, and came upon the partially devoured body of a calf about half grown.

"They pulled him down, because he wandered too far from the big bulls and cows," said Pehansan. "It may have been the king wolf himself that threw him. It was a foolish calf. His father and his mother had told him often to keep within the ring of their great bodies. They smelled the hungry wolves and saw them, but this silly calf was reckless. He did not obey and he paid for it with his life. Do you, Inmu, and do you, Waditaka, learn your lesson from it. I have seen the look on your faces when you came to the edge of the deep forest. You wanted to go into it, no matter what the wise Roka said, and hunt the panther."

"We admit the wish," said Will, "but we did not go. We paid strict heed to what the wise Roka said."

"It is well, but you might not have defied the temptation every time. Look again at what is left of the foolish buffalo calf, and think of his fate."

"He has suffered," said Inmu, "but in his death he warns us to beware of the great wolves. We have our lesson and our warning at the same time."

Returning, they stopped on a knoll and looked back

at one of the buffalo groups. Chance or, as Pehansan said, the direct purpose of Manitou, made them look, just when the king wolf himself pulled down another foolish buffalo calf. They saw the tremendous gray body of the monster distinctly, and they recognized him with certainty. Will did not believe there was another wolf in the world so large, and the sight gave him a chill. The chill was deepened when many other wolves rushed up and began to devour the calf.

"I do not care, Pehansan, how soon we leave our camp on the prairie," he said.

"It will be very soon now," replied the tall warrior.

CHAPTER VII

THE TRAP

THE new start was made the next morning, Capa's shoulder now being well on the way to recovery, and further delay being a waste of time. The forest into which they entered was unlike those they had left. It had the aspects of a vast northern jungle. The trees were large, but the soil was so deep and black that the undergrowth was astonishing in its extent and thickness. They made their way in the usual single file through a vast and intricate tangle of vines, bushes and creeping briars. The air was heavy with the odor of bloom, and they wondered at and admired the extraordinary display of vegetable and arboreal life, but neither Roka nor Pehansan trusted it. They knew that the great animals seeking their lives would find splendid ambush in these green depths. While the young warriors rejoiced at what they saw the two older men were wary and apprehensive.

A harsh scream startled them, but they laughed at themselves when they saw its cause. A huge lynx sat on the bough of a dead tree, spat at them and gave violent tongue to its hate.

"See, Inmu," said Hoton. "It is your brother, as it

154

bears the same name that you do, but it does not like you. It screams and snarls because another *Inmu* has come into the forest."

"No, it does not like me," said Inmu, "and I know what it is saying to us."

"What, Inmu?"

"It says: 'I scream and snarl and spit at you because I know I am safe. The wise Roka will not let you send an arrow at me. I am safe in the tree, and I show my contempt for you. I will not fight you myself, as I am something of a coward, but the great bear, the cunning wolf, and the sly panther are awaiting you in the thick forest. I will sit in a tree and scream my loudest when they attack you.' That, Hoton, is what the lynx is saying to us."

"Just like a cowardly animal. You, O, Inmu, are named for the Lynx because you are the exact opposite. The lynx makes a loud noise. You make little. The lynx is no warrior at all, but you are a great one."

The lynx continued to scream and squall, but they walked past him unnoticing, their attention now being devoted to choosing a path through the dense thickets. Will knew that the heavy vegetation was produced by a large rainfall. It was probable that the clouds passing over the lower mountains near the Pacific coast broke against those farther east and produced an uncommon and frequent precipitation, so creating this great northern jungle in which they found the traveling very hard.

Every one of the warriors glanced from time to

time at the spreading branches overhead, expecting, at any moment, to see a great panther crouched there. It was just such a place as would suit the tawny creatures best for an ambush, but they saw none. They saw instead, through the dense tangle of foliage, a darkening sky and heard the ominous roll of thunder in the south. It was evident that they were threatened with a spring storm, and Roka, the wise, not willing to have his men soaked with rain, put them all to work with their tomahawks building a brush shelter as fast as possible.

Their task was completed before sunset, and soon afterward the storm, after a tremendous display of thunder and lightning, broke upon them in a deluge. A part of it beat through the shelter, but with their blankets they were able to protect themselves and, eating cold food, they remained there all night. Will awoke several hours after the dark came, and he noticed that the rain had ceased. He could hear it no longer swishing among the trees, but he heard instead the sound of padded feet and heavy breathing. Inmu was lying next to him, and, as he moved a little, Will divined that he was awake.

"Did you hear?" he whispered.

"Yes, Waditaka," the young Sioux whispered back. "The great bears are walking about our house and are wondering what manner of creatures are inside."

"Do you think they will attack us?"

"No, they are merely curious. If we do not stir they will soon go away."

As Inmu had predicted, the shuffling of vast feet

and the heavy breathing ceased before long, but neither Will nor Inmu went to sleep again just yet. In a half hour they heard another and lighter tread, and they detected a strong, cat-like odor.

"The great panther, nay, two of them," whispered Inmu. "They, too, are merely scouting."

Will quivered a little. It was hard to lie still when huge and ferocious beasts were separated from him by only a thin brush wall that a single stroke of a great paw could rend from top to bottom. They, too, went away and the strong odor was replaced by the breath of the pure air. Then they heard a single tread, very soft, but suggesting an animal large and cruel.

"The king wolf," whispered Inmu. "The others came by chance, but he has followed us. He is counting us now."

"Counting us! What do you mean?"

"He is smelling us out to see if we are all here. If anyone is missing he might cut him off in the forest. Now he knows that none is absent and he is going away. I do not think, Waditaka, that we will have any more visitors tonight."

"Unless it's the birds. Such a forest as this should be full of immense eagles and owls."

Will was right, as within a few minutes they heard the flapping of heavy wings overhead, but he felt no quiver now, as he knew that beak and talon could not penetrate the brush roof. But he had received new proof that the great beasts were tenacious foes of the band, and perhaps he dreaded the huge and cunning wolf most of them all. The brain in the head of the king wolf seemed to him almost human, and much more cruel.

The day came without rain, but lowering and soggy, and reluctantly leaving the brush shelter, they pressed on through the dripping forest. About noon another heavy rain came up so suddenly that they did not have time to prepare for it, and they suffered a thorough wetting. When the rain passed the wise Roka, always with an eye to the comfort of his men, decided to build a fire, a difficult task in such a sodden wilderness, but they were master builders of fires.

A spot was selected and the young warriors went in search of wood. Tarinca bent beneath a great oak to pick up a fallen bough, and a huge, tawny body shooting down struck him squarely upon the back, pinning him to the earth. The devout Tarinca would have perished then and there, but Pehansan, who was standing not far away, saw the yellow flash in the air and the fall of Tarinca. Fortunately his bow was strung, and in a second he had fitted an arrow, letting it fly at the throat of the great panther.

There was another yellow flash in the air when the beast, leaving Tarinca, sprang at Pehansan. The tall warrior was aiming a second arrow, when the panther launched itself. He attempted to leap aside, but was not wholly successful. He evaded claws and fangs, but the great body, striking him upon the shoulder, hurled him heavily to the earth. Will, who was standing next, did not have bow or arrow in hand, but he snatched from his belt the loaded revolver, which he had not used hitherto on the journey. Driven by the desperate need, he put the muzzle of the weapon almost at the yellow brute's ear, and sent three bullets crashing into his brain.

The panther dropped dead almost at Will's feet, and he was fully as large as the first one they had slain. Pehansan and Tarinca arose, but the younger man struggled up with difficulty, the blood pouring from his back, where the claws of the beast had struck deep. Roka and Pehansan at once cleansed the wounds thoroughly and then bound them up. The others meanwhile built the fire, and they made it a big one, both for the sake of comfort and for protection from the wild beasts.

"I feared the stroke of the panther in so deep a forest," said Roka, "but we guarded against it the best we could. Nobody is to blame."

The roaring fire and plenty of food cheered them greatly, but in the night Tarinca grew feverish and by morning he was in delirium, with his wounds much swollen. Once more they were forced to stop, as they never dreamed of deserting a warrior, and Roka and Pehansan, who were skilled in Dakota surgery, bathed the wounds anew, searching the forest near by for herbs with which they could make poultices. But they went together, with strung bows and they never went far.

The poultices drew the fever from the hurts and rapidly reduced the swelling. In a day and night Tarinca was conscious, though weak, but it would be several days before he was fit to travel. Meanwhile they must do the best they could in the deep forest, where they were in continual danger of ambush by the fierce carnivora. They soon had proof that the peril was imminent, as Tatokadan was attacked by three wolves almost within the limits of the camp itself, and, before the others could come to his rescue and drive them off, he was bitten in the leg. Although it did not happen to be a deep wound, they applied to it all they knew of surgery, as there was usually much poison in a wolf's fangs. Tatokadan had a high fever for two or three days, but he did not become unconscious. Then, as with Tarinca, his hardy life and iron health prevailed. The impurities conveyed from the teeth of the wolf were ejected from his blood and the hurt healed rapidly and thoroughly.

But they were compelled to remain a week in the great jungle, and they were far from happy there. It reeked with damp, and they kept a big fire burning continually, as much to drive away miasma, as to protect themselves from wild animals. They had evidence every night that the fierce beasts were still watching them. In the darkness the pad of feet was heard again and again, and very near, and the fluttering of heavy wings in the branches overhead made them draw closer to the flames.

Roka became anxious. He had no words of blame for the two young warriors who had been hurt, as the fault had not been theirs, but he saw the gloom of the black forest and its many unseen dangers was settling down upon them. The Dakota, strong in the beliefs of their fathers, were sure now that the evil spirits were triumphant for the time, and that they were in great danger. The wise leader felt that they must give a demonstration of power against their foes, and he talked with Pehansan and Will—he had much respect for the clearness and strength of Will's mind. So, they arranged to teach the wild animals a lesson.

They proceeded as if their foes had human intelligence, which, in truth, the Dakota believed. A large piece of deer meat was left outside the camp, just beyond the circle of the firelight. It was not put down carefully, but dropped on the ground, as if it had been abandoned or lost, but the warriors marked its position well. Then after supper six went to sleep, leaving Roka, Pehansan, Will and Inmu awake. But the watching four counterfeited sleep, lying in their robes, but with their strung bows and arrows on the ground in front of them.

Roka had said it was the wolves that would come for the treasure trove, left casually just beyond the camp's edge, because they were more watchful than the other animals and their scent perhaps was keener, and Will was quite confident that the wise leader had predicted aright. He hoped so, and he hoped, too, that the king wolf might be among those that came. Lying almost flat he edged gently forward until his ear touched the ground instead of the robe. The earth is a splendid conductor of sound and he believed he could hear at a great distance the tread of any approaching animal.

The time was very long, but he had learned much

about patience from the Dakota, and he practiced it
well. The slight shifting of his fingers from time to
time along his bow was his only sign of eagerness.
But after the real night came, and the darkness moved
up like a circular wall about the fire, his ear told him
that the woods about them were well peopled. The
forest creatures had not gone to bed. Either they
were kept awake by nocturnal habits or by curiosity
concerning the bipeds who had invaded their domain.

He heard very light feet, not much more than the
fall of leaves, and he was quite sure it was the tread
of the large northern hare. The light feet came close
and then they retreated, as if curiosity had been amply
satisfied. A moment later he heard a swish of wings
and a faint squeak. One hare was gone and he pitied
the poor creature. A huge owl had swooped down and
had carried it away in its beak and talons. A terrible
price to pay for curiosity!

There was another tread as light as that of the
hare, but more cautious, withdrawing a little over and
over, but always coming on again. The fox, the
smaller cousin of the wolf! Will was quite sure he
would not fall a victim to the owl. His curiosity
might be as great as that of the hare, but he would
keep under cover beneath a veil of the thicket, where
beaks and claws could not reach him. The fox came
quite close. He must have divined that he was too
small for the arrows of the Sioux, as he made a complete circle of the fire, and then retreated, deliberately
but always under cover, into the depths of the forest.
A huge and hungry owl hovered overhead, but the

wise fox was as safe as if steel bars stood between him and the winged creature that craved his flesh.

A heavier step, and a rustling among the bushes came next. It was the snarling lynx, not snarling now, but filled with hate at these intruders upon the wilderness. A great bird, red of eye and steel of beak and claw, circled above it, but the lynx showed formidable teeth of its own and the bird, thinking better of its enterprise, flew away. Then the lynx, evil of heart and hot with rage, because it did not dare to attack the men by the fire, stalked sullenly into the forest.

Will heard the retreating footsteps of the lynx, but he was waiting all the while for another tread. The lynx might have taken the deer meat, though it was not bold enough to come so near, but the wolves would dare anything that would not bring them quite into range of the firelight. Another half hour passed, and he heard nothing from the earth, though there was a continuous rustling in the branches, which he was quite sure was made by huge owls.

At last he heard the tread which he knew instinctively to be that of *Xunktokeca,* very light, very cautious, advancing a little, retreating a little, circling to the right, then to the left, but always advancing, though ever so slowly. He surmised that the wolves were about four in number, and Inmu nodded confirmation to his questioning whisper. They were drawn, despite all their prudence, by the flesh of the deer. The savory odor, telling of physical delight to be won, had reached them afar, and now they were near enough to know that its source was just beyond the firelight, where cunning and wise wolves might steal it away, and yet incur no danger.

He who was at that moment Waditaka, the Dakota, rather than Will Clarke, the white lad, smiled to himself at that wavering but none the less determined approach. It was quite obvious that, however much they veered about, they would come to the place where the deer meat lay. That and that alone was their magnet. Gradually the course of the wolves became more direct, and, after a while, it bore straight upon the coveted venison. Roka raised himself softly upon his elbow, and then into a sitting posture.

"Now, my children," he said, "when you see me bend my bow do you likewise. When I let fly my arrow do you the same, and aim at the portion of the deer. Shoot thrice each. There will be no time for more, but it will be strange if some of our thirty arrows are not buried deep in the target."

A low growl came from the bushes. Inmu, who understood the language of the beasts so well, knew that it was a note of satisfaction from the wolves, who were now at the food. The powerful hands of Roka bent his bow, and the hands of nine others, also powerful, bent their bows in unison with his. Swiftly and with certainty they shot, and the thirty arrows struck so close together that the head of a small drum could have contained them all.

A terrific growling and snarling came from the bushes. An immense wolf, transfixed by two arrows, maddened by pain and fury, leaped into the light, rolled over, rolled into the fire and then rolled out again, to be despatched by the knife of Pehansan. In the bushes there was wild rushing about, and then the sound of running feet. The warriors laughed. They were all wild men, Waditaka too, and they had outwitted the wisest and most cunning of all animals.

"Now we will see if our meat is untouched," said Roka, taking a torch from the fire. "It was precious food that we put there, and although we were willing for the wolves to come we were not willing for them to eat what we left in the bushes."

They found the venison just as it had been, and, to their great delight, they saw another huge wolf lying dead beside it, a random arrow in his heart, his nose not six inches from the savory flesh. Hoton lifted up his voice and chanted:

"Truly I have won another great victory! Speedily did I avenge the wound that Tatokadan received! The wolf is great in wisdom and the wiles of the forest! For ages he has been learning, but I, Hoton, am wiser and more cunning than he! Lying by the fire in warmth and safety I have lured him within range of my arrow, and I have slain him."

"But it is my arrow that is in his heart," said Inmu. "Behold my mark upon it beside the feathers!"

"Truly it is your arrow, Inmu, but it was my wisdom and my mind that directed it. It was as really my shot as if it had been sent from my bow instead of yours."

"The credit is to us all, because we all shot together," said Roka, who had a very warm place in his heart for Hoton, the valiant boaster. "We will recover the arrows that found no living mark, and I think our enemies have received a lesson that will keep them farther from our campfire."

They found all the arrows except one, which they knew to be carried away in the body of a wolf, and returned to the fire, rejoicing over their triumph.

"We did better than I had hoped," said Roka. "To slay two wolves by shooting in the dark was the greatest of fortune. Surely our shafts were winged by Manitou himself. Now *Xunktokeca* has learned his lesson, and will not prowl within arrow shot of our camp. You can sleep well now, my children. Pehansan and I will watch the rest of the night."

Will lay down in his robe, but he put his ear to the bare earth again. Although he listened with great intentness he heard nothing. Neither the hares nor the fox, nor the lynx, nor anything else stirred in the great forest. There was no fluttering in the boughs above them. The great owls and whatever other night birds of prey had been there were gone away. It seemed that the fate of the wolves was a warning to all the smaller people of the wilderness. For that night, at least, man had triumphed completely, and Will, feeling intense satisfaction, soon fell asleep.

They had further proof the next day that the lesson was exemplary. Careful scouting showed that all the fierce carnivora had gone much farther away, and, as long as they remained in their present camp, they were not molested again. The hurts of the young warriors healed finally, and they pressed on anew toward the high mountains that loomed dimly in the east. Yet the great wilderness grew more matted and more nearly impenetrable than ever. The quantity of shrubs and briars and vines was amazing. At times they were compelled to cut a path with their tomahawks, but the thickets offered compensations, as they contained an abundance of spring berries of which they ate freely.

On the third day of their renewed march they came to a river, swollen greatly by spring floods, and melting snow on the mountains. Men less hardy would have turned back, but Roka, after a careful examination, chose a point that he considered best for the passage, and they made ready, putting, as usual, all their weapons, clothes and supplies in packs which they expected to carry on their heads while swimming.

Yet the river might have daunted even that chosen band. The wide current was swift, it carried much fallen timber, and despite the spring warmth in the air they knew that the stream, fed by snows, was almost as cold as ice. Roka gave strict orders that any swimmer who was about to be overcome by chill or cramp, or who was in danger of being swept away, must cry aloud at once for help, because to perish, like a stoic, would merely weaken the band. Then the ten let themselves into the stream, and took a diagonal course, going partly with the current.

Will shivered as the cold water enveloped his body, but powerful exercise soon drove away most of the chill. He had to swim with all his strength, as the current tugged at him with many hands, but he saw that he was doing as well as the others. Roka was on the right of the line, Will was next to him and Inmu was next to Will. The leader bore steadily farther and farther down stream, yielding like a wise man to the great drive of the waters, and avoiding the mass of fallen timber which was now coming in large quantities. Roka, turning his head a little, said to Will:

"Beware of the tree trunks, Waditaka. They are floating swiftly, and it seems almost as if they were alive and were seeking to crush us. A blow from a great log in this swift water is as dangerous as the bite of a wolf."

A tree, borne by some malicious current, came in a slanting course across the river, and drove directly at their line. In the minds of the Dakota it was impelled by the evil spirits of the air, and was sent by them to destroy. A shout from Roka and their line parted, five beating back up the stream and the other five going more swiftly down it. The jagged tree went through the breach without touching a warrior on either side, and then the line closed up again in triumph.

Roka, looking at the tree that had missed its mark, laughed in contempt. The Dakota, like the Iroquois, not only filled the air with spirits, but incarnated the trees, in truth, nearly all inanimate objects. This was an evil tree that had struck at them, but the blow had fallen on nothing. Will shared their beliefs, for the time at least, and he echoed the laugh of his leader.

They were now near the center of the stream and the current seemed to increase in power. It pulled at his feet and all his body, and the weight of his pack on his head made the fight with it hard and dangerous. Roka, sheering still farther to the right, now went almost with the current, and the others followed, the task becoming easier for the while, as the stream itself now bore them on. Yet they were coming but little nearer the eastern shore, and they could easily stay too long in the icy current.

Roka presently sheered in again toward the desired bank, and Will and the whole line promptly and gladly followed him, though they saw ahead masses of driftwood through which they must pass. Nevertheless they swam boldly, expecting to dodge past the dangerous obstructions. But these, too, were possessed by the evil spirits, and in a moment or two the Dakota found themselves surrounded by logs, boughs and great masses of heavy weeds torn from the soft banks by the flooded waters. They might have dived under some of these, but the packs on their heads precluded such tactics.

"Beware, Waditaka," said Roka, as he swept away with one hand a mass of brush that threatened Will's head, turning aside to do so. But as he turned back a heavy log struck him on the temple. Will, uttering a cry of dismay, seized him instinctively with one hand and clutched the log with the other. Roka was unconscious, and hung heavily on Will's arm, but the water sustained him partially, and, the lad with all the power of his other arm, clung to the log, holding both the leader's head and his own and the precious packs above the stream.

But while the log kept them from sinking, the evil spirit in it nevertheless was disposed to do all the harm it could. It floated into the swiftest portion of the river, rocked dangerously back and forth, and then shot downward with the stream at a great rate. Will's arm nearly broke with the strain, but he hung on to the log and to Roka, shouting meanwhile for help. All the warriors swam at once in pursuit, but the floating driftwood, which was coming thickly, interfered with them.

Will tried to climb upon the log, but its rolling kept him from doing so, and from fear of losing his hold on Roka he stopped the effort. Then he shut his teeth, prayed to the good spirits and held firm almost by will alone. His whole body seemed to have become numb. He was not conscious of cold or pain, but his will to save Roka grew stronger than ever.

He heard a shout and Pehansan, seizing the other arm of Roka, grasped the log, which he managed to steady. Hoton came next, then all of them, and in a few more minutes they arrived at the eastern shore, where they carried Roka up the low bank and opening his pack wrapped him hastily in his accustomed clothing. When they were dressing themselves, wet though they were, the leader revived and stood up, his eye clear and his figure erect again.

"I thank you, Waditaka," he said. "You have saved my life. It was your quick mind and strong arm that kept me in this world. I shall repay you some day."

Will was deeply gratified.

"I only did what I should have done," he replied. "Any of the warriors in my place would have done the same."

But Will knew that he now had a powerful friend in Roka, who, as leader of the band, was master of life and death, and, since no harm was in the final outcome, he was not sorry the accident had occurred.

They built a fire as quickly as they could, all helping in the task, and, taking off their clothes again, let the grateful heat soak into their bodies, until all danger of illness from cold had passed. Then they considered the further prosecution of their journey. Roka thought another day or two would take them out of the black forest, beyond which they might find a second region of little prairies, but ultimately they must cross very high mountains before they reached the great buffalo plains for which they were looking. The lofty ridges and peaks were an indisputable fact, as they saw them much more clearly now, their white crests showing in a serrated line against the sky.

"I think," said Roka, "that when we reach the other side of the mountains we will be on the great plains which run up from the Sioux country. I have heard from the old men that the plains go north in Canada hundreds and hundreds of miles, and that in the far north there are many great, cold lakes, some of them a week or two weeks' march in length. The buffalo is as plentiful on those plains as he has ever been with us."

"And perhaps," said Pehansan, "when we cross the high mountains the wild animals will cease to seek us."

"Maybe so," said Roka, "but then we will have to meet the Indians who hunt on those plains. They will regard us as enemies because we are strangers, and we shall have to fight. It is because red man fights red man that the white man has been able to advance over the plains."

Will walked to the edge of the firelight and took a long look at the white crests. He was not able to calculate the distance, but he knew that they were yet far off. They seemed, however, to nod to him, to beckon him on, and the lure was strong. It was the greatest ambition of his life just then to cross those mountains with his brave comrades. It seemed to him that he had been with them an age, and he had got into the habit of looking upon Roka as the best of men. He was seeking incessantly to excel in all the things in which the grave and stern leader was superior. His mind ran back over many incidents and then to his capture by the Sioux.

He thrust his hand into a small inside pocket of his stout deerskin tunic and drew out a parchment folded tightly. It was the map of the lost mine that his father had discovered, and opening it he looked at it, at first without full realization. Then his old comrades, brave and sympathetic too, came back with a rush. He wondered where they were, Boyd, the guide,

Bent, the valiant Little Giant, and Brady, the whimsical and valiant fur hunter. He had no doubt they were still among the living. Such men as they were not made to perish until they had attained fullness of years. Perhaps, giving him up for dead, they had gone on, and found the mine. Well, if it was so, it was all right. They were his heirs, and just then he thought little of money. But he had an intuitive feeling then, and not for the first time, that he would see his three white comrades again.

He refolded the map and put it back carefully in the little pocket. His absorption in the present returned. Once more he was Waditaka, the young Sioux, a member of Roka's great exploring band, and the problems of the band were his. He returned to the fire, where the warriors, in the fashion of Indians after great exertion, were giving themselves up to complete rest.

"What did you see, Waditaka?" asked Hoton.

"Only the far mountains," replied Will, not mentioning the look he had taken into the past.

"Waditaka was a brave man today," said Hoton, "and he deserved the praise the wise Roka gave him. He did almost as well as I would have done had I been in his place."

"What more could you have done, Hoton?" asked the pious Tarinca.

"I would have swum alone with Roka to the land. It would not have been necessary for me to hold on to a tree. But Waditaka's credit is as great as would have been mine. His strength is not equal to mine, and perhaps he is not quite so quick with eye and hand as I am."

"When we meet our next bear, Hoton," said Will, "I will shoot more arrows into him in a certain time than you can. I lay you a wager of a beaver skin on it."

"I will not lay a wager with you, Waditaka," said Hoton, grandly, "because I do not wish to rob you. It is the way of the very young to act rashly, and I will save you your beaver skin, because I am wiser than you are, and I do not wish to take anything from you so easily."

"Thank you, Hoton," laughed Will. "But we may not meet any more of the great bears."

"I think we will," said Hoton, looking at the far, white mountains with the eye of a prophet. "The monster bears love the high rocks, and they will be waiting there among the narrow passes for us."

"Our arrows will be ready for them," said the brave Inmu.

They came the next day to one of the little lakes, so numerous in the far northwest of North America, a deep, cool, blue bowl set in the green wilderness. The forest did not come down to the edge and the sward extended for some width all about it, a fact that gave them keen joy, as they were, for a time, out of the dense thickets which had produced so much hardship, gloom and dangers. The young warriors, when they came into the open space and saw the blue sky clear above them, looked at Roka.

"Yes, my children," he said, "we will stay here a

day or two and drive away the shadows in which the evil spirits have clothed us. We will catch fish in the lake, set traps for small game, and while Pehansan and I talk over grave matters the rest of you may bathe in the waters."

"But Waditaka should see that no wolf is here, watching him and keeping him from returning to the land," said Hoton, "because there is no island in this lake, and so no tree into which he can climb."

"But the wolf didn't get me, and he won't," said Will. "Come on, Hoton, you vain boaster, and I'll teach you how to swim!"

The eight young warriors were soon in the waters, which were not too cold for such hardy bodies as theirs, and, all fine swimmers, they splashed and ducked one another like so many little boys. Will did now know it, but while he had taken much from the Sioux, these members of Roka's band had also learned something from him. His had been a silent influence, but it had been pervasive, nevertheless. They had unconsciously imitated the gentleness and mercy that were inherent in his educated white blood. So, while they played together, their pranks were not cruel, and they never involved any danger.

When they came out they were glowing with physical buoyancy, and, running up and down the beach until they were dry, they resumed their clothing. Then the usual fire was kindled and they cooked their food. While they ate they saw they were not going to lack for supplies. Fish leaping up showed themselves in silver streaks just above the surface of the lake, and then splashed as they fell back. Now and then a huge bird of prey darted down and carried off a large fish in its talons. Flocks of wild geese and wild ducks of many kinds appeared, and they seemed tame and unwary enough to swim directly into the snares the Sioux meant to set. It had all the aspects of a place very pleasant to wild men.

"Are you not glad I brought you to this lake, Waditaka?" said Hoton.

"How did you know it was here, Hoton?" asked Will.

"I smelled the water two or three miles back."

"Come, Hoton! That's one of your big ones. You don't smell pure, fresh water like this."

"You must speak only for yourself, Waditaka. Your nostrils are not my nostrils. Many warriors cannot smell water where I can. The buffalo smells water afar on the prairie. The warrior's pony smells it, too, and I knew that the lake was here one, two hours before we reached it. I am a great warrior, Waditaka, not because I am so brave, for all of you are almost as brave as I am, but because I have so much wisdom, and I see, hear and smell so well."

"When we go up into the mountains, where the great bears are waiting for us," said Will, "we will send Hoton two, three miles ahead to smell them out."

"And I will go," said Hoton, more gravely than ever. "After I have slain more than half of them with my single arm, then I will come back, bring up the rest of you and let you share in what is left of the glory."

Thus spoke Hoton, the boaster, but a warrior of warriors, nevertheless.

CHAPTER VIII

THE BIG BISON

THE temptation to stay a while beside the new lake was so strong that Roka yielded to it. He reflected that, after all, there was no real reason why they should hurry, and, if his young warriors had plenty of food and rest, they would have more strength and endurance for the great hardships and dangers which were surely before them. The fish in the lake, of fine quality, were caught easily, and as they had foreseen, the wild ducks and wild geese fairly swam into their snares. Deer were to be shot when they came down to drink, but the young men kept out of the forest, of which they had seen enough for a while.

Roka and Pehansan put their heads together, and decided to employ the time in the further training of their young warriors, especially with the tomahawk and the bow. They were very fortunate in their tomahawks, which were of the finest steel, and they practiced for hours at a time in throwing them at trees, gradually increasing the distance. They acquired such skill that at ten paces or so they could plant ten tomahawks side by side deep in the trunk. But Pehansan could throw the tomahawk with deadly certainty at the greatest range. It was a sight to see him hurl his weapon and clip off a small bough, as cleanly as if it had been done by a saw.

So, first place with the tomahawk was willingly yielded to the Crane, who had the longest arm, which perhaps gave him superior skill, but leadership with the bow and arrow long remained in doubt. There was a certain artifice in bending the bow with the most power at a given moment, and all the Sioux had practiced it from earliest childhood. Hence Will in the beginning had been last in archery, despite the fact that he possessed the finest bow, but during the testing period he improved rapidly.

The Sioux, like other Indians of the plains, discharged their arrows with great accuracy and power, but at short distances. Their range did not approach that habitual to the English long bowmen of the Middle Ages, but in their stay by the lake they sought to acquire distance, chiefly due to the suggestion of Will, who had read about the great archery of white men before gunpowder came into use. Both Roka and Pehansan thought the idea good and gradually they lengthened the range.

As they had planted their tomahawks side by side in the trunk of a tree, so they now sank their arrows in a cluster in the same tree at a distance eight or ten times as great. They also shot at the stems of small bushes and once Inmu achieved a marvelous feat. Standing upon the shore of the lake with his arrow on the string and his finger on the arrow he watched until a fish sprang above the water snapping at a fly or a gnat, and so sure was his eye and so quick his aim that he transfixed the fish before it fell back into the water.

Nobody else was able to equal the Lynx's exploit, although most of them tried it many times. Hoton came very near it once, and was quite sure that his arrow had grazed the fish.

"If I could only find a slow fish like the one Inmu shot," he said philosophically, "I could send my arrow through him without any trouble. But all the fish that leap for me come up with great speed and go down with speed even greater. So it shows as great skill on my part to graze one as it did on Inmu's part to send an arrow through the body of his."

"Why, O Crow?" asked the pious Tarinca, "are your fish so much swifter in the leap than that of Inmu?"

"The reason is very simple, Tarinca, so simple that I am surprised you should ask it. They know that I, Hoton, the ready, Hoton, the great archer, am watching for them. An old, wise fish, that does not come up at all, says to the others, the young and the daring that are quick to take risks: 'If you leap into the outer air go and return with the speed of lightning, because Hoton is watching for you. I see him on the bank with his bow and arrow ready, and the danger is very great. He is the finest archer in the world. You need not pay much attention to the others, but watch him always. When the arm of Hoton draws back the bow dart down for your lives, my children, because only in that way can you save yourselves from him.' So, my comrades, the wise old chief of the fish talks, and you do not have his skill and cunning against you as I have them against me."

Nevertheless the prize was awarded by a hair's breadth to Inmu. All the others shot so close behind him that it was impossible to distinguish between them. Hoton, with generous warmth, congratulated Inmu on his official victory. As for himself, he said, he was cumbered with laurels and one more could not mean much to him, while it meant a very great deal to Inmu. He had been kept out of first place through the conspiracy of the fish, but conscious of surpassing merit and of his own approval he was content.

Roka also ordered a third exercise, in which, however, he and Pehansan did not share, acting instead as directors and judges. They had the eight younger warriors, starting from Roka and Pehansan, who sat on a little knoll, to race all the way around the lake, a full mile, broken, too, by rough ground and occasional bushes. It was a test of both wind and limb, and it aroused the greatest emulation. The first race was won by the pious Tarinca, and the second by Capa, Hoton finishing second on each occasion. But Will, proving that white blood with similar training was equal to any, won the third, and gradually established a superiority which he kept, receiving the prize, which consisted of words of approval from Roka and Pehansan. Hoton again offered congratulations.

"I could have won had I wished," he said in his

best grand manner to Will, "but as I saw that you had a chance I wished that you instead should take the prize. As you had the misfortune to be born white instead of red I thought it but fair to help you in this way."

"Thanks for the encouragement, Hoton," laughed Will. "It was kind of you and I sha'n't forget it."

They saw nothing of the wild animals until the fifth night by the lake when they hung the body of a deer that they had killed and dressed to the bough of a tree near the camp. The next morning it was gone and they found the tracks of a wolf under the bough. As the deer had been hung high to keep it out of reach of marauders they were quite certain that only the monstrous king wolf could have pulled it down, thus giving a new proof that he had no intention of abandoning their trail. They followed his traces some distance into the forest, a very clear path, as he had dragged the body of the deer with him, but the jungle becoming extremely dense they deemed it best to turn back, lest they walk into some kind of ambush.

Refreshed and feeling themselves stronger than ever, they pushed on anew toward the high mountains which were yet so distant that they seemed scarcely to have come any nearer in the last four or five days. Will knew, therefore, that the elevation of the ranges must be very great, and he looked for a hazardous passage across them, knowing that however pleasant it might be in the lowlands where they now were they would have to encounter once more vast fields of snow and ice. But for the present their way was easy, leading through a parklike forest, a great relief after their days in the thick northern jungle.

The next night they built their fire under a vaulted dome of young leaves that swept far over their heads, and, at twilight, they heard the fierce howling of wolves not far away. Roka listened attentively and then said:

"It is a chase, but they are not on our trail. It is a pack in full cry after game, a deer most likely. Such wolves as we find up here could pull down the great moose himself."

Will's blood quivered a little as he listened to the ferocious hunting cry. The old, primeval world came back once more. They had entered open forest again, but it was filled, nevertheless, with great, devouring beasts, and he was devoutly glad that he had such valiant comrades around him, and a big fire before him.

Roka divided the night into two watches, Will with the young warrior, Tatokadan, keeping the second, beginning it shortly after midnight. The fire no longer blazed up, but there was a great mass of glowing coals, which they had no intention of letting die out, as fire was now their great protection in the night against prowling beasts.

The wind sang softly overhead in the leafy vault, but Will and Tatokadan were watchful. They were not to be lulled by soothing sounds into any neglect of duty, and when they had been on post about an hour they heard voices above them which they were sure were not caused by the moving of air among the leaves.

"What do you think it is, Tatokadan?" asked Will, trying to pierce the darkness with his eyes.

The young Dakota, relying more upon ear than eye, waited awhile before replying.

"I think it is great birds," he said, at last, "flying above us, angry at our presence here, and trying to tell just what we are. Listen with all your might, Waditaka, and see if you do not hear the movement of wings."

"I think I do, Tatokadan. We were attacked by fierce birds once before, as you remember, and they may be planning for a second rush upon us."

"Perhaps. Not used to men they do not know we are creatures that have arrows and that arrows are sharp."

"It's a pity it's so dark against that roof of leaves. If it wasn't we might make 'em out."

"Look a little to the right, Waditaka, and you will behold an open place where the leaves of two trees fail to meet. The sky beyond it is bright blue, and, if anything flies there, we shall be sure to see it."

"And it's your idea to shoot whatever appears in that patch of open?"

"If we are quick enough we might send up an arrow or two."

"I think it's a good plan. We'll do it."

Each held his bow ready, the arrow on the string and attentively watched the blue expanse showing between the trees, although they heard the constant whirring of heavy wings in the thick gloom over their heads. It was a difficult task to wait. For all they knew, beaks and talons of steel might be dashed into their faces any moment, but, with the patience of the wild, they held to their task. A full quarter of an hour, and a dark figure appeared against the shield of blue, the outline of a hideous, misshapen bird. Quick as lightning the two shot, and they shot so close together that their arrows flew upward side by side. They heard a harsh scream, the sound of rushing wings and then a thud.

All the warriors were awake and up in an instant, but Tatokadan, snatching a torch from the fire, ran to the place where the body had fallen and disclosed a huge owl, vast beyond any they had ever seen before, still fluttering, but pierced by two arrows. It gazed at them a moment or two with fading eyes full of hate, and then died. Tatokadan pulled out the two arrows.

"It was good shooting," said Roka, approvingly. "Our practice has made us almost perfect."

"Do you think it would have attacked us?" asked Will.

"I know not, Waditaka," replied the leader, "but in this far northern region everything is so fierce and large that we cannot trust in the peacefulness of either bird or beast."

They left the body where it had fallen, and returned to the fire, Will and Tatokadan resuming the watch, and the others quickly going back to sleep.

The two sentinels soon heard a scamper of feet, coming and then going.

"The body of the owl has been taken away," said Tatokadan. "Wolves or foxes, I know not which, have done it."

They found the next morning that he was right and the trail leading from the spot where the owl had fallen was that of wolves.

"They may have been watching just beyond the rim of the dark while we were looking at the owl," said Pehansan. "They are ready alike to eat what we kill or to eat us, whenever they get a chance."

Yet they had several days of peace, advancing through the open wilderness while the great mountains now came visibly nearer. The ranges were clothed heavily with forest up to the snow line, and the keen eyes of the Dakota detected narrow white ribbons which they were sure were made by rushing streams. All of them were now eager to reach the first slopes and conquer the formidable obstacle lying before them, feeling, too, that when they had scaled those heights they would leave behind them the fierce carnivora that had been such a source of danger.

"When we are on the other side we will hunt the buffalo," said Hoton, grandly. "I think we shall find the greatest buffalo plains in the world, and, as everything seems to grow larger here, the buffalo will be bigger, too. But I, Hoton, the mighty hunter, will know how to slay them. Do you know, Waditaka, that in the fiercest winter, when no other warrior, no matter how old and experienced, could find the buffalo, I, Hoton, could find them? Perhaps it will be that way with us. When all the rest of the band fail I shall save you from starvation or some other extreme danger."

"Be sure, Hoton," said Will, "that while you are hunting the buffalo the buffalo doesn't hunt you. That fate has happened to the greatest hunters."

"It is so much the better, Waditaka. Let the biggest of all buffalo bulls come! I welcome him."

The ground now began to ascend and became very rough, interspersed with knolls and carved by deep ravines. Tracks were abundant, but they saw little game. It seemed to melt away before them, and their supplies of food became scarce Roka finally decided that it was necessary to go in search of it, and he sent out two parties of three each, Will, Inmu and Hoton being in one party.

Will and his comrades went toward the north, soon disappearing in the forest from the view of the others. The wilderness was now less open than it had been for the preceding few days, clumps of bushes appearing here and there, but they were not numerous enough to interfere with their progress. The leafage had increased to a great extent, forming such a roof over their heads that it was quite warm beneath it, and soon the three stopped on a knoll for rest and coolness. They had from that point a splendid view of the mountains which sloped gradually up from where they stood, the sun throwing back gleams from one lofty and glittering sheet of ice which Will was sure was a glacier. They also discovered when they looked back over the way they had come that they had already ascended a considerable slope. They were no longer in the valley proper, but they stood on the foothills leading to the lofty ranges.

The three felt the thrill of great explorers, of the intrepid Spaniards when they looked upon the mighty peaks of Mexico and Peru, and they were eager to scale the heights before them, but they soon brought their minds back to the prosaic task of finding food.

"If there is game here I shall soon discover its trace," said Hoton.

"Then Waditaka and I will take our ease," said Inmu. "Call us when you see the sign."

"Not so, Inmu. I wish you and Waditaka to go on with me, because when I kill the game I will need your help to bring it back. Since I have walked so far I do not intend to kill anything little."

"Bear in mind what I said about the hunter becoming the hunted," said Will. "It seems to me in such a country as this we're more likely to find big game than small. Maybe we'll meet the wolves or stir up one of the big bears."

Inmu was gazing intently at a bush on the edge of the knoll.

"What are you looking at so hard, Inmu?" asked Will.

"See the bunch of coarse hair, caught on the bush!"

"I see it now. From what was it taken, a bear or a moose?"

"Neither, Waditaka. That is the hair of the woods or mountain buffalo."

"Oh, a brother, perhaps, of the big fellow who gave us so much trouble near the village last winter. If he's around here anywhere I think we'd better let him have the right of way, and hunt something smaller."

"You show wisdom, Waditaka. We will leave the mountain buffalo alone."

They noticed the great prints of the animal's hoofs in the turf, and, following them for a hundred yards, saw that they led up the slope, and then they left them, content, as they had said, for the buffalo to go his own way while they went theirs. They preferred finding young bear to anything else. They had eaten deer so much that they were tired of it, and young bear, cooked in the skillful manner of the Indians, was always succulent.

"I think," said Hoton, "that the good spirits of the air will guide us to a young bear. We ought to find game sooner than the three who have gone toward the south."

"Why?" asked Will.

"Because I am one of the three who hunt here. I am a favorite of the good spirits. That is why I am such a fine hunter, and they will give to me the triumph."

But they did not yet find the trail of bear, nor even of the deer for which they did not care, and as they carried on the search they gradually ascended the slopes leading up toward the high mountains, finding as they proceeded that the clumps of bushes were growing more numerous, and that the ground was seamed and pitted more deeply by ravines and dips.

"A fine place for bear," said Hoton. "Dens are plentiful in rough, rocky ground like this, and they should be somewhere near it, looking for roots and berries."

A thicket, larger and denser than usual, lay on their right, and, as they approached it, Will caught a glimpse of something brown, followed by a gleam of sunlight on a polished horn. He was about to call the attention of his comrades to what he had seen, but he did not have time. The wind was blowing directly from the three toward the huge bull buffalo that lay in the thicket nursing his wrath against everything. He was made more angry than ever by the approach of these strange creatures who lay just beyond him in the woods.

The bull, a monster of the mountain or woods species, sprang to his feet, and with a puffing roar, charged. He had been so well concealed in the bushes that he was scarcely twenty feet away when Will caught that glimpse of his hairy coat. Filled with wrath, much larger and far fiercer than his cousin of the plains, he charged head down at the three impertinent intruders upon his rest.

They leaped aside, but he whirled with uncommon agility for so huge a brute, and rushed at them again, puffing forth his wrath and wish for vengeance. The herd, drawn by their leader, came also, trampling down the bushes and rushing forward, a formidable battalion. A kind of madness because the three figures had evaded him, for the moment, seized upon

the great bull and his herd shared his wrath. And
his anger was excited to a yet greater pitch when he
was struck by fiery, shooting pains. Stung into the
uttermost fury, he ran after the three figures. One
stumbled and fell in front of him, not having time to
rise before he was upon it. But the bull, with the
instinct of many animals not to trample upon anything strange and unknown, overran the prostrate
figure without touching it. When it whirled back,
the figure was no longer there. It had leaped up
lightly and darted to one side. Two other figures,
like the one that had fallen, were uttering menacing
shouts in the ears of the bull, and were stinging him
with little barbed shafts. His herd was puffing heavily and charging here and there but giving him little
real help, until a young bull almost trapped one of
the figures in a thicket, and might have trampled it to
death, but was turned aside in the very moment of
triumph by a shout from another figure. Foolish
brute! It did not possess the power of continuity
and was diverted from coming triumph by mere
sound.

But the herd instinctively began to gather into some
kind of order and charged in a semi-circle upon the
three figures that were leaping and dancing before it.
The big bull was now sure of triumph, but the human
creatures began to shout to one another, and suddenly
they disappeared from the sight of the bleeding and
annoyed leader. He stood for a few moments puffing and panting, and the herd, ranged behind him,
puffed and panted also. He was a fierce and terrible

sight. A dozen arrows stood out in his body, and, though the wounds were not mortal the pain was frightful. Great red bands of blood appeared on his hairy robe, and he puffed his anger to the whole world.

The rage of the bull was increased by his amazement. The three creatures that had taunted him and stung him with the barbs had vanished suddenly in a manner that was truly mystifying, in a manner that deprived him of all chance for revenge. A shout from above and he saw that the figures were now in trees. Other shouts came quickly and they were taunts. The bull felt them to be so, and he charged madly at the nearest tree, but he only hurt himself and another fiery barb, shooting down, was plunged deep into his shoulder. He drew off and the band drew off with him, the painful darts following them until they were out of range.

But the bull and his herd did not go away. Whenever one of the strange creatures that they now understood to be formidable, began to descend the tree they drew in again, making the full threat of a charge, and then the figure would go back up the tree. It happened over and over again. The rage of the bull was shared in no less measure by all the herd. They stamped and puffed and snorted, but they kept beyond range of the arrows, unless one of the human beings showed signs of coming to the ground. Then they advanced, with the usual result.

Much time passed, leaving the situation unchanged and then the fatal weakness of the wild animal developed. Instinct it possessed to a high degree, but forethought and continuity of action were lacking. The big bull was a monarch of his tribe. He feared nothing. The great moose of the north, even in one of his periodical spells of madness, had no terrors for him, the mighty bear did not care to dispute the way with him, and not until he was so old and decayed that he could no longer walk would the great wolves molest him. But the fierce little barbs in his body stung him. The blood dripped and the flesh around the wounds inflamed. He began to think of a good place he knew where he could wallow in the soft soil and cure his hurts. He had a vivid recollection of that sandy hollow, and the picture of it assumed deeper and more intense colors. The creatures in the trees that he had difficulty in seeing, because he did not look up so high, began to fade from his mind.

Now the break in his continuity of effort occurred. The attraction of the sandy hollow and its pleasures proved overwhelming. The human figures disappeared absolutely, and, uttering a puffing roar, he turned and ran away through the forest. The whole herd, puffing in like fashion, followed the leader, while Will, Inmu and Hoton, feeling immense relief, came down to the ground.

"I frightened them away at last," said Hoton, in a tone of intense satisfaction. "The great bull lifted his head, stared into my eyes and I stared back so hard that he lowered his tail and took to flight."

"If that's so, Hoton," said Will, "I'm sorry you

didn't stare him down sooner. It's tiresome work sitting up in a tree. I thought once my end had come when I fell and the great bull rushed upon me. But he went over me without treading upon me, for which I thank the good spirits."

"I think that the attack of all the great wild animals upon us is about to be renewed," said Inmu. "The buffalos charged us almost as if they had a plan, and we were not attacking them. Do you think, Hoton, that the king wolf could have been telling them what to do?"

"It is likely," replied the Crow, looking around with an air of apprehension. "I do not know, Inmu, that a wolf can talk with a buffalo, as I have never seen them do it, but I can well believe it. But if the king wolf and his pack had held us in the trees we know that he would not have gone away. He alone of the great beasts thinks and remembers like a man."

"And among the rocks and snows of the high ranges that we must cross he'll have a better chance for ambush," said Will. "You recall what happened the last time we crossed the mountains. The time has returned when we must be on guard every second of our lives."

"Truly spoken, said Hoton, "but it will not keep us from getting our young bear. Look, I have found his trail! Here go bear tracks down the hill, and they are fresh. He must have passed just before the buffaloes attacked us. I knew that I, Hoton, would be the first to find the bear."

THE BIG BISON

"But you did not find the big bull buffalo that came so near to destroying us," said Will.

"No, Waditaka, I did not find *Pteha* (Buffalo) because I was not looking for him. When I look for *Pteha* I find *Pteha* and when I look for *Warankxi* (Bear) I find *Warankxi*. I tell you also that the young bear we are following is uncommonly fat and tender, fatter and tenderer than any other we have shot on this great journey of ours. How do I know? O, Waditaka, do not ask me foolish questions. Maybe a good spirit in the air has put the thought in my head and the thought is knowledge. Maybe *Zica* (squirrel), chattering in the tree, has told me in his language, which I am permitted to understand. Perhaps *Maxtinca* (Hare) whimpering in his nest under the bushes told me, or it is even possible that *Wamduxka* (Snake), gliding in the grass, has hissed it to me. But it matters not how the news has come to my ear, Waditaka. I know it, and that is enough."

"Be it so, Hoton," laughed Will. "We shall see."

But all of the Crow's predictions came true. They followed a trail about a half mile and then dispatched a young bear in a clump of bushes with a single arrow. He had fed so much on early berries and roots that he was exceedingly tender, and they carried him back in triumph to the camp, giving to Hoton all credit as a prophet and as one to whom birds and animals gave good advice when he was hunting other kinds of birds and animals. The party from the south brought in several large hares, and the ten had an abundant and succulent feast

Roka and Pehansan listened with great gravity to the story of the encounter with the mountain buffaloes.

"You had a fortunate escape," said the wise leader, "and you, in particular, Waditaka, when you fell under the feet of the bull. The good spirits were watching over you, but the good spirits will not watch over us unless we also watch over ourselves. They are kind to those who have many sharp arrows which they know how to shoot straight. Our path will now lead upward, and tomorrow we will jerk some of the flesh of the bear, because we may not be able to find game in the high mountains among the snows."

When they resumed the journey they were well provided with supplies, and they also had warm clothing and furs for the icy pass. But, greater than food and raiment, they had high souls. There was not one among them who did not crave the adventure, whose spirit did not defy every hardship and danger, who was not filled with the most eager curiosity concerning the great lands into which they were penetrating. Tall, lean, strong, patient and enduring, they were the highest types of primeval man.

They advanced for a day through country broken and very rough. Although the general result was an ascent they had to cross now and then deep valleys or ravines, and it became evident that the passage would be one of great difficulty. But their ardor increased as the obstacles grew, and when they camped that night they built a fire of uncommon size, rejoicing in the leaping flames and great beds of coals.

The sky was so clear that it was almost as bright as day. The stars in myriads and of uncommon size hung low in that northern latitude and filled the whole sphere with shining light.

They saw the great valley that they were leaving rolling beneath them like a green sea, but before them towered the mountains, white, glistening and cold. They were already at an elevation where chill winds blew, and the character of the vegetation was changing into smaller and hardier evergreens that hang on the slopes of high ranges, before the snow line is reached.

They came the next day to a great chasm that seemed impassable, but, following along its edge, they found that it extended only about two miles to the south, and, passing around it they continued upward, choosing for their advance a point between two high white peaks. It was only a guess, but as the eye had a vast range in the thin, high air it seemed to be the most feasible place. The whole gigantic panorama before them though was soon shut out by a white veil.

"It is snowing on the slopes," said Roka. "We left one winter behind us to find another here."

The snow ceased in an hour or two, the entire white veil being cast aside suddenly, and once more the peaks and ranges came out sharp and clear in every detail against the blue sky. Living figures stood upon dizzy ledges, looking curiously at them.

"*Waxicantatokadan* (Mountain Goat) and *Tanicaxda* (Mountain Sheep)" said Roka. "They are far away, but we can see so well in this air that they appear to be near."

"I not only see them," said Hoton, "but I know what the great goat on our right is thinking and saying to himself about us. The breeze that blows down from the mountains brings me his words and I understand them. He says: 'They are Dakota warriors, of whom the most valiant and skillful is Hoton, save perhaps the wise Roka, their leader. Great is the fame of Hoton in the Dakota country, and great it will be here when he has done the mighty deeds that he has come to do. The ten Dakota will be in many dangers while they are crossing the mountains, but the courage and wisdom of Roka and Hoton will always save them.' "

"Is *Waxicantatokadan* saying anything about me, Hoton?" asked Wanmdi.

Hoton leaned his ear toward the big goat and listened intently for a full minute. Then he replied:

"Now he is talking of you, Wanmdi. His words are blown straight from his mouth into my ear. He says: 'The young warrior fifth in the line is Wanmdi (Eagle), named after the great bird that flies over the mountains. He is young and foolish, but time will cure his youth, and the company of Hoton, if continued long, will temper his foolishness. If he will only listen to the words of wisdom as they drop from the lips of Hoton he will become in time a warrior of some knowledge. The young warrior before Wanmdi is the merry Capa. He is obedient and worships Manitou and the good spirits, but he is not intelligent. It is one of the greatest tasks of Hoton, who is always kind, to teach him what to do in the forest and on the mountains, but Hoton will never give up the work, because he loves to overcome mighty difficulties. And the warrior who walks just before the pious Capa is the crafty Waditaka, upon whom Manitou put a terrible misfortune at birth. He was born *ska* (white), and though his skin is still *ska* he is striving with all his might to become a Dakota and his soul is turning *stanwe* (red). And it must be said for him that while the rest of us are born Dakota and could not keep from being Dakota, if we would, he is Dakota from choice. So the other warriors look kindly upon the crafty Waditaka, and when they have nothing else to do they teach him the things he should know, and, being crafty, he learns well.' "

The young warriors laughed. The invincible spirits of Hoton, the valiant boaster, were always a great tonic to them.

"Look!" said Will. "The great sheep on the other side of the chasm has gone."

"And there he is now on another ledge, two hundred feet below," said Inmu.

"I have heard," said Will, "that they plunge down lofty cliffs head foremost, and alight unharmed upon their horns, but I can scarcely believe it's so."

"No," said the wise Roka, "it is not. No animal could do such a thing. His horns would be smashed. But they do scramble down peaks that seem impossible. You see them walking like flies on the face of the mountains, and that is why the story of their dropping down on their horns started."

They said but little during the next hour, needing all their breath for the ascent, which now became very steep. But they were in no danger of falls, as they were not beyond the tree line, and there was plenty of dwarfed forest. Roka stopped some time before sunset, and they made a camp in a sheltered ravine in short but thick timber, where they had an easy night, although Hoton talked much in the evening about the great bears.

"We have known from what we have seen that they love best such slopes as these," he said. "The king wolf, who alone of all the animals thinks far, far ahead, has brought to them word that we are coming and they will lay an ambush for us. They know also which of this band is most to be dreaded and so I must be more careful than I ever was before in my life."

"We must all be more careful than we were ever before in our lives, careful as we have been in the past," said Roka, thoughtfully.

CHAPTER IX

IN THE PASS

WILL believed with Roka and Pehansan that the great buffalo plains of the far north lay beyond the lofty ranges that now confronted them. He remembered that the maps of America he had studied at school showed a sea of mountains along the Pacific coast extending far up into Alaska, and many of these mountains were known to be very high. Beyond question many of the peaks far overtopped those of Montana, Idaho and Washington, and he believed that the pass itself toward which they were going must be at least two miles above the sea level. The crossing they had made in coming from the smaller valley into the larger one was a light task compared with the mighty climb now before them. The Sioux were naturally a people of the plains, though small portions of them lived in the hills, but the members of the little band surveyed the formidable summits without fear.

They advanced two days without accident, though the path was surrounded with difficulties and dangers and their progress was slow, not yet taking them beyond the timber line. They encountered deep ravines which they crossed with infinite toil, and they came to several streams, every one flowing in a head-long current down the mountain and creating with its speed the white foam they had seen when they were far below.

Will admired these creeks, which he knew came from the glaciers and fields of snow high above, and, at one place where the ground was fairly level, they let down their lines, catching splendid mountain trout, much larger than usual and of a very delicate flavor. Will admired greatly their silvery beauty, and he was quite sure he and his comrades were the first human beings who had ever fished in those wild waters.

The space that sloped slightly did not extend many yards, but several of the young warriors were tempted, despite its coldness, to throw off their clothes and take a dip in the stream. Will was an inveterate bather, and, while primeval man was not particularly fastidious about his person, these mountain Sioux were neat and cleanly, and the young warriors like Will took keen delight in leaping and swimming in running water. Now they sought the deep places in the stream, and, fending off the cold with swift movements, felt exhilarating thrills, as they swam or floated on the current. Hoton in particular enjoyed himself.

"Behold me!" he called to Will, who was floating ten feet away. "As I am a great hunter so I am a great swimmer!"

"But I do not have to swim," said Will. "I merely lie upon my back in the current and let it carry me where I wish to go."

"And so can I," said Hoton, grandly. "Whatsoever you can do on the land or in the water, Waditaka, that I can do also."

He turned over on his back and floated peacefully with the stream. His violent exertion in swimming had fully counteracted the chill of the water, and his blood pulsed from his heart and back again in a pleasant and exhilarating current. It was very grateful to his tired muscles to lie thus at ease and to be borne swiftly. It was, in truth, the very poetry of motion to the son of the wilderness, and as he glided along he looked up at the great blue vault bending over him with such kindness and beauty and felt that he, Hoton, was the very incarnation of what he boasted himself to be, the flower and quintessence of the Sioux nation. He heard shouts from his comrades, but they only increased his satisfaction. They were shouts of admiration. Inmu, Waditaka and all the others were acknowledging vocally his wonderful skill in floating, without apparent effort, on the surface of a swift mountain stream. They saw his superiority and admitted it.

The shouts increased and the spirit of Hoton was fairly bathed in contentment. Seemingly he did not move a muscle. He was giving a most wonderful exhibition of floating. He knew that he was going fast, because, turning his head slightly on one side, he saw the bank receding at a great rate. He concluded that it was time to turn back. His demonstration had been sufficient. No member of Roka's band would ever again claim to be his equal in swimming.

He shifted to his side with the intention of going across the current, when, to his amazement and horror he made no progress, but was still carried down the stream. Nor was the water around him any longer silver in color. Instead it was foaming into white, and, from the rocky banks on either side, great coils and gusts of foam were dashed back. There was a roaring in his ears, so loud that it made the shouts of his comrades sound like distant echoes.

He managed to raise his head somewhat higher out of water and saw a current, with himself in the very center of it, running like a mad torrent to an awful place where, in a cloud of foam, it dropped off into nothing. Great though his efforts were they availed him not. The element that surrounded him was liquid. It slipped off his bare body and eddied around it, but it enclosed him as fast as if he were held in a vise of steel. Had his strength been ten times what it was he would yet have been powerless in the mighty current that was racing to the edge of the fall. Then, like wise men who resign themselves to the inevitable when they know effort is vain, he commended his soul, in his primitive, but none the less noble fashion, to the great unknown Manitou, who is merciful as well as just. He drew in his body compactly, shut his eyes, and the next instant, while the great waters roared in his ears, took the fall.

He had first a sense of wild dashings, a long, breathless falling as if from the clouds to the earth, a tremendous period of submergence followed by buffetings, and then, opening his eyes, he looked

benevolently at Inmu, Waditaka, Tarinca and Capa
who were working over him with all diligence.
They were rubbing his hands and his chest, and they
looked anxious, but the brave Hoton only smiled to
himself. He would soon calm their apprehensions.
He was not hurt. He had not really been unconscious. It was merely a little trick of his to heighten
the effect of a great deed. He had often seen the
medicine men with certain dramatic touches make an
achievement appear all the more wonderful. These
comrades of his, brave and daring though they were,
would have to admit that they could not shoot a great
waterfall as he, Hoton, the incomparable, had done.

"It is enough, my friends," he said, sitting up. "I
thank you for your care, but Hoton, the great swimmer, does not need it."

"You are alive then!" exclaimed Capa. *"Wica-
nagi* (the soul) was not dashed out of you by the terrible waters?"

Hoton turned upon him a gaze that was majestic
and reproving, though not unkind. Capa was very
young, but he was always willing to learn.

"Capa," said he in grave tones, "why should you
think the soul had left my body? Often after achiev-
ing a mighty task I lie down and rest. It is the way
of great warriors. Did you spring into the waters
after me, and Waditaka and Inmu and Tarinca with
you? I see that you did, but it does credit to the
goodness of your hearts, not to your judgment.
And perhaps I, too, am a little to blame. I should
have told you before that I always shoot a high fall

this way. I put my feet close together, my hands by my side, lift up my head a little that I may not be drowned in the foam, shut my eyes to keep them dry, and then go over like a great salmon. It is easy— that is, for me."

"You are a great swimmer, Hoton, but your mind is yet greater," said Will admiringly. "Farther on there is another fall higher than the one down which you came. We would see you shoot that also!"

Hoton rose to his feet and gave Will a lofty stare of disdain.

"Waditaka," he said, "when you are older you will know more. Understand then that a great man shows only once how a thing should be done. If those who see it do not learn, then it is their fault. One fall in one day is enough."

He walked in stately fashion back up the bank, noticing the fall out of the corner of his eye. It was really a high fall, and he wondered that he had come out of it alive. But then, Manitou was good to the deserving and he was grateful. Roka and Pehansan were sitting on the plateau above, and they welcomed Hoton's return with grave smiles.

"We are glad to see you back, Hoton," said Roka.

"I had no intention of staying away," replied the Crow. "I am attached to you, O, Roka, wise leader, and to all my comrades. Nor do I wish to cross the great mountains alone. The young warriors will need my advice and example."

"That is true, Hoton. Perhaps when we pass the crest we will find streams on the other side down which we can shoot even as you have done here, with Hoton himself leading us. It will save time."

"I am not one to dispute the word of the wise Roka," said Hoton, bowing low. Nevertheless he was willing to sit a long time by the fire, as he found some soreness in his muscles.

That night the snow fell again and they retreated deep into the scrub timber, where they built a new fire, and, wrapped well, lay beside it, listening to the roaring of the wind, which at that height had many voices, all high and shrill.

"The winds warn us to go back," said Inmu, after listening a long time. "They are hostile. The evil spirits ride on their edge and shout at us. They say that men have not been on these mountains before and that they cannot cross them. They threaten us with great suffering and final death if we go on."

"Are you in favor of going back, Inmu?" asked Will, knowing well what the answer would be.

"As we have fought the wild animals, so will we fight the winds," replied the Lynx.

"I knew you felt that way and so do all the others."

The winds died presently, as if, having given their warning to the foolish human beings who scorned to heed it, they refused to say more, and the still air became intensely clear. The peaks, now that they had come nearer, seemed to increase in height, the white crests piercing the blue void. All the ten had a sense of awe, which, however, had in it no tincture of fear. The white peaks were a line of majestic sentinels guarding their promised land and they seemed to offer a challenge to those who could to pass them.

They climbed a steep slope and stood upon a shelf of stone to rest. The mountains towered above them as high as ever, and apparently they had made no progress, so little was the distance they had come compared with that which they had yet to go.

"Look!" said Will, who had turned and who was gazing back into the valley.

Far in the southwestern corner the edge of a gray shield was appearing above the horizon. Higher and higher it rose, and broader and broader grew the dark circle. Then a flash of light burst from the center and a low sound, almost like the moan of a distant ocean, came to them.

"A great storm!" said Roka. "It will sweep over the valley but it will not touch us!"

Will, always interested in the mighty manifestations of nature, watched from above while the air in the valley darkened. He had often gazed at storms from below but seldom from above, and now he found the gathering of elemental forces unspeakably majestic. The thunder, at first only a groaning on that dim horizon, began to rumble heavily, and the gorges of the mountains all about gave it back in many sinister echoes. The clouds increased, the green in the valley narrowed until it was only a strip and then it was gone altogether. Banks and columns of white vapor floated along the edges of the clouds, but at their center, where they were darkest, the lightning shot in long, flaming streaks, red, or blue, or white, but intensely vivid in any hue.

"It is a mighty storm, and it passes almost at our feet," said Roka.

"As if to prove to us how tremendous nature can be," said Will.

"The storm knows us not," said Roka. "In its presence we are but flies on the mountain side, no, we are nothing. Think, Waditaka, that storms may have been occurring here for thousands of years and that we may be the first men who have ever seen one of them! It does not matter to the Storm God whether we see or do not see."

"The storm has many spirits besides the great Storm God himself," said the pious Tarinca, "and most of them are good."

"Perhaps the good spirits and evil spirits fight together in the clouds," said Inmu, "and they hurl the thunderbolts and the lightning at one another. We think ourselves warriors, but it is not for mortal man to share in such mighty battles."

They watched the storm more than an hour. When it reached its zenith the air was dark as night on the mountains, and nothing could be seen in the valley below save by the lightning stroke. The roll of the thunder was so great that the peaks and ridges seemed to shake, but the Sioux were not afraid. The storm was not concerned with them. It did not touch them. The good spirits and the evil spirits fought in the valley at their feet and passed them by.

"The good spirits win," said Inmu. "The thunder sinks and the lightning dies!"

The clouds floated away with amazing rapidity. The lightning flashed for the last time, the thunder became a murmur and then nothing, the whole valley, vast and vivid, sprang out into the light, and there below them waved the great forest, deep green with the silver bands of its rivers cutting across it. The storm vanished as if it had never been.

"It was a great sight," said Roka. "I am glad to have seen it."

"And I," said nine other voices all together.

"We have not been alone in watching the storm," said Pehansan, pointing across a gorge. "Doubtless he has seen many such, because he goes about his business undisturbed."

The gorge was three or four hundred yards across, and beyond it was an easy slope on which grew sparse and dwarfed vegetation. A huge brown bulk prowled among the bushes, digging for roots or ants. Will recognized at once the monstrous bear of the north, evidently in his own home, engaged in the chief business of his life, the pursuit of food.

"I wonder if he knows we are here," he said.

"If he does, he does not care," said Pehansan. "Like *Tateyanpa* (Wind) he thinks we cannot cross the mountains, but I will tell him we can."

He made a hollow of his two hands, and shouted in loud, piercing tones:

"O *Warankxi* (Bear)! O *Warankxi!*"

The bear went on with his hunt for roots and

grubs. Pehansan's voice rose and carried far across the gorge.

"*Warankxi! Warankxi!*" he shouted. "Look up! Do not pretend that you do not see us or hear us! Your brethren in the valley and on the lower mountains said that we could not cross the mighty ranges and reach the great buffalo grounds, but we have beaten them every time we met them! Look up! Look up, *Warankxi,* and behold your masters!"

The bear could not ignore that fierce summons, which was at once a taunt and a challenge. He raised his head and Will knew by the wrinkling of his lips that he was growling.

"What is he saying?" he asked of the imaginative Inmu. "Does a good spirit bring you his words through the air?"

"He tells us that he accepts our challenge," replied the Lynx. "He says that no man has ever yet crossed these mountains, and that his tribe is here to see that we also fail. He adds, too, that the wolves, the panthers and all the great animals also are on watch. See, he rises on his hind legs and stands up like a man, shaking his fore paws at us!"

The monstrous bulk of *Warankxi* was upreared and it seemed to Will, imaginative like Inmu, that he had made a threatening gesture intended directly for them. Presently he lowered himself, but without haste, and shambled away.

"We do not fear him," said Pehansan, "but we know we shall have to fight him. And now look,

Wanmdi, the bird after which you are named, is watching us too!"

A dark speck appeared in the blue arch, enlarged rapidly, and then shot down with amazing rapidity. A few hundred yards above them it sheered away, crossed the gorge and alighted on a blasted stump near where the bear had stood, its beaked head and great wings quivering slightly, as if in menace.

"It doubles the eagle of the south in size," said Roka. "I think it could carry away a young goat or a young mountain sheep in its talons. I should not care to meet it on these heights without my bow and arrows. Speak to your brother, Wanmdi."

The young warrior, whose name meant the eagle, made a trumpet of his hollowed hands as Pehansan had done and shouted across the chasm:

"O *Wanmdi,* you sit there on the blasted stump and threaten us, but we are not afraid! Though I bear your name I am man, and you are not, and I am your master! Your beak and talons are great and sharp, but my arrows are sharper. I, Wanmdi, whose name is the same as yours, have come to cross your mountains, and you cannot stop me! Leave your stump, come near and my arrow will tell you how much greater my power is than yours!"

The eagle rose from the stump, spread his wings and circled high above the heads of the ten, saying very plainly that he accepted the challenge.

"May I let fly an arrow at him, Roka?" said Wanmdi.

"Yes, Wanmdi," replied the wise leader, "but the mark is too difficult."

Nevertheless the young warrior sent a shaft straight up at the hovering shadow, but the arrow, flying to a great height, came back and rang on the stone shelf beside them, where Wanmdi picked it up again. The sinister shadow hung over them a moment or two longer, and then the eagle flew slowly away toward a high peak.

"You did not hit him, Wanmdi," said Roka, "but it was a good shot for so great a height. The arrow almost touched his wing. You said to him that while he could threaten we could strike. He will not forget it. Now, I think it would be well for us to build our fire on this shelf and pass the night here."

The night was cold, but very bright, and in its silvery light the ranges and peaks seemed more tremendous than ever. Before any of them went to sleep they heard a long, melancholy cry come from a deep gorge. Roka turned to Hinyankaga (Owl), one of the youngest of the Sioux warriors.

"Wanmdi's brother who, nevertheless, hates him, came to see him in the day," he said, "and there, Hinyankaga, is yours calling to you in the night."

Hinyankaga, noted for his high spirits, replied:

"If I may, O wise Roka, I will talk with my brother, who does not like me any more than Wanmdi's brother liked him."

"Talk as much as you wish."

Hinyankaga pursed his lips and uttered a hoot so piercing and of such wailing quality that Will, who

sat beside him, was startled. The mournful lament
passed in echoes through the mountains and died.
Back from the gorge came the hoot of the real owl
and Hinyankaga rejoiced. For several moments they
talked together, wail for wail, and their voices had
many inflections, now rising in anger, and then sinking in lament.

"What were you saying, Hinyankaga?" asked
Roka, when they ceased.

"Nothing that was friendly," replied the happy
youth. "Like the bear and the eagle the owl warned
us, he told me these mountains belonged to the great
animals and the great birds, and that we must turn
back or our bones would lie to eternity frozen in the
ice of the lofty peaks. I told him we would go where
the wise Roka led, and that he meant to lead us over
the pass."

"Manitou himself makes no threat against us," said
Roka, "and so long as he does not we need not fear
the menace of the animals."

Although the air at that height was quite cold, the
young warriors felt snug and comfortable as they lay
in their robes before the fire. The scrub pines extended for some distance up the slope, and, as usual in
those undisturbed regions, plenty of dead wood was
lying about. Now and then, when someone brought
a fresh bole or trunk and threw it on the bed of
coals, a bright blaze sprang up and the area of light
widened. It was Will's turn after a while to fetch
wood, and he went twenty or thirty yards along the
slope, where the little pines grew in a dense cluster.

He found what he wished and was turning back with his burden when his attention was attracted by a light rustling, a faint sound, not much more than that made by two leaves rubbing together.

Will, gazing into the depths of the pines, from which the light noise had come, saw two red sparks, and as he continued to gaze with the greatest intensity, he traced the outline of a large and menacing form. Then he knew that the red sparks were eyes. Although he could not see it clearly, he felt instinctively that this was the king wolf, still following them, and, with a tenacity that was more human than animal, meaning to follow them to the end.

He was not afraid. Although his bow and quiver were left by the fire, the loaded revolver was in his belt and it was sufficient to meet a rush. But he did not believe the king wolf meant to attack. Instead, he was there to watch and threaten. He was too wise, even had the chance offered, to spring upon Will with the others so near, and the lad, standing stiffly erect and motionless, stared at him with the human eyes that are so much more compelling than those of the beast.

A kind of pride possessed Will. He had at that moment a great feeling of power. In the long duel between him and the king wolf he had been victorious so far, and he believed that he would continue triumphant. The eyes of the wolf were fierce and burning. They seemed red, then yellow, then green, like those of a panther, casting off sparks of malice and menace. But Will was exalted by his pride in being human. He was superior to any wolf or to any animal, no matter how large and fierce. He felt his figure swell and grow more powerful. He took a step forward. Nor did his hand go to his revolver. Instead, both, empty, swung by his side. But the great wolf, daunted by that human gaze, fixed and fearless, gave back. The eyes, red and yellow and green, with changing lights, shifted from his and became irresolute. He advanced another step, never relaxing that relentless gaze. The eyes of the wolf shifted again, he uttered a low, uneasy growl, and, turning suddenly, slid away among the bushes.

Will, triumphant, still stood stiffly erect, but a cold sweat broke out on his face, and then he felt limp and relaxed. It required a great effort of his will to keep his figure from sagging, but he managed to hold himself together, and, going back, he cast the pine bole on the fire.

The dry wood flamed up the moment it touched the bed of coals, and blazed across Will's face, revealing a great pallor which did not escape the sharp eyes of Roka.

"What has happened to you, Waditaka?" he asked. "All the blood has left your face."

Will laughed nervously.

"I saw our old friend in the bushes," he replied.

"What old friend?"

"One that has followed us, one that I know is possessed by a demon, and is bent upon our destruction."

"The king wolf?"

"None other, O wise Roka. I saw his red eyes in the dusk and stared into them. It was not because of any courage or greater hardihood of mine, but because I was a human being, that I at last stared him down. He went away, but I know that he and his pack will always be near us, waiting their chance."

"I was sure that it would be so, Waditaka. They will go with us over the mountains. But we will not fear them so long as our eyes watch and our arrows are sharp."

Soon all slept but Roka and Pehansan, and they sat long, making a strong rope of knotted strips of rawhide, which they felt sure they would need before they climbed much farther on the slopes. In the morning they set out in a day that bade fair to be clear, but, before it was two hours old, a cold, drizzling rain began to fall. Nevertheless, they did not allow their spirits to be depressed, although danger was added to discomfort. The narrow ways became slippery, and, now and then, they were compelled to pass with much caution along the edges of great gulfs. But as they were not yet beyond the range of dwarfed timber, they were aided most of the time by the bushes, although the rawhide rope was put to good service.

The test, however, was severe. The chilly water soaked through their leggings and moccasins, and their muscles began to ache from the steep climb. Despite every effort spirits would flag, but the indomitable Hoton cheered them anew.

"The big white peaks ahead are nodding to one

another," he said, "and they are saying: 'Lo, the band of Roka comes! His warriors are brave and at any time they would gladly fight other warriors who should try to bar their way, but they cannot forever fight snow and ice, and bitter rain! Their wills would grow weak if they did not have with them Hoton, Hoton the bold, Hoton the wise! However high we may be, although our crests touch the top of the sky, he will climb over us!' "

Thus the valiant boaster chanted as he went along and his chant was uplifting. The air grew colder and the rain turned to hail. The wind rose and, moaning and shrieking around the peaks and through the gorges, it sent the rain in gusts like the spraying of shot into the faces of the ten. But the warriors, bending their heads to the blast, went on, and above all the lash of wind and rain rose the mighty voice of Hoton in his brave chant:

> "The warriors of Roka come,
> The cunning king wolf they fear not,
> Nor the great bear of the cold north,
> Nor the huge panther on the bough.

> "Over the snow mountains they go,
> Up the steep, icy cliff they climb,
> The winds cannot turn them back,
> O, brave men of the Dakota.

> "Wild beasts and mighty peaks warn them,
> The fierce storm rages over their heads,
> Bitter hail beats on their faces,
> On, warriors of the Dakota!"

It was a gallant song, because they were not now facing wild beasts, but the fierce spirits of the high mountains, over which they had no control, wind, hail, snow and ice, which they could not conquer with weapons, only with deathless souls. The hail began to beat so fiercely that they were compelled to protect their eyes with their uplifted arms, and they moved very slowly over their slippery footing, lest they be hurled into fathomless gulfs below. But always the mighty voice of Hoton boomed out, chanting his bold song, and the others joined with will and power in the chorus:

> "Wild beasts and mighty peaks warn them,
> Fierce storms rage over their heads,
> Bitter hail beats on their faces.
> On, warriors of the Dakota!"

And on they went, in spite of all the elements that were conspiring to drive them back. There might have been passes, lower and wider and safer, but they knew them not, and they climbed along the best path their eyes had shown to them. Luck favored them in one respect, as they were not yet beyond the timber line, though very near. Little evergreens grew here and there in crevices between the stones, where a few inches of soil was lodged, thrusting up brave heads only a foot or two but often thick of stem, and they made a welcome hold to the climbers.

At far intervals the gusts of hail ceased for a full minute or more and they caught glimpses to the south of great, deep valleys set close with tall timber, but as well as they could judge these valleys were like bowls without any visible outlet. All around them circled the high, white peaks.

"We must look for some place in which to pass the night," said the wise Roka to Pehansan. "Our young warriors are brave and enduring and will try everything we bid them do, but we must save them as much as we can."

"We may find some shelter in the cliffs," said Pehansan. "Stone mountains are always full of hollows and caves."

"If we find one, we must retreat into it and lie by until the hail passes."

But it was a full two hours before they found a cleft in the rock big enough for their purpose, running back eight or ten feet, and, with the floor sloping outward in such fashion that melting snow or hail would not enter. It was crude and rough, but in the dim past myriads of men had probably slept in shelter no better, and with thanks to the good spirits, they drew into it. The floor was rough and the roof was so low they had to bend, but no matter how the wind shifted the hail could not reach them at the far end, and they crouched there, wrapped in their robes, until the numbness departed from their bodies.

Then they ventured forth, and managed to gather a little timber, just a little, because the vegetation ceased entirely a few hundred yards farther on, and managed, with great skill and infinite pains, to build a small fire in the hollow. The smoke from it would have troubled them at an ordinary time, but they did not mind it now, and hovered over the low flames, rejoicing in the grateful heat. Then up rose the voice of Hoton once more in his defiant song, and all the warriors, even the wise Roka and the tall Pehansan, joined in the chorus:

> "Wild beasts and mighty peaks warn them,
> The fierce storm rages over their heads,
> Bitter hail beats on their faces.
> On, warriors of the Dakota!"

Their voices thundered in the narrow cave and a deep gorge somewhere gave back an echo that they heard above the swish of hail and moan of wind. The soul of Will leaped within him.

"It is our voices triumphant over everything," he said. "It is a sign. The good spirits have willed that we shall be victorious over all."

"Those triumph who refuse to be put down, and the good spirits are always on their side, Waditaka," said Roka. "Now we are all warmed well and we will put out the fire, because there is but little wood and we do not know how long we shall have to stay here."

Several of the young warriors would have liked to keep the fire burning, not alone for the heat but for the courage that was to be drawn from the light of the flames, but the commands of Roka were to be obeyed, and they extinguished the coals. Then, crouched close once more, and wrapped thoroughly, they listened to the tales of the valiant boaster. Hoton never talked better. The legends of the warlike Dakota nation, passed on from father to son through the generations, had been caught by his vivid mind and stored in his retentive memory. Now he told of mighty hunting expeditions and of great battles with other tribes before the white man came. Outside the swish and rattle of the hail gave place to a softer sound, and Roka, going to the entrance of the hollow, announced that the hail had given way to snow.

"It is well," said Pehansan. "The snow is not so treacherous. With it under our feet our heads will not be where our feet were a moment before."

"And on mountain heights a fall is dangerous," said Roka. "A warrior who goes down never knows where he will stop."

They had warmed food over the coals before they put them out, and after a while they ate supper, having decided to remain in the cave until the next day, as Roka and Pehansan agreed that it was dangerous to venture forth while the snow was driving so hard.

After supper Will dozed. Shelter, food and warmth kept him in a happy frame of mind. Now and then he roused himself to listen to Hoton, whose tongue ran on pleasantly like the murmur of a river, but the intervals between such moments of consciousness grew further apart, and at last he slept. The next morning they found the snow banked high before the mouth of the cave, but they broke a way through it, and looked upon a world clothed everywhere in gleaming white.

Roka sent the warriors in different directions to

seek a good path up the slope, everyone carrying, as always, his blankets and full complement of weapons. Will and Inmu turned to the left and went along the slope. But when they came to a vast rock with a path on either side they separated, one on each side.

Will was not far from the edge, and, by leaning a little, though he did not dare much, he saw the mighty valley far below and white domes which he knew were snow on the lofty tops of the evergreens. It made him dizzy to stare into the gulf, and leaning back the other way he continued to pick his path with great caution. Then he felt something tremble, but at first he believed the effect to be purely mental. His nerves had been shaken by looking into the great depths, and, steadying himself, he took two more steps forward. The shaking came again. The snow beneath his feet began to yield, a terrible fear shot through him, the whole bank on which he stood gave way and slid down the mountain. There was a mighty roaring, a white flood poured over him, he had a sense of falling into infinity and then he became unconscious.

CHAPTER X

THE UNSCALABLE CLIFF

WHEN Will returned to earth, after wandering for a space in vast unknown regions between the worlds, he was conscious of lying on something soft. The feeling, vague at first, was not at all unpleasant. For just a minute, perhaps, he did not remember what had happened, and then it all came back, the terrible sliding beneath his feet, the roaring in his ears, and the fall into the abyss.

Then he wondered why he was not dead. Perhaps he was and this was *Wakantankatipi* (Heaven) of the Dakota. If so, it must be a glorious place, worth looking at, and he opened his eyes. But he saw only walls of snow, and when he undertook to move he found that he was imbedded in snow to his waist. Then he knew that he was not in *Wakantankatipi,* but that he abode yet a while on *Maga* (Earth). He was pleased with the knowledge. Heaven must be truly a magnificent abode, but he was young and before he went to heaven he wished to live his allotted span in the world into which he had been born. He felt that he had work to finish before he went away.

He struggled to pull himself out of the snow, and then he became conscious that he had not escaped all injury in his fall. He felt bruises all over his body, but he strove on, nevertheless, and managed to raise himself until the snow only came up to his knees. Then he became exhausted and his head grew dizzy. Leaning against the snow bank, he rested and looked upward, where he saw nothing but a rift of sky. He had no way of telling how far he had fallen, but he knew that it must have been far, the great mass of snow skidding with him as he went down and acting as a pillow when he struck. It had been a mere chance that he had fallen on top of it instead of under it, but he took the result as a direct interposition of the good spirits. There was other proof of it, his splendid horn bow and quiver of arrows hung on his back unharmed, his revolver was safe in his belt and his pack of food had not been disturbed.

It was surely a miracle, and he would rejoice in the telling of it, when he rejoined his comrades an hour or two later! Perhaps they could come down and help him out of the snowy chasm, and he began to shout at the top of his voice, repeating his call over and over again. There was no reply save a fall of snow from the crest of the bank, and its soft swish as it rolled down to his feet. He realized that the current of air, set in motion by his voice, had been sufficient to cause the fall. Hence he was in a situation in which he must move with extreme caution. He might be on a shelf in the side of the cliff, or he might be in the valley itself. It was a vital problem, and, for the moment, he did not know how to decide it.

Although he had been imbedded in the snow, he was not cold. He realized instead that he had cause to be very grateful for snow. Whether he was on a shelf or in the valley, his fall had been great, and only a vast amount of snow could have saved him. Nothing else could have helped. He worked again at the process of extricating himself, until he stood entirely free upon the snow, which his exertions had now packed under his feet. His success, even in a small way, encouraged him. Why should he despair? He was Waditaka of a valiant band of the Dakota, led by the wise Roka, a band that had overcome superhuman hardships and dangers, and it was not for him to feel depression. Moreover, he had just been saved by a miracle, and he would soon be back with his brave comrades, who beyond doubt were now looking for him. The fact that his weapons, as well as himself, had escaped real injury was proof that the good spirits still watched over him, despite his fall.

He raised his voice once more and sent forth long calls, but his comrades did not answer. As before, snow fell beneath the wave of air set in motion by his voice, and he concluded that the wall in front of him must be thin. His belief, growing into a conviction, he began to push at it, taking care, in case it fell, not to fall with it, and soon he saw it toppling. Then he stood back, and the embankment went over with a crash, showing him, to his great delight, that he was really standing on the floor of the valley, and that the high wall he had overturned had been formed by snow falling from above and outward.

He drew long, deep breaths of relief and stepped out among the trees, which here grew thick and tall. It was upon their snowy domes that he had gazed down and now he looked up to see how far he had fallen. He was amazed at the distance. It was four or five hundred feet and a vast quantity of snow had come down under him to soften his descent so far. He tested himself thoroughly, and found that the pain from his bruises was departing. He had lived a life of such hardihood and endurance that in an hour he would forget them entirely, and, sitting down on a fallen log, he ate some of the jerked venison from his pack, thinking at the same time upon his position, and of a possible way out of it.

He was in a deep valley, or rather in a great well in the mountains. From his seat on the log, and owing to the absence of underbrush, he saw very clearly that it was almost round, and that its diameter was about half a mile. It was grown up everywhere with trees of great height and size, and a small brook of bright green water, evidently formed by melting snows on the mountain, flowed down its center. As the cliffs rose on all sides to the height of about five hundred feet, he surmised that the little stream went back into them through some rocky opening.

Despite the wintry heights that surrounded it, the little valley was attractive. The peaks and ranges themselves protected it. The tops of the trees, covered with snow, were like vast white umbrellas, but as they rose to a height of two hundred and fifty feet or more, the ground beneath them was in places almost bare of snow and green grass was showing. The whole aspect of the place was inviting and Will thought it a little Eden. After eating, he knelt and drank of the brook's cold, sweet waters. Then, sure that his comrades must be somewhere on the rim above him, he began to shout.

"Roka! Roka!" he called.

"Pehansan! Pehansan!" he cried.

"Inmu! Inmu!" he sent up from the valley.

"Hoton! Hoton!" he summoned.

They came not for his call, nor did they answer. For a moment apprehension stabbed like a spear at his heart, but he put it aside. They would not leave him. They were off on a false trail, but they would come back soon to the true one. Why should his hopes decline? He was unhurt, he was well armed, and he had food for several days. He resumed his seat on the log, and waited patiently until the face of a Dakota should appear, peering over the edge of the cliff. He wondered which would show first, but he believed it would be Inmu, with whom his comradeship was the closest.

He saw the tops of the trees moving a little under the wind, and the snow fell from them in flakes. A brilliant wintry sun blazed overhead, but it came through the snowy domes, transfigured and softened, until the red was almost pink. The beautiful delicate colors fell across the earth in parallel bars, and Will admired them. Surely his first impression was right, and, in very truth and reality, this was a little Eden.

Although the floor of the valley seemed to be level,

it had, nevertheless, a smart slope toward the east, as the brook running in that direction flowed with a swift current. Clear, running water was always grateful to Will's eyes and he had never seen a finer little stream. Its waters, which at first had appeared a sheer green, were now tinted violet and pink, where the transfused rays of the sun fell upon them. He surmised that noble trout might be found in deep pools farther on, but it was not a matter into which he would look now, as his comrades would be waiting for him and he must discover a way up the wall.

It was hard to decide where to try the ascent first, because the whole circle about the valley seemed to rise up straight like the side of a house. But he knew that difficulties were seldom so great as they seemed, and a wall that looked perpendicular from afar might lean much when he stood at its foot.

He finally decided to follow the stream, but, when he had gone a few steps, a hovering shadow darkened the air above him. He looked up. A vast eagle flying below the snowy umbrellas of the trees was circling about him, and his imagination instantly became so vivid that he was sure he saw the beak and claws of steel and the ferocious red eyes flaming down at him. He strung his bow and took an arrow from his quiver. The great eagle did not attack, although it flew lower and lower, but when it was forty or fifty feet above him it began to rise, going higher and higher, until it was lost from his sight.

Will felt a chill and his heart sank suddenly. Was the shadow of the eagle's wing a dark omen? As he looked up he no longer saw the beauty of the valley's floor, but the lofty stony walls and the rim of snow beyond. He refused to let his courage decline, merely because black wings had hovered over him, and turned his eyes back to the green waters of the stream, shot in the shallows with pink and blue tints. It flowed in many a curve, and he saw, at intervals, the deep pools that he had expected. In them, too, he beheld the great trout that he had felt sure would be there, but he did not disturb them now, following the current until it disappeared, as he had foreseen, under a low arch of stone and into the depths of the mountains, through which it probably passed in its subterranean channel to some river, and then on into other rivers, until it reached its haven in the universal ocean. An easy passage for the water, but none for him!

He watched the green stream as it passed under the stone arch, taking the plunge into the dark with a pleasant sigh and gurgle, flowing on forever, fed always by the eternal snows. Then, with a sigh of his own that his way should be so much more difficult, he left the mouth of the brook and continued his walk around the valley. As he had surmised, the walls were not perpendicular, but they were far from having slope enough for a climber. In many places, he might have gone high by crags and pinnacles, but always they failed at some point, leaving a smooth surface beyond which no strength or skill of his could lift him. He had almost completed the circle and despair was replacing hope, when he came to a rift in the stone wall where the path sloped back, and a sparse and dwarf vegetation grew in the crevices. Hope sprang up with a great bound. It was a poor trail and dangerous, but by great exertion he might work his way out there and rejoin the Dakota. As it was now growing dark in the valley and night would soon be at hand, he felt that he must postpone the effort until the next day. A single false step in the dusk would send him crashing to the floor of the valley, to lie there, every bone shattered.

Marking well in his mind the place, he retreated to the green brook, chiefly for the sake of company. The mountain and the valley itself were now so quiet that he liked to hear the pleasant murmuring sound of the swift waters. They talked to him, they told him of the cheerful journey they were going to take through the limitless caverns, through open rivers to the infinite sea, and of all the wonderful things they would see on the way. It was a soothing song and murmur, and looking down at the green waters he envied them once more.

The sun blazed in red splendor for a moment on the western rim of the mountains, and darkness rushed down, filling the valley like a well. The air became cold and he resolved to build a fire there by the stream that talked to him incessantly and so cheerfully. It was not a difficult task for one trained as he had been. Like his comrades of the Dakota, he was never separated from his flint and steel, and soon a heap of dead sticks was sending up a bright blaze, irradiating a circle perhaps twenty yards in diameter, beyond which the heavy darkness hung like an impenetrable curtain.

As the ground was damp from the melting of the light snow around the fire, he secured enough dry boughs and sticks to make a flooring before the trunk of one of the great trees, and he sat down upon it with his back to the tree and his face to the flames. Then, wrapped closely in his robes and with his bow and quiver across his knees, he waited for sleep. The sticks were of tough wood and would burn long, for which he was glad, as with both the stream and the fire near he would not be lonely. Both were talking in merry fashion.

The waters sang of the great leap they were going to take in the dark, though they feared not because the sunshine lay beyond the dim caverns, and the flames chattered back. They would die, but before dying they would send up sparks to be taken by the winds and swept away into the bright heavens. Will's dozing brain comprehended all they said and he listened to the pleasant chatter of fire and water.

"I flow on forever," said the water. "The great ocean receives me at last, but I am not lost in it."

"I send my sparks toward the heavens," said the fire, "and they are taken into the bright clouds which pour back in gold over the earth."

"I am clean and joyous of heart," said the water. "I harm no one. I am life."

"I drive away cold and I warm the soul. I, too, am life," said the fire. "I bring light into the dark."

"The grass and the flowers spring up under my touch," said the water.

Will felt that the claims of both fire and water were justified. Each was vital, each was life, and theirs was a noble competition. The fire began to sink a little, but as the sticks of wood were damp and they were many, the heap would burn a long time. The water ran on, unchanged in volume, and he knew that its pleasant trickle would still be there, neither louder nor softer than it was in the night. But in the darkness the fire was worth more to him than the brook. It gave light and heat and therefore physical comfort in a night that was uncommonly black. Looking up from the floor of the valley as from the bottom of a well, he saw a dark, brooding sky, unflecked by a single star. All around him the circling blackness was moving up closer and closer as the light from the flames dwindled and was less able to push it back.

Yet Will felt comfort of both body and spirit. His bruises were forgotten. He remembered only the miracle that had saved him in so great a fall, the vast bank of snow plunging down beneath him and receiving him like a huge feather bed in its bosom. It was a good omen. He would climb the steep path the next morning and surprise the Dakota by appearing among them alive and well. What a tale he could spin! Not Hoton himself could boast of having fallen five hundred feet to alight with just a few bruises.

His eyelids drooped and then he dozed, the fire wavering dimly before him and the black forest seeming to move up, as if it would circle his throat and compress it. He came suddenly out of his drowsiness. Ice flowed down his spine and the hair on the back of his neck stood up, straight and stiff. His heart stopped beating for a moment and then leaped wildly. He became conscious, not through eye or ear but by some sixth or even seventh sense, that he was not alone in the valley. He did not know by what process of divination he knew it, but he never felt a doubt. A mighty effort of will and he steadied his leaping heart. His hands crept to his bow and quiver, but otherwise he did not move. His dark figure blended with the mighty trunk against which he sat, and only a careful observer would have noticed him.

Not a sound came to him. Eye and ear registered nothing, but still he did not doubt. The warning had been given, how he knew not, but perhaps it was one of the good spirits telling him in a wordless voice to beware. Slowly he bent the great elkhorn bow and fitted an arrow in the notch.

Ready to shoot on the instant, he watched the darkness beyond the fire, and on the right and left. The massive trunk of the tree, seven or eight feet through, put ample protection behind him. At last he heard a light shuffling noise, but, trained in the ways of the wilderness, he knew that it was made by the feet of a great animal put down slowly. No doubt it had scented its prey and was coming for it, stalking it with the caution of all the great carnivora.

At first he could not place the sound definitely. It might be beyond the fire or at one side. It is hard even for a trained ear to locate a light noise, but, concentrating every faculty upon the task, because dire necessity was pressing hard, he decided that it was just across the coals. He watched there with all the power he could put into his eyes and slowly a darker figure detached itself from the general darkness, the vast, hulking form that belonged to the great bear of the north, a flesh eater, if flesh were near, and all the more dangerous because, unknowing man, it had no knowledge of man's weapons.

Will's blood ran cold. How he longed for his comrades, the valiant Dakota! With Inmu on one side of him, the brave boaster on the other, and the rest nearby, he would have defied anything, but it was wholly different to be alone in the dark, at the bottom of a great well, with this frightful beast just across the fire from him.

He saw the bear stare at the blaze, draw back a little, and then slouch toward the right. He hoped that it was going away, but it was merely moving slowly around the circle, and, in time, it would come to his tree and to him. He knew now that the animal had been drawn by the odor of flesh; that it was hungry and that it had no intention of departing without what it wanted. He did not yet rise, because he was in a good position and he kept his arms free. The temptation to shoot at the tremendous shambling bulk was almost overpowering, but he remembered all the lessons of Roka and Pehansan. When one's life was at stake one must strike at the right time, or the stroke was lost, and life with it.

The great bear came on around the circle, beginning to puff a little as he drew in his heavy breath, and Will, able to see his red eyes, rose slowly to his feet, his back to the huge tree, and bent the great elkhorn bow. His body felt fear, it was cold with it, but his will controlled and his arm was never steadier, as the splendid bow bent slowly back. Choosing the throat, he sped the arrow, and, snatching another from the quiver, he shot in an instant at the throat again.

He did not expect to inflict a mortal wound with one arrow or with two, but he hoped to stop the rush of the mad brute. The bear reared to its full height, growled horribly and dripped with blood. But it stood only for a second, then it dropped upon its four paws and lunged forward at a speed marvelous for a beast so large and apparently so awkward. Will leaped to one side, circling swiftly about the fire, which he knew now was his chief ally, and shot arrow after arrow into the monstrous bulk. The bear at last, blinded by its own blood and wild with pain, plunged directly into the fire, knocking the brands in every direction and almost putting them out. A horrible smell of burnt hair and flesh arose and the huge brute, now wholly mad, charged at random beyond the circle of firelight and into the dark woods, Will planting two more arrows in its body as it went.

He heard the monster panting and growling, the tearing of vines and bushes, and then a silence in which, his muscles and spirit relaxing, he sank down by the remains of his scattered fire. He did not remain in that attitude long. He was too conscious of his danger. The wounded bear might come back, or he might have brothers or cousins, just as terrible, who would come in his place. He hastily put the burning sticks together again and then built another fire about twenty feet away, and even went so far as to put a third on his right. He would be surrounded by flames and no beast on earth would cross that barrier to reach him.

Work and the certainty of safety brought back his strength and spirits. His mood even became exultant. Once more he had defeated the great bear. *Watakapa* (Bow) was his deadly weapon, and *Peta* (Fire) was his defender. With *Watakapa* to attack and with *Peta* to stand as a wall before him, he was more than a match for *Warankxi,* no matter how large and strong. He was so buoyant and so confident that he lay down within his fiery circle and slept soundly until dawn.

When Will awoke a flood of gold was pouring into the great well, at the bottom of which he lay. The snow, loosened by the warmth, was falling in lacy flakes from the white umbrellas above him. The stream of green water chattered and sang as pleasantly as ever of the long caverns and great rivers through which it would pass, until it found its home in the infinite sea. What was the huge bear of the north or any other kind of monster to it? It flowed by them all, unnoticing.

Will drank of the cold water, warmed his food over the fire, and ate breakfast. He was glad the day was bright. He had been a victor in the night, but he did not like the darkness while he was alone there in the valley. He remembered how his blood had chilled and his hair had stood up at the first faint sound of those shuffling footsteps beyond the circle of firelight. He did not want to go through such an experience again, and he meant to start in a half hour for the path he had marked in the wall.

He noted great spots of blood that the bear had left and he followed them forty or fifty yards until they entered the stream. Probably the beast had tried to assuage his pain with water and he may have waded a long distance with the current. At another time Will's curiosity might have made him follow, but he was too anxious now to climb out of the valley. He returned to his camp and scattered the coals of his fire. The green stream was still murmuring joyously and he understood it very well. It said to him anew to be of good heart, and that all things were won by the brave.

He fastened his pack, which yet contained food enough for three or four days, securely on his back and adjusted his bow and quiver over his shoulder, as he would need both hands in climbing. The revolver, hatchet and knife were in his belt. He had lost nothing from his equipment and he would return to his comrades, as fit in strength and in weapons, as he was when he left them so suddenly.

Although he anticipated no attack in the brilliant morning, he kept his hand on the butt of the loaded revolver. If there was one great bear in the valley— and he knew there was one—there might be two, or more, and he was on his guard against a sudden rush from the bushes. He reached the place where the steep trail, not much more than a crevice between the rocks, led up, and at once began the ascent, difficult in the extreme and made possible only by the dwarfed shrubs that grew in the shallow soil accumulated along the ledges. He had never undertaken a task slower or more strenuous. He tested every new shrub to see if it would bear his weight, before loosing his hold on an old one, and now and then he grasped a projection of rock in order to draw himself up. Surmounting a crag larger than the rest, he sat upon it with his legs dangling, and his body pushed back against the wall.

He took one glance downward from his slender support and was amazed to find that he had climbed not more than twenty feet. The look upward was easier, because it did not make his head swim, but the crest of the cliff seemed as high as ever. The distance he had come so painfully counted in the total as nothing. He refused to be discouraged. He recalled what Roka or Pehansan or Inmu would do under the same conditions, and, after a rest of a few minutes, he resumed the dangerous ascent.

He had about doubled the distance when he was conscious of a hovering shadow over him, and very near. He looked up. There was the huge eagle again, vast in sweep of wing and with fierce head poised. He felt a shiver of horror. He was quite sure that it was going to attack him, and he was nailed against the wall of stone, almost helpless. He shouted, but the great eagle, circling and swooping, came nearer and nearer. The rush of air from its wings fanned his face, and the beak and claws, sharp and hard as steel, cut alarmingly near.

Will paused and clung tightly to the cliff. One foot rested in a small crevice, the other was supported by a slight projection, and his left hand clutched a small shrub that grew in a crack of the stone, where earth had been deposited by the winds. The other hand was free, held in reserve to meet the rush of the eagle. It passed near him, then circled below him, although he did not dare to look down for fear of becoming dizzy, and he hoped that it would go away, but he soon heard the heavy sweep of its wings again.

The eagle, as the bear had been, seemed mad with fury. Did it look upon him as something to be eaten? Did it regard him as an interloper and therefore an enemy in a secluded valley, or was it a female with a nest near by and in fear for its young? Whatever the cause, Will, on his perilous perch, recognized that it was extremely dangerous.

The eagle was over his head now, and it swooped down, not making a direct attack, but he was struck on the shoulder by one of the heavy wings. The blow was no light one, and his whole figure shook. But his left hand gripped the bush with the clutch of death, and his toes fairly dug into the stone. Then a fierce anger seized him that he should be assailed thus by a bird, when he meant no harm to anybody or anything, and mingled with it was humiliation that he should be almost helpless clinging to the side of a cliff.

It was impossible for him, in his situation, to use bow and arrow, and he remembered the loaded revolver swinging in his belt. He drew it with his free right hand, and then apprehension and mortification alike gave way to a fierce sense of coming triumph. It might be an eagle far beyond the average in size and ferocity, but it knew nothing of bullets. It would soon learn. He steadied himself against the stone and waited. The eagle was flying in undulating curves several hundred yards away, as if it were gathering impetus for a tremendous swoop. Will's spirits had come back with such a bound that he challenged it vocally.

"Come on, *Wanmdi!*" he cried. "I've a comrade of your name, but he isn't like you! He's good and true! He would not attack anybody who was engaged in a struggle to save his life and who wasn't harming him! But make the biggest and swiftest swoop you can! I've a little piece of metal waiting for you and you won't like it!"

It was evident that *Wanmdi* was going to take him at his word, as the undulating curves brought it nearer and it poised itself for the final swoop. Will, feeling his imminent peril, gave his will absolute command over his body, and, holding the revolver firmly but lightly, waited. He would not fire at the head. He could not hope, hanging as he was, to hit such a small and fleeting target, but he would aim at the center of the great feathered mass that was the body.

The eagle, having risen above him, suddenly came down with a slanting rush, and, with amazing power over his nerves, he waited until it was so close he could not miss. Then he pulled trigger and sent his bullet directly at the target he had chosen. The assailant was so near that he fancied he heard the thud on the feathers. A harsh screaming followed, the great body dropped, recovered, rose slowly and wheeled in aimless circles, while Will distinctly saw drops of blood falling from it. Again fierce exultation seized him. His life had been sought, and he had saved it.

"I warned you, *Wanmdi!*" he shouted. "I told you I meant you no harm! I was merely seeking to escape from this valley! You would come against the metal pellet, and now that you have got it in you how do you like it?"

It was evident that the eagle liked it not at all. Despite its vast sweep of wing, it wavered as it continued to wheel in aimless circles, but at last, gathering strength, it rose above the rim of the cliffs, and disappeared in the east with a welcome from Will for its going. He returned the revolver to his belt, rested himself a few minutes, and then resumed his slow climbing. He now saw that thirty or forty yards above him the ascent became less steep. The bushes grew more thickly there and seemed to be stronger. He felt that when he reached it he would be in a haven and the rest of the ascent would be easy.

He was a full half hour in covering the distance and when he came to the more gradual slope he plunged among the bushes, where there was plenty of support, and breathed great sighs of thanks. Snow was there, but he did not mind it, and he lay at least five minutes, allowing strength to flow back into his tired muscles, and the overstrained nerves to steady themselves. He had divined that the ribbon of bushes would lead to a broad shelf and that beyond the shelf the ascent would be easier than ever.

When he felt himself fully restored he began to climb, now almost on hands and knees, but before he had gone many yards he noticed a faint, hostile odor tainting the pure mountain air. It seemed to come from above, and looking up he saw, as he had expected, that the slope of bushes ended in a shelf. But sitting upon the shelf, regarding him intently with evil eyes, was a monstrous figure, that of the great king wolf.

Will was struck with horror. He saw the malignant triumph in the eyes of the huge brute, as he barred the path, the only path that led from the valley. Then he went quite mad himself. It was surely a demon beast that pursued him with so much malice and pertinacity, but he was not in such an awkward position as he had been when he lay against the cliff beating off the attack of the eagle. He fixed his feet firmly against the strong stems of the bushes, and, half lying, half sitting, drew an arrow from the quiver and bent his bow. In his anger he called out:

"O *Xunktokeca,* you are the largest, the most powerful, and the fiercest of your kind, and you undertake to bar my way, but you can't! The metal pellet drove away the eagle, and the sharp shaft of bone that I have here will bite into your heart!"

The wolf did not stir, but still gazed down at him with eyes of malicious triumph. To the straining youth below his form continually grew larger, but he bent the bow and placed the arrow. Then the wolf drew back suddenly, and became invisible. Will realized that the shelf was broader than it appeared to be from below, and the last approach to it also was so steep that he would have to use both hands there for climbing.

He credited the wolf at once with full human wisdom and more than human cunning and malignity. Whenever he aimed an arrow the beast could take instant cover, and, if he tried the last climb to the shelf, he would be at the mercy of those monstrous teeth and claws. He broke into a cold perspiration as he recognized the fearful ingenuity of the brute's plan. It had probably been sitting there, all the time, while he fought with the eagle and had wished him to win the combat in order that the wolf himself might have his full triumph. Will saw everything through the eyes of a primordial being who credited animals with a cunning as great as his own.

"Come out, you coward!" he cried in his ungovernable anger. "Why do you hide, *Xunktokeca!* Only cowards hide!"

But *Xunktokeca* was no coward, neither was he foolish. He remained invisible, while Will waited in vain for him to reappear. Then the baffled youth understood that taunts would be of no avail. He looked around for some other point to which he could climb, but there was none. Nor could he remain forever on the side of a cliff. But one path was open to him, and that was the descent that led back to the valley.

Burning with rage and mortification, he replaced the bow and quiver over his shoulders, and began with infinite care the dangerous slope. Two steps and he looked up. There was the wolf, standing on the shelf again, and gazing at him with those eyes of ferocity in which he now also read malignant triumph. Clinging tightly with the other hand, Will clenched a fist and shook it at him.

"It's your hour, O *Xunktokeca!*" he called. "You have barred the way! But remember that my arrow may yet bite deep into your vitals!"

The wolf stood there, unmoving, while Will made the descent, which was more perilous than the ascent had been, and the latter was dangerous enough. He refused to look up again, until he stood once more on the floor of the valley, and then he collapsed in a heap, lying there a long time, until the spell had fully passed.

But it was not in the nature of him whom the Dakota called Waditaka to remain despondent long. The heights were barred to him, but there was the valley, and somehow or other he would find a way out of it, sooner or later. He rose to his feet, pulled himself together, body and soul, and surveyed once more the lofty and circling rim of stone that walled the valley in. He could not see the wolf on the ledge nor the eagle in the air. Both *Xunktokeca* and

Wanmdi were gone, but he knew that *Xunktokeca,* at least, would be on watch should he try the steep again. And it was likely, too, that *Warankxi* was loose in the valley. It might not be the same great bear that had attacked him, but his brothers and cousins could come.

Nevertheless, Waditaka was not afraid. Standing on the level ground, he had ample room for the use of his bow and arrows, and, in the last resort, there was the revolver in his belt, with plenty of cartridges. He went back to his place between the big tree and the stream, and built his fire anew. Fire never failed him. It always stood between him and his foes, and before night came he would light two more fires, thus making an inviolable circle, in the center of which he might sleep in safety. But he knelt first by the green stream. It had talked to him pleasantly, and had given him assurance of success before he assailed the cliff. What was it saying now?

"Be of good faith, O, Waditaka," murmured the green waters. "The time will come when you shall escape from the valley, even as I do, though not by the same path. One failure does not daunt the brave, nor two, nor three. Wait and hope, Waditaka."

"I not only wait and hope, O *Mini* (Water), I know," he replied. "I never doubt for an instant that I shall scale the cliffs and rejoin my friends."

Mini laughed. Will knew it was so, because the voice of the stream grew louder. Many bubbles, flashing in yellow and green and purple and all the other colors of the rainbow, formed on its surface and broke merrily. If that was not laughter, encouraging laughter, then he did not know what laughter was.

"I thank thee, O *Kadusa* (Stream). You have put new heart into me," he said. "Even as you go under the mountain, I will go over it."

"And what is more," he said to himself, as he turned away, "I will take my line and hook out of my pack tomorrow and catch some of those big trout I saw in the deep pools."

While he had been tremendously shaken by his experiences on the cliff, he was in fine trim now. If he saw no way out of the valley at present, surely his comrades would come there and find him. The Dakota would never desert him, and he did not understand why they had not come already. They must be searching for him now, and, to help them, he built his central fire to a great height, piling on vast quantities of wood, which was abundant everywhere, until it sent up a lofty column of smoke, rising far above the valley, and tapering into a blue spire high in the heavens. It was a splendid signal and it had beauty also, making a strong appeal. It seemed to him that he was setting his banner in the skies for all to see, and he wondered why he had not thought of it before.

While the tall bonfire burned he went along the stream to the point where it had been entered by the bear. The big spots of blood remained on the bank, but, though he followed the current for some distance, he could not see any place at which the great beast had emerged. But as the shores were rocky farther on he concluded that the fact had hidden the traces from his eyes. Doubtless the bear had a den in the rocks at the foot of the cliff, and, if there were others of his kind, they would be hidden away in the same manner. He would not make any diligent search farther. If they let him alone, he was more than content to leave them alone.

He took hook and line from his pack, found the usual bait in the soft earth under a stone, and went to one of the deep pools in the stream. He meant to have trout and he had no doubt these were among the most splendid of their splendid kind. He had striven fiercely with bear, eagle and wolf, but now the milder ambitions of the fisherman were roused within him, but he did not forget caution. When he dropped hook and line into the stream, he also placed the loaded revolver by his side on the bank. He did not intend to become a trapped fisherman.

Although no line had ever before been dropped into those waters, the trout were as wary as Waditaka himself. But his acquired gift of Indian patience stood him in good stead, and one bit at last. Playing him skillfully, he landed him, and, as he soon caught a second, he considered two quite enough. He broiled them on the coals before his great fire, and nothing that he had ever eaten tasted better.

"I may be a prisoner in your valley," he said to the green stream, "but you will always bring me plenty of food of the finest kind."

"We hold you, but we do not treat you ill," the

pleasant waters murmured back. "I shall always have fish for your taking, O, Waditaka. There are worse places in the world than this green valley of mine. Again I bid you be of good cheer, O, Waditaka."

And Waditaka responded:

"I had no thought of being otherwise, O, joyous waters!"

Then he did more work on his fire, building it higher and higher until it seemed to him that the blue spire rising into the topmost heavens must be visible over a circle of fifty miles. Surely Roka and the others would see it, and he would be discovered by tomorrow night at the farthest.

Having dined well and being warm through and through, he fell asleep, wrapped in his robe, between the fires, and so sound were his slumbers that he never stirred once during the night. The great bear that he had wounded came back through the woods, licking his hurts, and eager for revenge, and another came with him, but when they saw the edge of light from the fires, and smelled the burning wood, the monstrous beasts, that feared nothing living, were afraid of this terrible red thing that might be torn into countless pieces, and yet every piece would continue to inflict frightful pain. To attack it merely meant to make a thousand indestructible foes where only one existed before.

The wounded bear felt the man smell strong in his nostrils. He knew that it was the odor of the creature who had shot the arrows into him, and he was anxious to rush in and tear him to pieces, but the red flare held him back. With his comrade he advanced slowly a few paces, their huge hulks making no noise, and then they paused, gazing with frightened eyes at the flames which roared and crackled and said to them very plainly:

"Come on, *Warankxi!* You are monstrous and powerful! You can pull down the greatest buffalo that ever lived, then why do you hesitate when you see us? We are often little and slender. A wind may make us vanish into nothingness. We have neither hoofs nor claws nor horns. We cannot shoot arrrows like *Wicaxta* (Man), who lies sleeping surrounded by us. But you dare not touch us, and you dare not touch *Wicaxta,* who kindled us into life. And because he has kindled us into life we protect him against *Warankxi, Xunktokeca, Inmutanka, Wanmdi* and all the beasts and birds of prey! Come on, *Warankxi!* Are you afraid of a thin red spire that is little more than air itself, and that the next puff of wind may send forever into the dark? Are you a coward, O *Warankxi?* Look, *Wicaxta* is asleep! He is like one dead! You might be upon him before he could reach for his bow or his pistol! His strength compared with yours is no more than that of a weed in a storm! Only we protect him because he has made us rise out of nothingness and dwell for a little space in the good air. You are a coward, *Warankxi,* you and your comrade, too! Look! You give back! You turn and you will run!"

The two bears were withdrawing fearfully. They understood very clearly what *Peta* (the Fire) was saying. The desire to seize upon *Wicaxta* and tear him to pieces was immense, but he was guarded around by the little red spirits, flitting and wavering, but omnipotent. Of all the gods known to *Warankxi, Peta* was by far the most powerful. In truth, he was invincible. No bear or any other beast that ever lived had ever conquered him or ever would. They drew back beyond the faintest gleam from the fire, but *Peta* only laughed in disdain.

"Are you gone, O *Warankxi?*" *Peta* roared and crackled. "As we said, big and fierce as you are, you are a coward when you face us! Never will you take *Wicaxta* when we stand about him!"

And *Wicaxta,* known to the whites as Will Clarke, and to the Sioux as Waditaka, awoke at dawn from a night of deep peace and perfect safety.

CHAPTER XI

FIRE AND WATER

MADITAKA rose, restored fully in both body and mind, although the dawn was far from bright, the sun being hidden by drifting clouds, while the air was raw and chilly. But the fires, though they had sunk much, were still burning, and they threw out a consoling warmth. One of the trout was left and he put it over the coals.

"Now, *Hogan* (Fish) you have passed the time when it will hurt you to make a better acquaintance with *Peta*," he said, "and, since the closer contact will serve me better, you must make it."

The fish was browned delicately, and he ate it along with several slices of venison, following them with a cool drink from the friendly green stream. Then he saw the great tracks of *Warankxi*, stopping just where the firelight threw its farthest edge, and his nature had become so thoroughly primordial, so closely linked with that of the great beasts, which early man hunted and which hunted early man, that he laughed as if a human being seeking his life had been balked in the effort.

"O, *Warankxi*," he said, "you tried to steal upon me like a coward in the dark, when I slept, and I see that you brought your brother with you. But I had put *Peta* on guard and you were afraid of him when he licked out his red tongue at you. Both of you ran away like scared rabbits. Is it not so, O, *Mini?* You are here always, both by day and by night, and you saw."

"It is so, *Wicaxta,*" gurgled the water.

Will felt an immense satisfaction, and he resolved that he would never let *Peta* go out while he was in the valley. He would show his gratitude by prolonging as much as possible the life of a vanishing element. Prudence also was added to gratitude. The drifting clouds were becoming stationary, and they had thickened greatly. The sky was dull gray and gloom gathered heavily in the valley. He collected, at speed, great quantities of fallen wood to feed *Peta,* and then he rapidly cut down brush, with which to build a rude wickiup, just before the largest fire, using the trunk of the great tree as one side and chief support. Now and then as he worked, he glanced up at the clouds, and he was quite sure that they would soon open, letting down an immense volume of snow. But before the first flakes fell he succeeded in putting on the crude roof of poles and brush, and, after heaping fresh wood on the fire he sat down, inside on his narrow bed, also of brush.

Then the snow came, as if it were resolved to fill up the whole well of a valley, and Waditaka, from the open side of the wickiup, watched *Peta* fight with *Wa* (Snow). At the opening attack of *Wa, Peta* cowered down. The great red flames, wavering back and forth and so full of life, quivered and sank, sputtering with wrath. But *Peta* was not conquered nor even dimmed for long. Taking fresh grip on the wood that continually fed his strength and life, back he came, crackling and roaring, rising in triumph as high as before, or higher, shaking his lofty red crest in defiance at *Wa*.

Wa came down all the faster, pouring streams of great white flakes, but loftier and loftier grew the red spires of *Peta*. Waditaka, lying in his wickiup, which had one side open to the fire, felt their penetrating warmth and rejoiced in the certainty that *Peta* would be the victor. A thing could be so strong that victory over obstacles merely made it stronger, and such was *Peta*. Much of its roaring and crackling now came from triumph over *Wa*.

Wa was not ignoble in himself. The oceans of flakes contained both beauty and grandeur. Many of the flakes were long and lacy at the edges like feathers. As they came down they formed, too, a white veil through which everything was magnified and glorified. The trees grew white and the whole valley was filled with a white light. But young Waditaka felt that at present *Wa*, despite his beauty, was hostile to him. One could perish easily in a great fall of snow and so the success of *Peta* meant life. He knew now that the flames would rise steadily many hours, no matter how hard *Wa* might wage war, and he felt immense satisfaction.

The primordial youth was, in truth, happy just then. He had all that the primordial man spent most of his

life fighting for—food and shelter—and the victory of
Peta over *Wa* had been due to his own forethought
and preparation. *Wa* came out of the skies, *Peta* had
been created by his own hand, and the fire was surely
beautiful to look at, with its broad base, and red cone
tapering into a lofty spire, from which the sparks in
myriads, like fireflies, shot boldly upward through the
falling snow.

He felt warm, safe and happy. He never doubted
for a moment that he would find his comrades, or that
they would find him. His stay in the valley was
merely an interruption, not a misfortune. It was so
soothing and comfortable in the wickiup that he dozed
a while, and then awoke to find *Wa* falling as hard
and steadily as ever, and *Peta* crackling and roaring
away in triumph, just as before. Beyond the firelight,
and almost hidden in *Wa's* white veil, he saw three or
four great, shambling forms, and he knew that *Warankxi* had come to see. The grizzly bear was *Rota*
in the language of the Sioux, but *Warankxi* was the
generic name for the bear, and as the immense bears
of the north were not grizzlies the members of the little
Dakota band called them *Warankxi*.

Waditaka felt so little alarm at the presence of the
bears that he did not reach for his weapons. *Peta*
not only fought for him against *Wa,* but also defended
him from *Warankxi*. He was quite sure that *Peta*
crackled and roared with unexampled fury when
Warankxi appeared in the shadows beyond. Fancy
was so strong within him then that he saw the great
tower of fire lean toward the bears, and send off

255

showers of sparks in their direction. The bears shivered and drew back until their figures were mere shadows. Waditaka laughed, and his laugh was a compound of delight and derision.

"O *Warankxi*," he called through the driving snow, "I see you, come again, hiding there in the shadows! A coward you were and are! I am lying here where you can see me, but I do not reach for *Itazipe* (Bow) and *Wahinkpe* (Arrow), and *Mazakanptcedan* (pistol) lies untouched in my belt! I know that *Peta*, who has conquered *Wa* in my behalf will take care of me against *Warankxi*! Now, while you slink there in the shadows, I go back to sleep!"

He kept his word. *Ixtima* (Sleep) took him in the next five minutes. The bears were still in the shadows and the man-odor of the slumbering youth came to them. They were hungry and the most powerful of all their instincts pulled them on, but before them stretched *Peta*, a wall of terror, and at last they drew away, seeking the great hidden caves in which they made their dens.

Old *Inmutanka*, a huge yellow panther which lived on the western edge of the valley, also detected the succulent odor of man, and came to look over the scene, but did not find it to his taste. *Peta* was truly a terrifying guardian, so tall, so red, so fiercely hot, and all the while crackling out threats, too.

While *Inmutanka* looked on *Peta* suddenly bent over with a shift of the wind and sent a shower of sparks in his direction. Dozens of them lodged in his yellow coat, and one, tremendously alive and active, struck him in his left eye. Uttering a shrill, almost human, scream of pain and anger, *Inmutanka* fled into the forest, completely defeated by *Peta,* plunged into a snow bank to rid himself of the fiery little darts that were burning into him, and then resumed a rapid flight for his lair.

The sudden gust of wind passed and *Peta* straightened up, still crackling. Had Waditaka been awake he would have said that the crackle was a laugh. *Peta* was laughing at his easy victory over *Inmutanka.* One attack by his flames, with a shower of sparks thrown out as skirmishers, was enough. *Inmutanka* had run away like a frightened rabbit before that charge. Now, the great animals having had enough of it, the combat was left to *Peta* and *Wa.* They had the field alone, and, like valiant warriors, they fought all through the afternoon and all through the evening that followed. *Wa,* always beaten, never failed to come on again. Hour after hour he poured his white columns down on *Peta,* who merely gave his crackling laugh and devoured all the flakes that struck him. In the morning, when Waditaka awoke, although *Wa* was yet bringing up his battalions, *Peta* was still the victor. The supply of wood was so great that the flames were as bright and high as ever.

Young Waditaka arose, stretched his muscles and was pleased with himself, although the flakes of snow were coming down in such dense columns that he could see but a little distance beyond *Peta's* rim. He ate of his venison, and, with a stout stick, knocked the snow off the roof of his wickiup, lest the brush and

poles fall in beneath the weight. Then he stood by
the fire a little while, basking in the glow. Beyond the
melting touch of the fire's warmth the snow lay a
full three feet in depth and more than a foot of it lay
over the tracks left by *Warankxi*. Nevertheless, as
he made a circuit, wading in the snow, he found coarse
hairs left on some bushes and he knew that *Warankxi*
had been there.

He read the whole story as clearly as if he had seen
it enacted. The bears had come for him, but *Peta,*
red and blazing, had stood in the way. He had saved
it from vanishing in the dark, and it had saved him
from tooth and claw. While the score might be even,
he was none the less grateful on that account.

"O, *Peta,*" he said, "you are my champion and defender. You and *Mini* fight always on my side. I
thank you and I promise you in return that as long as
I am in the valley you shall not vanish into nothingness. The wood on which you feed, and, without
which there is no life for you, shall always be here."

He felt about in the snow and dragged up vast
quantities of fallen brushwood which he heaped near,
food for *Peta's* throat whenever it should be needed.
He consumed the whole morning in the task, and then,
after more venison, broke a way through to his other
great friend, *Mini,* the green stream. He expected to
find it frozen over, or choked with huge heaps of
snow, but the air was not cold enough for ice, and the
swift current, cutting its way through, flowed on,
laughing as pleasantly as ever, brilliant bubbles breaking on its surface, as if they were there for decorative

purposes, and to please the eyes of young Waditaka. It was a brave stream. *Wa* had failed to conquer *Peta,* and by just as much had he failed to conquer *Mini.* On the contrary, the faster *Wa* fell the more *Mini* was enlarged by the flakes, taken into its bosom, and turned into water.

"Between you two, *Mini* and *Peta,* I shall be saved," said Waditaka, speaking directly to the stream. "*Peta* will keep me warm, and *Mini* will feed me, and the time may come when one or the other of you will show me the way out."

The last was a word spoken at hazard, and forgotten a moment later for the time. He never dreamed then that it would come true. But he was sure since *Wa* had not triumphed over *Mini* that he could catch enough trout for food, as long as he stayed in the valley, no matter how long. He had venison and bear meat enough to last a week, and he devoted the remainder of the day to strengthening his wickiup, cutting many slender poles for the sides and roof. When the snowy twilight came he put another great heap of wood on the big fire, gave it full encouragement for a second night's battle with *Wa,* and then, creeping into his reënforced wickiup, slept, absolutely confident that loyal *Peta* would protect him, no matter what came.

The next morning showed no tracks in the snow about his little home. If *Warankxi* still felt inclination to devour him his fears of *Peta* had kept him away. The fire, moreover, was still burning finely. There had been plenty of wood to feed *Peta* well all through the night, but *Wa,* giving up the battle, had now ceased to fall. Nevertheless, the snow lay a full five feet in depth over the levels, and much deeper in the dips and gulches. It was with difficulty that Waditaka broke short paths through it, one down to the brook, and others into the forest where he might obtain more firewood, which, by good fortune, was in great abundance.

But he did not wish to go far. He had no reason for doing so. Under the conditions now prevailing it was impossible to try the ascent of the cliff again, even if the king wolf should not be on guard there, and so he remained most of the time beside his bonfire, which he built to a great height, still having a hope that his loyal Dakota comrades might see that lofty red spire, or the blue smoke issuing from it. The heavens themselves appeared to nurse this hope, as he had never seen them clearer. The whole dome was a dazzling blue, against which every trace of smoke showed at a vast height. It was a signal that he had sent far into the vault, but he must wait patiently to know whether it would avail him anything.

He might have been discouraged had it not been for the fire. Never was there a braver, or more cheerful or more talkative fire. Fully a Dakota now, he became thoroughly steeped in their beliefs, while he was a captive in the lone valley, and he was subject to Dakota emotions and impulses. The fire was incarnate. There was a good spirit in it, or rather it was a good spirit itself. How could anyone doubt a fact so manifest? And the spirit of the fire talked through the crackling of the flames as they ate into the wood which he supplied to them. Everything combined to develop an imagination extremely lively and sensitive at any time, and *Peta's* talk translated itself to him.

"Fear not, O Waditaka," *Peta* repeated. "Lo, I have conquered *Wa!* He ceased to fall, and I burn more merrily than ever! You have kept me alive, and in return I warm you and hold the soul in your body! Fear not, O, Waditaka, brave young warrior! It is the patient and persevering who win!"

Peta was so soothing and clothed him around with so much warmth and light that Waditaka was quite content to sit in comfort and wait. While a prisoner in the valley he was able now to admire its beauty and magnificence under its deep white covering. The great domes of the trees bent over a little beneath their weight of snow, the bushes everywhere were delicate and intricate lace work, and the air was so pure that it seemed to fill his lungs with a vigor he had never known before.

He communed with *Peta* nearly all the morning, but in the afternoon he took his hook and line, and went down to see what *Mini* had to offer. He knew the stream would be swollen yet more by melted snow, but he was quite sure he could catch trout in the nearest deep pool. But *Mini* was far larger than he had expected, already overflowing his banks nearly everywhere, while his song was much louder and much more rollicking in tone than it had been before the great snow fell.

"See me grow! See how large I am!" sang *Mini*

in Waditaka's ear. "My stream has become twice as deep in a day! I eat fast at the snow on my banks, and I flourish on what I eat!"

The swift current gave a triumphant swish. Little pools and backwaters, swirling and eddying, chattered in minor tones the same victorious chant. Unquestionably *Mini* was feeling puffed up in spirit as well as fact, and Waditaka was in full sympathy. *Mini* reminded him somewhat of Hoton. *Mini* boasted like Hoton, but, like Hoton, *Mini* had something to boast about.

"By fire and water I shall be protected and saved," said young Waditaka, remembering his former inspiration. "Now fire has shown how it protects me, but water has not yet shown how it will save me! O, *Mini,* how will it be?"

But the green waters merely foamed and tumbled and sang as they raced away, and did not answer. Then the lad devoted himself to his work in the deep pool, and again caught two fine trout, one of which he ate for supper, saving the other for breakfast. He slept very warmly and in great comfort a second night in his wickiup under the protection of *Peta,* and finding the next morning so much colder that he did not sink very deeply in the snow he took his weapons and went forth to explore. He had been about the valley several times, but he did not know what changes had occurred since *Wa* had poured down so hard and long.

He found nothing until he came near the southern end. Then he heard a savage growl behind a clump of bushes, and, drawing back, he made ready with bow and arrow. One of the monstrous mountain wolves appeared, struggling in the deep snow, and, standing at a safe distance, Will slew it with three arrows. He withdrew the precious shafts, and, at another time, might have taken the skin, but he could not carry such a heavy load now, and he left the body to the scavengers. The incident made him very thoughtful. Wolves were in the valley now, and he was quite sure none had been there when he arrived. Bears were there, also, but they might make it their permanent home. Not so the wolves. How had they come? He thought upon the problem a long time, but, as no solution presented itself, he gave it up, and turned his mind to other matters. He did not have much fear of the great animals while the snow was so deep. The bears most likely would keep to their hidden caves, and if any more wolves appeared they could only flounder in the deep snow, while he picked them off with his arrows.

An entire week passed. Now and then he built his fire to unexampled height, sending lofty signals into the heavens, but, as no reply ever came, he reached the regretful conclusion that his comrades had wandered to so great a distance that smoke, no matter how high, could not be seen by them. His spirits refused to sink. If they showed any tendency to do so *Peta* and *Mini* always raised them up. He kept his promise to the fire. Throughout the week he fed it nobly. There was always plenty of wood for the flames to eat and crackle over joyously, and *Mini,* the stream, grew and grew and grew. The pools con-

tinued to furnish all the trout he needed and life might
have been very comfortable for one who had returned
to the primordial state, but he felt that he had over-
stayed his time in the valley. If he was to help Roka
and the others find the great buffalo ranges of the far
North it was time for him to be moving.

The snow was melting fast. It fell in showers from
the great domes of the trees, and, thundered, as it
rolled in avalanches down the cliff. Putting his pack
on his back and taking all his weapons, young Waditaka went forth once more to explore. By some
chance, he had let his fire sink lower than usual,
lower than ever before, and, as he turned away, it
seemed to him that the crackling of the flames was no
longer merry and joyous. Unless his fancy was so
intense that it deceived him, *Peta's* note was that of
farewell.

"Good-by, Waditaka!" sang the flames. "We have
warmed you and protected you from the great wild
beasts, and, as long as you could stay here, you kept
us alive! You did not let us vanish into the dark and
nothingness! Now we die, but we die only to live
again elsewhere!"

Waditaka stared at the fire. Was it true that he
was not coming back? Surely *Peta* would speak
nothing but the truth. And if he did not come back
Peta, of course, would vanish into the dark and nothingness. But it might be true that one fire could be
a reincarnation of another, and it might be true, also,
that one life was a reincarnation of another. Alone
in the wilderness, one often had solemn thoughts, and

the Dakota theology was molded in accordance with the great facts of nature. He must not leave *Peta,* who had been such a powerful friend, without a proper and grateful farewell. There was a great heap of wood on one side and he threw it all into the flames, which crackled and roared and leaped higher than ever, sending up myriads of sparks and a spire of blue smoke that pierced the very center of the heavens.

"And now, farewell, *Peta,*" he said. "I've created for you a right royal funeral pyre, one that will give you a glorious departure into the dark, and that will serve you well until your next reincarnation."

He walked down to the green stream, now swollen beyond its banks by the melting snow, deep and swift, rolling tumultuously and rejoicing in the large and vigorous life that had come to it. It was beyond its banks everywhere, and, throwing off portions of its surplus waters, was cutting little new channels through the earth and snow. To young Waditaka, the Dakota, the spirit of the waters was alive and leaping. In his Dakota belief all things, the inanimate as well as the animate—because the inanimate were only seemingly so—were incarnated, and he was pleased at *Mini's* clamorous song. He liked to see the stream enjoy its abounding life, while it could, because in time it would have to sink back into its natural channel, just as a human being, after momentous days, returns to the ordinary current of life.

"O, *Mini,*" he said, "it is your hour, and I see that you appreciate it and enjoy it to the full. Now, *Peta* has done his work for me. He has kept me warm and has protected me until I feel that it is time for me to go. And you are to save me. How do you intend to do it?"

The water bubbled, and, as sure as there were eyes in his head, he saw it boil into little fountains and cascades directly in front of him. And as sure, too, as he had ears, he heard its song increase in volume.

"Follow me! Follow me!" chanted *Mini*. "I have given my promise and I will save you! Be thou of brave heart, O, Waditaka, and follow!"

Nothing could ever persuade him that he did not hear the words, said especially for his benefit, and he took his course by the side of the stream, making his way through the deep and slushy snow, and leaping the rivulets that branched off from the main current. And *Mini* never ceased to chant in his ear his song of encouragement and to bid him follow on. Three quarters of the way to the enclosing cliff and *Mini* suddenly shot off a stream fully one-third his own in volume, pouring it down a little ravine that was dry in ordinary times. He had followed the main current until it plunged into the low mouth under the stone, a mouth that must be choked now by the swollen waters, and partly the cause of this overflow. He would follow the new channel and see where it led. He walked a few steps down the side of the ravine, and stopped, listening. Would *Mini* bid him come back?

There was no chant of recall. The new stream, instead, although much smaller, sang a song of its own for him, and it was more than a song of welcome.

It also bade him come, and ran swiftly to its unknown destination. Waditaka's heart began to beat hard. He could feel the pulses in his temples and wrists leaping. As *Peta* had kept his promise to him so would *Mini*. He followed, as fast as the deep and sodden snow would let him, and saw that the current was leading directly toward the circling cliff. It was running now through the open forest, but would soon plunge into a thick mass of bushes that grew at the base of the mountain wall.

The water was not banking up against the wall, and his pulses beat faster. He rushed forward, forcing his way through the bushes by the side of the stream, and came almost face to face with blank stone. But the water turned around it, and then he saw that the power of the stream had torn away a mass of bushes that had thoroughly hidden a narrow opening in the main wall. Not even the eyes of Roka or Pehansan would have seen that crevice. It was *Mini* alone that knew of it, and *Mini* was waiting for a vast increase in growth and strength when he could show the way.

Waditaka never doubted, for an instant, that he was saved. The spirit of the waters had been true and had kept the promise. He followed into the crevice, walking gingerly on a narrow ledge between the water and the stone. He expected to go into the dark and that he must feel his way, but it was merely a twilight, and he saw that he was under a natural bridge with a roof fully forty or fifty feet above him. Nor was the bridge long. He discovered clear daylight ahead, and he knew that he would soon come into a great ravine or cleft in the mountain. The way of escape lay straight before him. He looked down at the rushing and singing stream.

"O, *Mini,*" he said, "I thank you! As *Peta* kept his promise to warm and protect me, so you have kept your promise to save me! Never will I forget Fire and Water, my best friends!"

The ledge on which he walked soon broadened and the traveling was easy. He had nothing to guard against save slipping on the wet stone, and in a few minutes he passed under the arch, coming into the great cleft, which was thickly grown with spruce and pine and cedar. Then *Warankxi,* mighty in his size and wrath, rose up in his path, but he was not afraid. His natural courage and strength were reënforced by a great exultation, and, bending his bow, he fitted the arrow to the string.

"Now, *Warankxi,*" he shouted, "I've a friend, *Itazipe* (Bow) who fights for me, even as *Peta* did. *Itazipe* stays in my hands, but his child, *Wanhinkpe* (Arrow) will bite you deep! Come, you growling monster, face the three of us, and see what will happen to you!"

His voice rang in the deep cleft and came back in many echoes. The spirit of Hoton was upon him and, like the valiant boaster, he welcomed his enemy. The great bear seemed to be puzzled by the wild, chanting creature that confronted him, and reared upon his hind legs, revealing all his vast height, far greater than that of a man. A deep growl issued from his throat, and, after a moment or two of hesitation, he dropped back upon his four paws, lurching forward to the attack.

Waditaka's skill and strength were equal to his spirits. The air hummed with his arrows as he planted them in the throat and flank of *Warankxi*. It seemed to him that the spring of *Itazipe* was more powerful than ever, and that *Wanhinkpe* whistled with eagerness to reach the target.

"Come, *Warankxi,* come!" he shouted. "I am waiting for you! Why are you so slow? The path is narrow here, and we two cannot pass! Come and fight with me for the right of way! What, you hesitate? Does little *Wanhinkpe* bite too deep for you? O *Warankxi! Warankxi!* You have stopped! Did I not warn you that *Itazipe, Wanhinkpe* and I would be your conquerors? Now you tremble and would turn, but it is too late! *Wanhinkpe* has bitten too deeply, great as you are! He has severed the cord of *Wiconi* (Life) and you pass into *Tokata* (Hereafter). Farewell, *Warankxi!*"

The great bear rose again upon his hind legs to his prodigious height and he was a terrible sight, with the blood pouring from him in streams, where the arrows were planted deep, gave a last growl more ferocious than all the others, shivered all over, and then fell with a crash upon the stone. Young Waditaka, now a Dakota in every sense, advanced with a shout of triumph and contemplated the mighty beast that he had slain, surely a member of the most monstrous tribe that roamed the American continent.

He had no doubt that both the bears and wolves

had pushed their way into the valley by means of the crevice and through the bushes, and probably more of them would have come for him in time had he remained, but that caused him no fear now. His problem was solved. It was painful to a true Dakota to leave the vast pelt there, to be torn by wolves, but he had no choice. Such a skin could have been carried away only on a horse and, after cutting out the arrows, he walked on, his faithful bow ready in his hand. Before he was out of sight he heard a rush of feet and a snapping. Looking back he saw the wolves already at work, while overhead dark figures hovered, waiting for their share of the feast, when the stronger were done.

Waditaka saw that the cleft ascended gradually and that it was choked with evergreens from the summit. A stream of water from the melting snow flowed down its center and joined the overflow from the valley, the united current losing itself somewhere in hidden caverns below him. But he was now wholly pleased with his situation. As he climbed, the evergreens would give him shelter from the cold, and if he needed it, plenty of wood for a fire. It seemed to him that it was only a matter of time until he rejoined his comrades.

The ascent, however, was extremely slow, as he had to pick his way over rough boulders, and he was in continual fear lest he might slip upon a wet stone. A broken ankle would probably mean death alone there in the wilderness. But his spirits remained at the zenith. However pleasant the valley had been, it was a prison, nevertheless, and now the wide world was his own. He was free, and freedom was the most glorious of all things.

He toiled slowly and patiently upward, carrying his heavy pack and quiver on his back and his bow and one arrow in his hands. Now and then, where there were no boulders, the snow was so deep that he sank into it to his waist, and in other places he pulled himself along by means of the dwarfed evergreens. He thought it likely that he might meet one of the great wolves in the cleft, or the king wolf himself, but he saw nothing more than huge eagles soaring above him in the clear sky. His anger rose at sight of them. One had attacked him with beak and talons when he was making his perilous climb up the cliff, and his defense then had been handicapped by the necessity of saving himself from being dashed to death, but here he would have free play for his archery, just as he had enjoyed it when he met the great bear.

"O *Wanmdi*," he shouted up into the heavens, "you rushed at me when my hands were not free. Come down now and have a taste of *Wanhinkpe! Warankxi* has tried it, but he was a big target, and he had to stay on the ground, but I promise you, *Wanmdi*, although you may swoop and circle, that you, too, shall learn how sharp and swift is *Wanhinkpe!*"

But *Wanmdi* did not come down. Perhaps from some convenient height he had seen the amazing death of *Warankxi*, slain from a distance by a human creature less than one-tenth his weight, and he and his comrades decided that it was not wise to attack when

271

the human being stood on level ground and all his limbs were free. They flew in slow circles at a great height, and then sailed gracefully away beyond the mountains and out of sight. Waditaka, indignant at such cowardice, went on his way up the difficult slope.

It was well toward nightfall, when he reached the crest and looked upon a vast expanse of country, lofty peaks and ranges and valleys between, blue lakes shining here and there, and many clear streams. He concluded to send up another signal, and, laboriously gathering wood he built a big fire that rose, a mighty column of red, in the night. Then, thoroughly exhausted, he wrapped himself in his robes and fell asleep beside it.

In the morning his fire was still burning, but, no answer having come to the signal, he decided that he would travel as fast as he could in a general easterly direction. The great buffalo plains of the north lay that way and his comrades doubtless, having given him up as dead, had continued their original search. While the mountains were covered with snow all the valleys that his eyes reached were deep green, uniform in character with those they had passed, heavily wooded with trees of great height, and, beyond a doubt, abounding in game. An adept in the forest he would be in no danger of starvation, and if, by any chance, the animals escaped him the innumerable streams would yield abundant food to his hook and line. By day he felt that his bow and arrow would protect him from attack by the wild animals, and, at night, fire would be his guardian on the mountains, as it had been in the valley.

Full of confidence, he began his descent into the next great dip, which was of much greater width and extended a long distance to north and south, containing several small blue lakes. He judged that it lay a full three-quarters of a mile below him, and, as the slope was gradual, it would take him a long time to reach it. He went on, keeping a wary eye for *Warankxi* or *Xunktokeca,* and seeing traces of both on the soft ground.

Before night he was in the valley, which he found clear of snow and warm, but without sign of human habitation. Ripe strawberries grew on low vines in the grassy openings, and he enjoyed them as only one can who has lived a long time on an exclusively meat diet. He saw several small black bears feeding not far away on the berries, and he could easily have slain one with a single arrow. Black bear, moreover, was tender, but he did not even bend his bow. These bears were quite different from *Warankxi.* They were little, good-natured, and infected with the comic spirit. They had never seen human beings before, and they raised their noses, reddened with juice of the berries, cocking their heads on one side in an amusing manner, as they gazed at young Waditaka.

"Go on with your berries," called the happy youth. "I'm your friend, not your enemy. You've nothing to fear from me."

The bears took him at his word, and continued with the feast, varying it at times to romp with one another. Waditaka looked at them with amusement. These little black bears, that is little compared with the others, were his brethren of the wilderness and he hoped this valley would remain forever immune from men, both white and red, in order that it might furnish safe harvest and sport for the comedians of the forest.

He meant to make his camp the next night beside one of the blue lakes, but before the twilight he made a great discovery. He came unexpectedly upon a small bush, the top of which had been cut out with the keen blow of a tomahawk. He believed it to be a sign left by his comrades in the faint hope that he was yet alive, and, by some amazing chance, might see it. If so, another bush marked in the same manner would be not far away, and after some search he found it, and then a third. The course seemed to lead along the southern side of the lake and towards the east, but, as it was too late to go any farther that day, he prepared for his camp. Hook and line were brought into use once more and the fish tumbled over one another in their eagerness to get at the bait, thus proving to his own satisfaction that these waters had never before been fished in by man. It was a kind of salmon that he caught, not so delicate as the mountain trout, but good enough for anybody.

He built his fire high, not merely for the sake of warmth but to send forth the signal anew. Then, lying between it and the lake, he fell asleep, knowing that *Peta* and *Minidi* (Lake) would keep away all harm. He felt the pleasant kind of weariness that does not overstrain, but which makes the passage easy to *Ixtima*. He did not fall into slumber, he slipped away, easily and gracefully, and he did not stir all through the night. When he awoke at dawn Roka was broiling slices of venison over the fire that Waditaka had built, Pehansan was roasting a fat partridge on the end of a twig, Inmu was taking a short swim in the lake, Tarinca was scraping away at an arrow head, Wanmdi, Capa, Tatokadan and Hinyankaga were lying at ease on their robes, while Hoton, the valiant boaster, stood before him.

Waditaka looked at them sleepily, even with a certain air of reproach in his lazy glance.

"And so you've come at last!" he said. "I waited a long time for you. Have the feet of the Dakota grown heavy that they are so slow?"

Then he closed his eyes again and apparently was off to the pleasant land of *Ixtima*. But he roused himself with an effort because Hoton was speaking, and, as it seemed to him, in a tone of reproach.

"Waditaka," said the Crow, "you went away from us and you did not tell us why you were going, or where. We would never have seen you again if it had not been for the wonderful skill and the watchful eyes of the great trailer, Hoton. Now you upbraid us for wandering from you, when it was you who went. Where have you been, Waditaka?"

"It's a great tale, Hoton. I've had wonderful adventures, and I've overcome mighty dangers, beneath which you would have sunk, but it would take too many words for me to tell it now. I'll go back to sleep, and, while I'm sleeping, be sure, Hoton, that you cook me the best of breakfasts, because I'm going to be a great chief, and I must be served well."

He shut his eyes once more, and kept them shut tightly, although Hoton began to declaim with vigor and fire. At the end of five minutes he opened them again and said languidly:

"Are you still talking, Hoton?"

"Yes, Waditaka," replied the boaster. "I am telling you that in the night I smelled the smoke of your fire, even when we could not see it."

"It is true, Waditaka," said Roka. "It was Hoton who first detected your signal and we came an hour ago. You were sleeping so soundly that we did not disturb you, but Manitou knows how glad we are to see you again. Now, your venison is ready."

"And you are not more glad to see me than I am to see you," said Will, rising and joining the others at breakfast.

CHAPTER XII

THE WILD PEOPLE

THE Dakota warriors made no demonstration, but Will knew that their joy at his recovery was great. The best of the food was offered to him, and he took it without hesitation, knowing that he would please them by doing so.

While he ate, Inmu told what had happened to them. When he and Waditaka parted before the big rock, the Lynx turned to the right and was caught in a snow slide which carried him a considerable distance down the mountain. He rejoined his comrades with much difficulty, and finding no trace of Waditaka's trail they thought that he, too, had gone down the same way. Positive in the belief they had wandered farther and farther from the great well into which he had fallen. Finally they had returned on their trail, and, during the fierce snow storm, had looked into the valley in which he was a prisoner, but seeing nothing there, save a deluge of falling snow and the impossibility of descending into it, they had gone in the other direction again, believing that he had been lost under an avalanche, but cherishing a faint hope that he might be alive, and seeking they turned toward the east.

"And what of yourself, Waditaka?" said the wise Roka in a deep voice. "Your face tells me that strange adventures have befallen you."

"Aye, Roka," said he, "adventures so strange and dangers so great that I could not have overcome them had not I been aided by the spirit of the two elements, greatest and most friendly to man."

"Which do you mean, Waditaka?"

"Fire and Water, O, wise Roka."

Then he told his story to the Dakota with all the power of imagination, and certainty of belief, and they, listening with eager curiosity, had implicit faith in every word he said. The circle about him never interrupted, but he heard many a long breath and sigh of approval.

"A warrior who trusts the good spirits," said the wise Roka, when he had done, "has more to rely upon than mere weapons. When bow and arrow and tomahawk and knife fail, then the spirits may come to the help of one whose heart is true. In your great peril, Waditaka, you called upon *Peta* and *Mini,* and they did not fail you."

"They did not, Roka. I did but little myself. I avow it here before you all. I was saved by Fire and Water. Have you and the band suffered much while you were looking for me?"

"But little. *Peta* and *Mini* were ours to command whenever we needed them, and *Can* (Wood) was always lying around for the taking. And now that you have eaten and rested we will start once more on the great journey."

But at the end of a day's march they came to such a pleasant country that they decided to spend a while there, replenishing their supplies of food and making new arrows. Roka and Pehansan insisted that the warriors should not only maintain the number of their shafts but increase them. They had an idea that when they crossed the next range they might come among men, and, among wild men, strangers were always enemies. Hitherto, they had fought only with wild beasts, fierce and dangerous though the latter were, but since they were likely to meet human foes their caution and preparation must be redoubled.

"What people do you think we are likely to meet beyond the mountain?" asked Hoton.

"Indians like ourselves," replied Roka; "but of what nation I know not, though it is certain they will not belong to any tribe of the Dakota. It is the misfortune of our race that we should always be fighting one another and we cannot expect to escape it here."

"Let them come with their bows and their arrows and their lances!" chanted the valiant boaster. "They will attack because they do not know that Hoton is in the band, Hoton, the great runner, Hoton, the great archer, Hoton, the great hunter, Hoton, the great warrior!"

"A great runner, Hoton," said Inmu, "may run as fast from the enemy as toward him."

"But I look only one way, Inmu. My face is always turned toward the foe. I bid you now, when the battle comes, to follow me and do what I do, as well as you can. Then you will learn how to become a great warrior."

"I promise, Hoton."

Game was abundant and spring had advanced so much in this sheltered portion of the deep valley that the trees were in full foliage, wonderful cones of the most vivid green, wild flowers nestled in every hidden place, and there were great red banks of early berries, very welcome to the young warriors, who feasted upon them, varying their perpetual diet of game.

"Later on, we will find many wild fruits," said Hoton, with enthusiasm, "and I will show you where they are. I always lead the way to what is good."

Will thought it likely that Hoton might be true to his word. He had a wonderful facility in finding his way toward the edible, but for a while they were concerned more about the living creatures they were likely to meet. On the second day after they left the pleasant places they made a discovery that startled them. It was Inmu's keen eyes that alighted upon it, the faint trace of a human footstep, an old imprint made by a moccasin. The ten gathered around it in a circle and studied it. They recognized its full import. Human beings were or had been in this valley and they might be near now. It was wholly likely that they would have to fight fierce human foes, before they reached the great buffalo plains of the north.

There was no trail, as time had faded all the other imprints. This alone, sunk deeper than the others, remained to tell them a warrior had passed.

"It is not probable that one man only has been here," said the wise Roka. "Warriors from the east would come only in a band and they may be hunters, but, whether hunters or not, they will be no friends to the Dakota. Now we must stay close together. No one must leave the party unless he is sent on special duty. Ten we left, and ten we wish to return."

They went very slowly now, in Indian file, and in the usual order, and, late in the afternoon, they came upon the ashes of an old camp, made perhaps a week gone by, but the Dakota, with their almost superhuman skill at reading every sign, knew with certainty that about a dozen warriors had been present, and that the moccasins worn by them were not known to the Dakota tribe. They were broader and flatter than those of the nations farther south.

"They may be directly ahead of us," said Roka, "and if so they will give us trouble."

"And if so," said Hinyankaga, otherwise the Owl, "have we not many shafts and do we not know how to shoot them straight and hard? Are ten men of the Dakota, the greatest of all the red races, afraid of twenty men of any other race?"

Roka smiled. He was not at all displeased. He liked enthusiasm on the part of his young men. It was easier to keep it within proper limits than to create zeal where there was none. But the wise leader knew the value of prudence.

"It is true," he said, "that a Dakota band would never fear twice its numbers, but we did not come upon this great journey merely to fight. If we should

go back to the village and the chief, Xingudan, should
say to me, 'Where is Hinyankaga?' and I should have
to reply to him, 'We buried him in the unknown mountains after a battle with the wild warriors of the
north,' Xingudan would not like it, nor would I. We
will camp tonight without a fire and the warriors
whom I put on watch must keep guard with all their
eyes and ears."

There was no protest from the young men, as they
knew that Roka was right, and, even if they had not
known it, they would not have objected, as Roka,
however wise and kindly, was a stern leader who
would not allow his commands to be disobeyed. The
camp was chosen at nightfall in an open grove, by the
side of a small stream, and they made their supper of
cold food. Inmu and Tatokadan kept the first watch
of four hours, and, obedient to the instructions of
their leader, they watched with eyes, ears and the
faculty of the Indian in the forest, which may almost
be called divination, that is, a rapid and correct infer-
ence from small signs that others might not notice.
But nothing happened. They were succeeded by
Tarinca and the buoyant Wanmdi. Wanmdi's mind
always floated aloft in a light and gay manner, just
as the eagle, after which he was named, sailed easily
and naturally on high.

Wanmdi felt particularly happy because they had
recovered Waditaka, whom they all liked and whom
they had all mourned as dead, and because, foreseeing
action, his warrior soul was pleased. He had instantly translated the faint footstep in the turf into a

powerful band that meant to attack them, and the old campfire had made it a certainty to him. The attack could not come too soon to please his sanguine mind. He was a Dakota, a member of the mighty red nation of the west, and the hostile tribes, roaming about in the far north, were inferior peoples. He looked down upon them haughtily.

"Do you think they will await us in an ambush?" he said to the pious Tarinca.

"Manitou alone knows," replied the Deer, "and he veils the knowledge from us. We can do nothing, Wanmdi, but watch and wait."

"And have our bows and arrows and our tomahawks and knives ready. It is they that serve the warrior."

"It is true, Wanmdi, if Manitou so wills it. But if Manitou does not put his blessing on our cause then all the bows and arrows and tomahawks in the world will avail us nothing."

Wanmdi did not dispute it. Like all the Dakota he had the greatest respect for the medicine man and Tarinca, who thought so much about the spirits, which are everywhere, would certainly be a mighty medicine man some day. In truth, a little awe was mingled with his esteem for Tarinca.

"Then you believe, Tarinca," he said, "that it was not his own skill, but the will of Manitou, that brought Waditaka back to us?"

"I know it, Wanmdi. Waditaka knows it, too, and says so. Was it his bow and arrows, was it his tomahawk or his knife that protected him while he slept in the sealed valley? It was none of them. It was

Peta. Nor did they show him the way out. It was *Mini.* All the courage of all the warriors in the world would not have made Waditaka see the hidden passage, but *Mini,* flowing smoothly and singing on the way, showed it to him. And who and what are *Peta* and *Mini?* They are but instruments in the hands of Manitou, who ordered them to save Waditaka. Weapons are not all, Wanmdi."

"I know it, Tarinca. I know that the chief who makes good medicine is often more powerful than the one who leads in battle. But did you hear anything moving among the bushes to our right?"

"The wind is stirring there a little, Wanmdi, but I thought I heard something else, as the young new leaves rustled together. I am glad the bushes are beyond arrow shot of us."

"The wise Roka would not have pitched a camp in any other way."

"That is true, but I think I hear again the slight sound that is not the sound of the new young leaves rubbing together. Neither is it *Warankxi,* nor *Inmutanka,* nor yet *Xunktokeca.* I think it is *Ikcewicaxta* (savages) in the bush."

"*Ikcewicaxta* it surely is."

It was wholly typical of both of them, proud members of the Dakota race, to speak of the Indians of this wild northern land as "savages," and what is more, they thought it.

"Shall we awake Roka?" asked Wanmdi. "Perhaps he will lead us in battle, if they are in the bush. Do you think Roka would let us go into battle now?"

The pious Tarinca smiled. He appreciated the zeal of Wanmdi, but he knew also the prudence of Roka.

"I reply 'no' to both your questions," he said. "Roka would not let us attack in the dark, because we might run into an ambush, and we need not awake him since we can wait in patience and safety to see what the *Ikcewicaxta* do, as long as they are beyond bowshot. I can see they will not attack, for their numbers are not great enough. Look, Wanmdi, did you not see the low green bush with the heavy foliage move?"

"Yes, Tarinca, and, while the wind is blowing toward the north, it bent to the south."

"Which proves that one of the *Ikcewicaxta* is behind it. It proves also that he is a fool. Did he think to bend a bush against the wind before the eyes of a Dakota, and that the Dakota would not notice it?"

"He is truly a fool, as you say, Tarinca. But what else could you expect of the *Ikcewicaxta?* That is why they are the *Ikcewicaxta.*"

"I can see more bushes moving now, Wanmdi. At least four or five of the *Ikcewicaxta* are in the thicket, eager to attack us, but afraid."

"Shall I send an arrow at random into the bushes, Tarinca? It might strike a target among those spying upon the Dakota, who are seeking to harm nobody."

"No, Wanmdi. The wise Roka would not like it. We are not to seek a quarrel with anybody. If the *Ikcewicaxta* wish to spy upon us let them spy, but if they attack that is another matter."

But the young Eagle found it hard to control his warlike impulses. His hand moved restlessly along the string of his bow, and every arrow in his quiver was eager to leap forth and fit itself to the string. He knew, however, that Tarinca was right, and the two, standing close to the trunk of a great oak, where the night shadows blended them with its bark, continued to watch the bending bushes. There was no fear in the heart of either. The proud Dakota had never heard of any warriors to the north of them who were the equal of their valiant selves, and, if these inferior peoples felt like attacking, Tarinca and Wanmdi awaited the onset with full confidence in their band.

The bushes ceased to shake by-and-by, though the leaves still rustled lightly under the west wind. But the keen eyes of the Deer and the Eagle noted that the leaves bent the way the wind blew.

"They are gone?" said Wanmdi.

"It seems so," said Tarinca, "but to make sure we will search the bushes now."

They approached very cautiously, bows strung, and crossed the thicket from side to side. Nobody was there, but they noticed broken and bruised stems in several places, and they knew they had not been mistaken. They could not look any farther, as they had to maintain the watch, and they returned to the camp, where they remained vigilant sentinels until dawn.

"Has it been peace through your watch?" asked the wise Roka, as he awoke and stood up.

"There has been peace," replied Tarinca, "but it was only a peace with a threat in it."

"What mean you, Tarinca?"

"The *Ikcewicaxta* were in the thicket, spying upon us. Wanmdi and I did not see them, but we saw the bushes moving against the wind, and we saw afterward bruised stems where they had passed."

"Then, since the day has come and no ambush is possible, we will look again."

Half of the band, Roka at its head, went fearlessly into the thicket, and, in the brilliant sunlight of the early morning, they were able to trace the imprints of numerous feet. Beyond the thicket they merged into a trail that led into the forest, but the Dakota did not follow it far. Roka felt only contempt for those who had prowled by night about his camp.

"They are truly the *Ikcewicaxta*," he said. "Dakota spying upon their enemy would not have left such a trail, nor would they have broken and bruised the stems in the thicket. It has pleased Manitou to make them an inferior people. Yet, we must beware of their cunning. As the prairie wolves sometimes pull down a buffalo, so a great Dakota warrior may be trapped and slain by the *Ikcewicaxta*."

"Let us trail this band and give them a lesson, O, wise chief," said Hoton.

"No," replied Roka, firmly. "We have not come here merely to make a war. It is likely that we may meet them in battle, but they must first bring the fight to us, we shall not carry it to them. Remember what I have told you. We must keep close together on this march, and no one may leave the band for any purpose, unless he is sent on duty by me."

"We will remember it, O, wise Roka," said nine willing voices together, and they bore it in mind as they resumed the march through ascending country, thickly clothed with forest, not now open, but, to their disadvantage, abounding in thickets and wide areas of bushes. The thickets were made up mainly of great clumps of briars, many of them bearing berries already ripe, and they usually circled about these, but they made their way through the bushes, watchful of eye and ear, and ready of hand. With mind and muscle strained to such a pitch, travel through the primeval wilderness was exhausting work, and they were glad of a long rest at noon in a wide opening. Some of the younger men wanted to search the surrounding forest. Tatokadan and Hinyankaga were particularly eager, but again Roka would not allow it. He was all for prudence.

After a rest of full two hours, they resumed the advance through country that presented many opportunities for ambush, and Roka and Pehansan were exceeding wary. Both soon became convinced that the *Ikcewicaxta* were in the bush on either side of them and keeping pace. They noted it, because birds started suddenly from distant boughs, and faint but unusual sounds came to their ears. At a nod from Roka, Pehansan dropped back to the end of the line— they always went in single file, after the Indian fashion—and the glances he sent to the rear were full as keen as those Roka darted ahead. If the *Ikcewicaxta* attacked it was likely that they would come from behind, after the manner of inferior people.

Young Waditaka noted the precaution, but he said nothing. He shared the feelings of Tatokadan and Hinyankaga, and, since the *Ikcewicaxta* seemed to want it, he was anxious for the clash of arms to come at once. It could not be denied that the Dakota band was favored by the good spirits. He thought that the wonderful manner in which *Peta* and *Mini* had protected and saved him, whom he considered the least deserving of Roka's men, proved it. But the savages could not know that the Dakota were a chosen people, and so they would have to receive a lesson. It would be well to give it to them quickly.

The afternoon march was a severe trial to all the young Dakota warriors, and perhaps it was none the less severe to Roka and Pehansan themselves, though they did not show it. Emboldened by the failure of the Dakota band to take notice, the *Ikcewicaxta* soon increased the evidences of their presence. Bushes well beyond bow shot and on either side were moved purposely. Now and then a top rising above the others was twisted and flaunted about in a most insulting manner.

The Dakota band, Roka leading and Pehansan guarding the rear, marched steadily on, but the muscles of all were quivering and every heart was beating with rage. The hands of the young warriors moved restlessly over their weapons, and now and then the perspiration stood out on their faces. Their souls were being tried in the fiery furnace. Although they knew it would be in vain, they looked longingly at Roka for a signal. The leader marched silently on, his eyes searching the undergrowth in front, and to right and left.

Now, the tops of the tall bushes moved more fiercely than ever, and sometimes when one on the right shook, another on the left shook as if in answer and in confirmation. Then distant shrill voices on one side began to chant, and voices on the opposite began to chant in like fashion. The eyes of the young warriors fairly flashed fire, and their hands clenched on their weapons. They knew that they were being derided, that they were being called *Canwanka* (cowards), *Sinkpe* (Muskrats) and, worst of all, *Manka* (Skunks). Their blood was as fire, and their strong teeth were bitten hard together. And this to them, of the haughty nation of the Dakota, lords of the western plains! This to them, the Dakota, from the *Ikcewicaxta,* savage and inferior people who hid in the bush and would not show their faces!

"I pray you, O wise leader," said Inmu, "to let us send a few arrows into the thickets! Are we warriors that we are called upon to endure this?"

"Hold your hand and follow on!" said the leader sternly, though Inmu, a valiant lad and uncommonly wise for one so young, was dear to his heart. Roka neither increased nor decreased his speed and the others, so straight and regular was their file, stepped exactly in his footprints. Yet their hearts were swollen with rage and mortification. They could not recall that ever in their lives before had they listened to such a chant. They walked straight on after Roka, but a mighty power pulled at their feet, striving to draw

them into the forest after the *Ikcewicaxta.* Doubtless
Manitou looked down on them and pitied their agony,
but there was the wise Roka, unyielding as he was
wise, leading them on, and the fierce Pehansan, cast
in the same mold, who brought up the rear, would not
spare them if they broke from the line.

Louder and louder came the chant of the *Ikcewicaxta,* from the bushes on the right, from the bushes
on the left, and the sounds, fierce and biting, filled
the ears of the Dakota. Then, when the young warriors felt that they could endure it no longer, Hoton,
the boaster, Hoton, the valiant, came to their aid.
Clear and thrilling his voice rose in a challenge:

> "You sing a song, O, wild people.
> You taunt us much, O, wild people.
> But you hide deep, O, wild people,
> In the bush you lie, wild people.

> "We are the warriors of the Dakota;
> Fierce wolf and great bear we fear not,
> Our faces we turn to the day.
> No foe we dread in the open.

> "Come forth, O, wild people,
> Taste our arrow and knife.
> Be you ten or a hundred
> To combat you are welcome."

The songs of Hoton were satisfying to the soul
when they were put to such uses. The taunts of the
wild people were given back to them. They might not

understand the words, but they could not mistake the tone. Even the stern Roka and the crafty Pehansan felt the defiance and they joined with full voice in the challenging chorus:

> "Come forth, O, wild people,
> Taste our arrow and knife.
> Be you ten or a hundred
> To combat you are welcome."

The *Ikcewicaxta* remained hidden. The tall, fierce warriors, powerful of chest and limb, long bows in hand and terrible tomahawks and knives in their belts, were not men to meet in open combat, and they preferred the dense covert. Roka felt that it would be so. The song of Hoton was really a weapon and the stern leader felt anew that they should be grateful to the valiant boaster who, like Inmu, was dear to his heart. His own soul, which had been stung with grief and rage, felt a mighty relief and, throwing his shoulders farther back than ever, he strode steadily on, though all his senses remained perfectly attuned, and his caution was not relaxed a particle, while all the time above the thickets boomed the fierce challenge:

> "Come forth, O, wild people,
> Taste our arrow and knife.
> Be you ten or a hundred
> To combat you are welcome."

The song sank after a while, but the Dakota felt better, far better. The taunts of the *Ikcewicaxta* were now darts without a point. Be they ten or be they a hundred, they had been invited to come into open battle. They had not come, and they had surely understood! Nobody on earth could mistake Hoton's song, the song of the Dakota. When the last echoes of the chant died away in the forest, the *Ikcewicaxta* began to call to one another again in derision, but the young warriors no longer felt grief. Instead, mockery was theirs and they hurled it at their hidden foe.

Hoton began to laugh, and all the others laughed with him, even the wise Roka and the cunning Pehansan. Up and down the line, and back and forth, and back and forth again swept the derisive laughter. The *Ikcewicaxta,* crouching low in the thickets, could not fail to understand it. The warriors of the Dakota were laughing at them. Shrill cries came from the bushes, but Roka's men merely laughed the louder and once more sent forth the dauntless battle cry:

"Come forth, O, wild people,
Taste our arrow and knife.
Be you ten or a hundred
To combat you are welcome."

"They will not come in the day, that is sure, though they may come by night," said Inmu to Waditaka, who walked just behind him.

"The sooner they attack the better," said Waditaka. "We can drive them off, no matter how many they are. I know that Roka would have had peace with whatever tribe he met in this region, but, since they've chosen otherwise, we'll give 'em war to the uttermost."

"We're strangers, and so they look upon us as enemies," said Inmu. "We ten will have to stand together against all who come."

The song of defiance sank to a hum, a fierce hum, though, and they heard above it and anew the cries of rage, and cries that were signals. It was Will's belief that more of the *Ikcewicaxta* had arrived, that at least fifty of them might now be in the bush on either side of the Dakota. He knew that the situation had become dangerous, that the extensive undergrowth favored the enemy, but he believed that the powerful bows carried by the Dakota exceeded any weapon of the wild people, and would keep them at a distance. Yet the kind of march they were making was tremendously trying on nerves, and he wondered how long Roka, stern and immovable, could lead on.

The thickets sank away, and they came to a wide stretch of forest, free from undergrowth, gratitude for this favor of Manitou appearing in the heart of every Dakota, though they gave no voice to it. They entered the park-like expanse, still in single file, and near its center came to a small brook of clear water running directly across the way. Roka signed to his men to kneel and drink and they did so, the cool stream soothing heated body and brain alike. The shouts of the *Ikcewicaxta* now came from thickets far beyond bowshot, but they were again taunting. Their cries said plainly that, like wolves trailing the much larger moose, they would follow the Dakota until, by force of numbers, they pulled down game greater than themselves. And they were cunning, too, like the wolf or the fox. So far Roka's warriors had not seen a single one of them, not the passing glimpse of a body, not a feather in the hair, not the gleam of a weapon. They had heard only the taunting cries, so hard to bear.

Roka and Pehansan put their wise heads together, while their young warriors sat by the stream, and, like good generals, they considered their situation. They saw ahead of them high hills, sloping up toward the ranges, and one of them seemed to be bare. There they would pitch a camp for the night, if they could but reach it, and, judicious leaders that they were, they gave the young warriors a long rest, after which they resumed the march in the usual single file.

The thickets soon spread across their path again, and the *Ikcewicaxta* once more came near with their irritating cries, running through an extraordinary series of variations. They imitated eagle and hawk and owl and crow. They growled like the bear or screamed like the panther, they sent forth the grunt of the buffalo or the snarl of the wolf, and they snapped like the fox or uttered the neigh of the wild horse. Will had never before heard so many notes, and, all the while, those who threatened yet remained invisible. It was weird, uncanny, and as Will, the white youth, suddenly merged again and wholly into Waditaka, he was assailed by a great fear.

"How do we know it is the *Ikcewicaxta* at all?" he

said to Inmu. "Perhaps the evil spirits have overpowered the good, and it is they that are in the bush, seeking to frighten, and perhaps to destroy us?"

"It is the *Ikcewicaxta,*" said Inmu. "Those are human cries, though the cries of deadly foes. We have not caught a single glimpse of their bodies, it is true, but perhaps we may soon have proof that they are men, as the thickets ahead of us now grow much more dense."

They reached a region not merely of bushes but of vines and briars also, affording passage only to those who had consummate skill in the ways of the wilderness. Yet Roka entered it without hesitation, gliding through the obstructions in an extraordinary manner, and the others followed in like fashion. Now, as Inmu had foreseen, the *Ikcewicaxta* came much nearer, and their cries redoubled. Every kind of beast or bird howled or barked or screamed about the Dakota. The warriors, watching with eyes trained to pierce the undergrowth, kept their powerful bows ready, and the *Ikcewicaxta* made no rush. But there was a light swishing and the gleam of something falling. They saw arrows striking in the thickets on either side of them, but all dropping short, as if the savages did not yet dare to come near enough. The Dakota saw that the arrows were shorter and smaller than their own, concrete proofs that the wild people were inferior to themselves, and they gave back the taunts of their enemies in the same wild fashion. They, too, growled like the bear and screamed like the panther, but with a fiercer and deeper note, as if the sounds were sent from mightier chests. It was also the note of invitation, of welcome to battle.

It was a scene from dim antiquity, the superior, trailed and assailed by numbers, challenging the inferior to come forward and give battle, man to man, and the inferior, knowing its inferiority in strength and courage, resisting the taunts, and trusting always to cunning, numbers and pertinacity. And the great leader, Roka, knew all the time, while the arrows were falling short on either side of them, that he could not draw the *Ikcewicaxta* into pitched battle. He knew, too, that the danger was formidable and pressing. Cunning and powerful as wolf and bear had proved themselves to be, man was more so, and the *Ikcewicaxta* would follow with surprising patience and endurance the noblest game that they had ever found. Even the spirit of Roka, so strong in self-restraint, began to show irritation. He fingered his bow restlessly. He sought in the bushes on either side for a sight of the pertinacious foe, and had he caught a single glimpse of a brown body his arrow would have gone straight and true, but, look as he would, he had no reward for eye and spirit. The *Ikcewicaxta* never ceased their cries, and at times sent flights of arrows, but they remained invisible.

The little shafts of the wild people began to fall nearer. They pierced leaves and cut twigs not two yards away. Then one struck at the very feet of Pehansan, and, the next instant, another passed directly between Waditaka and Inmu. Warriors of lesser fiber would have been thrown into a tumult, and would have begun to fight, shooting at random, perhaps, but fighting, nevertheless. But Roka gave the supreme proof of unflinching courage and steadiness, and he still led his men on, straight toward the desired hill, while not one of them dared to loose an arrow until he gave the word.

The thickets thinned out for a while, and then closed in again. The patter of arrows from the wild people on twigs and leaves was incessant. A shaft scraped the shoulder of Inmu, but he did not utter a word. One lodged in the pack of Pehansan. He pulled it out and threw it on the ground, and marched on in silence, though the cries of the *Ikcewicaxta* were now triumphant and closer. Until now Roka had never looked back once. Turning, for a moment, a face flashing with wrath he said to Inmu, who was just behind him:

"The time is at hand when they will dare too much. Be ready with bow and arrow. Pass the word!"

Inmu passed it, and it went down the line until it reached Pehansan at the rear, and, as it was sent from man to man, the souls of the Dakota were lifted up. Every pulse leaped with joy. They were going to give answer to the foe who had assailed them so long with taunt and shaft. Their own fierce song had told that they would fight, but that was like the voice of a herald, it was not good until action made it true. Now shaft would answer shaft and the wild people, the savages, the *Ikcewicaxta,* would know what it was to fight with the great Dakota. And it was true that young Waditaka, who had been born white, was not the least eager among them.

It happened also that Waditaka was the first to catch a glint of brown in the bushes. His great elk-horn bow bent to the uttermost and his arrow shot forth, a flash of light. The death cry coming back showed that it had not been launched in vain, and the Dakota gave fierce approval. Hoton, who had been silent for a long time, began to shout forth his tremendous song:

> "Come forth, O, wild people,
> Taste our arrow and knife.
> Be you ten or a hundred
> To combat you are welcome."

And all the ten joined in the song. They knew that Waditaka's arrow had gone true, and they were glad. Their wild instincts were alive and leaping. The taunters were learning what it was to come too near the Dakota. Pehansan suddenly uttered a terrific shout. He, too, had caught the brown glimpse, and, quick as lightning, his arrow went to the target, carrying instant death. Inmu wounded a third and Capa a fourth. The cries of the *Ikcewicaxta* ceased suddenly and they drew back, knowing now what it was to attack the picked warriors of a superior race. Hoton, in thunder tones, upbraided them.

"Do you flee, O *Ikcewicaxta?*" he cried. "Do you flee, *Canwanka?* Do you flee, *Manka?* We are here, the Dakota! We are but ten! You are many times our number! You are on either side of us! Your arrows have fallen at our feet! They have struck in our clothing! They have grazed our bodies! But we flinch not! We neither stop nor do we run! The wise Roka leads us on at the appointed pace to the place where we would go! Come again! Come close as you did before, and we will teach you another and yet greater lesson! O *Ikcewicaxta,* is it possible that you are going to fail us! You will not come! The Dakota have had but one battle in one day, and true warriors of our nation cannot sleep well unless they have had at least three! O *Ikcewicaxta,* are you so hard of heart that we must lie awake tonight?"

Waditaka knew well that the hearts of the *Ikcewicaxta* were consumed with rage. As before they might not understand a word of Dakota, but the tones and inflections of Hoton were unmistakable. Only the certainty of death could keep back those who had heard such a challenge, and the *Ikcewicaxta* did not come.

The forest about them became absolutely silent. The wind ceased to blow, and not a leaf or a twig stirred. The ten as they marched on at the same even gait made no sound, so light were their footsteps. Their hearts were light, too. Roka felt an immense relief. If the *Ikcewicaxta* had pressed the attack there in the thickets, reckless of losses, the Dakota must have gone down, no matter how great their courage and strength. But superb archery and a dauntless front had driven them off, for a while. Now he prayed silently to all the good spirits of earth and air, of fire and water, to give them soon open forest, where the enemies could lay no ambush, and where the ten, with free arms and bodies, and shooting so fast that eye might not follow hand and arrow, could drive off any number of these wild and inferior people of the great northern wilderness.

But the *Ikcewicaxta* held back, for the time at least. Now and then the Dakota heard a distant shout, but no more arrows fell near them. The hill that they had chosen for their camp of the night drew near, and Roka, who had first seen it with the eyes of a general, knew now that his hopes were confirmed. Summit and slopes were clear of trees and undergrowth and from a rocky part of the slope flowed a fine little brook. They had ample food for several days which, in a pinch, they could make last two or three times as long, and it would be strange, in truth, if ten such warriors as they could not hold the crest.

"Behold the hill that is waiting for us," said Roka, in even tones to his men. "It rises up, a tower of might, and we will make our home there for a while. But do not hasten. It is not seemly for the Dakota to flee, or to have the appearance of fleeing, before the *Ikcewicaxta*."

He marched gravely to the brook, where he knelt and drank, and, when everyone had drunk copiously in turn, they proceeded toward the crest of the hill, after Hoton had issued a thundering but unanswered challenge to the *Ikcewicaxta* to follow.

"Here we rest, and, if need be, fight," said the wise Roka.

CHAPTER XIII

MAHPIYA'S PROMISE

IT was a hill, sloping down gently and evenly in all directions, with no underbrush on any side for a distance of several hundred yards, the spring at which they had drunk being well within the open area, and it had all the aspects of a fortress that might be defended indefinitely by brave men. The Dakota warriors, despite their courage and warlike training, felt enormous relief. All lay upon the grass, drawing deep breaths, except Roka and Pehansan, who stood erect watching the bushes for the first sign of the *Ikcewicaxta.*

But the wild people did not come. They had already obtained a taste of the Dakota quality, and they did not like it. They sent jeers from distant coverts, but did not show themselves, and then Roka and Pehansan also sat down, their old contempt for the savages returning. The taciturn leader seldom showed his feelings, but he was willing to prove now to the *Ikcewicaxta* how little his men cared for them.

"You have had one good drink," he said to the warriors, "but you can now go back to the spring and drink again. But take your weapons with you."

The young warriors caught the spirit of it, and ex-

pressing supreme contempt for their foes, they saun-
tered carelessly down to the water, drinking their fill
a second time. Then they dipped their heads and
hands in the pool, and, retiring to the crest of the
hill, where they sat in plain view of the savages hidden in the bushes, began to comb their hair with
little combs that everyone carried in his pack. Will
suddenly remembered the old story of the three hundred Spartans at Thermopylae, sitting placidly in the
sunshine and combing their long hair in the face of
the Persian hosts, as a sign that they would meet the
attack, though outnumbered a thousand to one. The
ten were like the three hundred to him, not less valiant,
and he was proud to be their comrade. He, too, had
a little comb, and he sat with them, combing his long
hair as they did theirs. The ordinary eye could not
have noticed that he differed from them in any respect, save that his hair was brown and fine while
theirs was black and coarse.

Will liked the spirit of the challenge, and he knew
that it was thoroughly genuine. The Dakota, sitting
on their hill, would have welcomed a rush by the
Ikcewicaxta. They had yet shot but few arrows.
Their quivers were full, and not in vain had Roka
trained them so carefully in archery. If the *Ikcewicaxta* charged across that open ground not a Dakota
arrow would go astray.

An hour passed and no demonstration came from
the thickets. The locks of the warriors had been carefully arranged long since. Their dress was smoothed,
their faces were calm and composed. If battle were

offered, they would enter it like guests going to a feast. But Roka became confident that it would not be offered, at least while day lasted, and, wise general that he was, he began to make preparations for all emergencies.

"Do you, Tatokadan and Hinyankaga," he said, "gather fallen wood for a fire, and Capa and Tarinca can slice venison for the broiling. Pehansan and Inmu will watch the thickets, and the remainder of us will rest on the grass until supper is ready. We will take our ease and we will show that just now these savages do not exist for us. You think, Waditaka, that *Xunktokeca,* the king wolf, still follows us?"

"I do, Roka," replied Will, "and in some ways I dread him more than the *Ikcewicaxta* down there in the bush."

"It is because the wolf does not forget. Perhaps he alone among the animals does not forget."

"How do you think he happened to be on the shelf waiting for me the time I tried to climb out of the valley?"

"Perhaps he had some secret way of entering the valley, some narrow gulch that you did not see. You know that *Mini* showed you the way out. The wolf is very crafty and very wise, and he may have known of another path. Do the *Ikcewicaxta* stir in the thickets, Inmu?"

"No, O wise Roka, and they must have drawn back to some distance, because at the edge of the bushes I can see birds fluttering about and darting from one bough to another."

"Good proof that you are right, Inmu. Now, the odor of the broiled venison is very pleasant and all of us will eat."

A small fire had been built quickly and Capa and Tarinca were broiling the venison in such fashion that every member of the band was assailed at once by a fierce hunger. There was enough for all, and they ate in a leisurely manner, like gentlemen of the wilderness. When they had finished they wiped their hunting knives carefully, and returned them to the sheaths. Then they went down to the spring, and drank a third time. It was now almost sunset and they put out the fire. The most dangerous period was drawing near, and they knew it, but forest warriors never awaited an attack with prouder or bolder hearts.

"The night," said Roka, studying the skies attentively, "will not be very dark. The *Ikcewicaxta,* hidden by the grass, may creep within fifty or sixty yards of us, from which point their arrows will reach, but even if we cannot see them we must hear them."

"Why not roll these old, fallen logs into a sort of circle?" said Will, who had the white man's instinct for fortification, "and from their shelter we can beat five times our number of the wild people."

"Yours are wise words, Waditaka."

They put the tree trunks into place, making a barrier that would be a great help in forest warfare, and then they crouched behind them in a circle, facing all the slopes of the hill, Will sitting between Inmu and Hoton. The sun set swiftly behind the ranges, and the night came on, as Roka had predicted, neither absolutely bright nor absolutely dark. Their eyes, trained to the dusk, could easily detect an enemy close up, but for a foe farther away they must depend upon hearing, which necessity had developed to such an extraordinary degree. They doubted whether the *Ikcewicaxta* would try a rush, but, in any event, they were supremely confident, and knowing that they would have to wait long, they made themselves as comfortable as they could behind their logs.

"If the leaders of the *Ikcewicaxta* would only come out and talk to us," said Will to Hoton, "not an arrow need be fired by either side. All we want is a passage through this country which may or may not be theirs."

"But they won't come out," said Hoton. "That is why they are savages, inferior people. Observe, Waditaka, that the lower breeds always take the higher to be their enemies. We would not harm a single one of the *Ikcewicaxta,* but they will not have it that way. Folly rules as often as wisdom."

"Hoton speaks truth," said Inmu. "If all the red races had made friends with one another, and joined against the white people, who were once yours, Waditaka, the beaver streams and the buffalo plains would remain ours forever. Can you see anything stirring in the thickets, Hoton?"

"No, it is too dark there. All the bushes blur together until they make a black wall, nor do I hear anything creeping toward us. And remember, Inmu, that if I, Hoton, do not hear it, nobody hears it, and remember also that if I, Hoton, do not hear a sound, the sound is not made."

"I shall remember it, O boaster, and remembering it, I wonder why Roka keeps the rest of us on guard. You would hear the *Ikcewicaxta* first, and you alone would defeat them."

"But it would not be seemly, Inmu. What would Xingudan say when we went back to the village, if it were told to him that nine of his men left Hoton to fight a savage horde alone?"

"The reason is a good one, Hoton. Boaster you are, but valiant is your heart, and your tongue is one that never tires."

Will heard the Lynx's low laugh, but the serenity of Hoton was not disturbed in the least.

"Hark, I hear the twitter of a bird," he said, "and the bird is not one that flies from bough to bough."

"It walks on the ground, and it carries bow and arrows in its hand," said Inmu.

"True, Inmu, and its heart is filled with hatred of the Dakota, who have done it no harm, save in self-defense."

"And the answering twitter comes from another bird of the same kind."

"Shall we tell Roka?"

"No. He has already heard and he knows."

All the Dakota understood the signals, and, raising themselves a little behind their defenses, they gazed intently, trying to pierce the dark. But they were not as yet able to trace human figures.

"Don't you think it likely they will try to wear out

our patience?" Will said to Inmu. "I've noticed that usually the wilder people are the more patience they have."

"It is true, Waditaka, and it is because they have so much time. The *Ikcewicaxta,* having little to do and think about, can afford to wait long. It is a weapon which they consider as good as ours, although their bows and arrows are inferior."

Nevertheless, the patience of the Dakota themselves was almost infinite, and in this trial they proved to be the equal of the *Ikcewicaxta.* Several of them lay fully an hour behind the tree trunks, without stirring. The moonlight came out and silvered their bronze figures, but they were as still as the dead. White men would have found such long waiting past all endurance, but it was a part of the lives of the Dakota, and, knowing its need at this vital time, they did not mean to be outdone in it by the *Ikcewicaxta.*

The twittering of birds in the woods ceased, and then came the hoot of owls, the barking of foxes, the snarling of wolves and the growl of bears. The sounds were on all sides, but the Dakota warriors only looked at one another, and smiled contemptuously.

"Do they expect to scare us with noise?" asked the pious Tarinca, "and do they think we are so ignorant that we do not know the noises are made by the *Ikcewicaxta* themselves?"

"The wild people are foolish," said Hoton, "they do not know who the Dakota are. They do not know our prowess, and they do not know that I, Hoton, am here. They do not know they are trying to stalk the greatest of all Dakota warriors—save, of course, the wise Roka, our leader."

Roka himself smiled at Hoton's last and diplomatic touch, but he let the valiant boaster whisper on. He knew that the men liked to hear him, that Hoton was always an optimist, and that the talk of an optimist was like a trumpet to those going into battle.

"When do you think the attack will come?" asked Will of Inmu after a while.

"Not before midnight, Waditaka; perhaps much later."

"And midnight itself is a good two hours away."

"But as a Dakota, Waditaka, you can wait patiently twenty hours, if need be."

The chattering sounds in the forest ceased again, and after midnight the skies began to darken. The dimmer stars danced uncertainly and then went away. The face of the moon became dusky. The black wall of the circling forest merged into the general blackness, and the heavy shadows came closer to the little force on the hill. The Dakota range of vision, although their eyes were used to the dark, did not extend above fifty or sixty yards now, and that was within bow shot. Will felt sure that the attack would come soon. All the conditions now favored the *Ikcewicaxta,* and he continually examined the open space about them for the sight of creeping forms. Nevertheless, like all his comrades, he relied in the crisis more upon ear than eye. No wind was blowing and the Dakota would be able to hear any sound made upon the earth.

The cries of beasts and birds in the thickets suddenly burst forth anew and in much greater volume. Wild animals were growling, snapping and barking in the whole circle of the forest, and the owls hooted in weird and melancholy unison. Will was astonished. Why this demonstration? Did the *Ikcewicaxta* merely wish to prove the power of their lungs and their skill in imitation? Then, in a flash, he divined the reason.

"It is the cover for an attack," he whispered to Inmu. "They wish to draw our attention to the thickets, and also to drown out light sounds made by their creeping warriors."

"As sure as the moon is in the heavens! And now, may the good spirits watch over us."

A light swish, and an arrow, passing over their heads, was buried in the ground beyond. Will noticed it as it stuck upright, the shaft still quivering. It was smaller than the arrows of the Dakotas, and not so well made, proof of their inferiority. A people was to be judged by the quality of its weapons. A thud, and another arrow was buried in the defending tree trunk. Three more buried themselves in the wood, and two others passed beyond. The hands of the young warriors became eager and restless, but the wise Roka, sweeping the circle with his eyes, compelled them to withhold the reply yet a while.

"They are there, but you cannot see them," he whispered. "We must not shoot until we know the target. Let them waste their arrows, because they are the *Ikcewicaxta,* an inferior people, but we, the Dakota, will not speed our shafts in vain."

The volume of sound from the forest became amaz-

ing. It seemed to Will that at least a hundred warriors must be there, sending forth cries of bird and
beast from their throats, and perhaps as many more
were creeping forward in the deadly circle. The arrows were whizzing all about them, sticking in the
tree trunks until more than a score stood out there,
but mostly passing in a stream over their heads and
beyond. Roka arranged his men carefully, facing all
sides of the circle, and now bade them, whenever they
saw a creeping form, to shoot.

It was the fortune of Hoton to make the first reply
for the defense. He saw a dark shadow detach itself
from the darker earth in order to bend a bow, and,
quick as lightning, his own shaft sped straight to the
mark. Then Inmu shot, and in another minute the
entire circle was in action. The circumscribed space
within the fallen trees was filled with the twanging of
bows, the whistling of arrows, the heavy breathing of
men, the low commands of Roka and Pehansan, and
now and then the fierce, triumphant shout of Hoton,
which Roka made no effort to check, knowing that it
was a bugle call to his young warriors.

"Come on! Come on, O *Ikcewicaxta!*" cried the
valiant boaster, "and learn what it is to attack the Dakota! You pay high for the knowledge, but it is
worth the price! Why do you creep? Stand up!
Face us like men! You are a hundred and we but
ten!"

Although they did not accept Hoton's invitation to
stand up, the *Ikcewicaxta* were not lacking in courage. Their arrows pelted like hail upon the little circle

of defense. They had an advantage, too, in knowing just where the Dakota were, while the Dakota must rely upon fleeting glimpses in the dark for their targets. They clung to the ground, creeping closer and ever closer, and they believed that, where so many arrows of theirs were falling, some must surely strike home.

Thankful were the Dakota now for their shelter of logs. The good wood received scores of arrows intended for their own breasts, and in all the excitement and fury of the battle they obeyed the strenuous injunctions of Roka and Pehansan to expose no more of the body than was necessary for the bending of the bow. And despite the darkness and confusion the Dakota never shot better. Figure after figure fell before their swift arrows, but they were not escaping now without harm themselves. Roka himself was grazed by an arrow across the chest, Capa was wounded slightly in the side, and a shaft stood out in the shoulder of Totokadan. Fortunately it did not penetrate deep, and, pulling it out, he bound up the wound hastily, going on with the battle as if he had not been touched. An arrow shot high and, falling within the circle, struck Hoton in the foot, but, snatching it forth, he fitted it to his own bow and returned it to them.

"I give you back your present!" he shouted. "These are gifts that the Dakota like, arrows and yet more arrows, and yet more arrows, and hoping that you, too, will like them, they send them to you in return! Come closer, and yet a little closer, O *Ikcewicaxta!* Let us see the color of your eyes! Come into our circle! We are but a few, but we are enough to give you a welcome that will last you a hundred moons!"

The *Ikcewicaxta* obeyed. They came nearer, but now the good spirits favored the Dakota. A sudden unveiling of the moon revealed them with distinctness, and the Dakota shot with such deadly swiftness that, uttering howls of terror, they gave up the attack, fleeing for the shelter of the thickets.

The cries of beasts and birds ceased suddenly. The Dakota warriors themselves sank down exhausted, and an oppressive silence succeeded the sounds of combat. It was broken by Roka.

"The *Ikcewicaxta*," he said, "are not Dakota warriors, but they have borne themselves well in the battle."

"They might now be within our log circle if I had not frightened them," said Hotoṅ.

"You shouted well, O Crow," said Roka, "and you shot no less well."

"But we never could have driven them back had not the good spirits helped us," said the pious Tarinca.

"Tarinca speaks the truth," said Roka, and all the Dakota devoutly gave thanks, though not neglecting meanwhile to help themselves to the uttermost. The watch was never relaxed for an instant. Slight wounds were bound up anew or for the first time, and Roka served food. Then Inmu and Hinyankaga, scaling the barrier and creeping about in the dark, scouted the open ground thoroughly, reporting that no enemy was

313

now there. The *Ikcewicaxta* had carried away all their wounded and dead, save two.

"If they return for the two," said Roka, "we are not to fire upon them."

Later in the night they heard creeping noises, but not an arrow was discharged. At dawn the two bodies were gone. Then the young warriors in turn went down to the spring and drank deeply, those who had wounds bathing and cleansing them also. No sign came from the thickets, but they felt sure the *Ikcewicaxta* were still there.

"Since they suffered so much in last night's attack," said Pehansan, "they may conclude to use patience, of which they have as much as we."

"What do you mean?" asked Will.

"To keep a circle about us, not to rush us, but to hold us within our logs. They know that our food and arrows cannot last forever. They may sit in the thickets a week, two weeks, and wait until we have to come out."

The prospect made no sort of an appeal to Will. He thought himself as well supplied with patience as those who were born Dakota, but the calmness of Pehansan when he announced the probability seemed to him wholly unwarranted.

"Two weeks would be a long time to wait," he said.

"But think how young you are, Waditaka," said the Crane, grimly. "You would not be an old man, even when the *Ikcewicaxta* came to the end of their patience. And bear in mind, too, Waditaka, that you are yet alive, that all of us are alive, and that as the good spirits helped us last night, so they may help us again."

"Every word you say is true, Pehansan, and I am grateful for the favor that is shown to us."

"You will notice, too, Waditaka, that the spring flows on, that it will probably flow forever, and that its water is cool and very pleasant."

"I notice it, Pehansan; I notice also that it flows for us, and again I am grateful."

Will, despite the belief of his comrades, was hopeful that the wild people would go away that day, but he soon saw that Roka and Pehansan did not cherish the same idea. When they were all refreshed they set the warriors to work, strengthening the fortifications, putting more fallen logs into position, and also helping out the breastwork with loose stones that were scattered about. The leader examined the food in every pack, and announced the size of the ration for every man, about half the usual amount, a severe trial for such sturdy young warriors, but enough to keep life in their bodies. All that Roka and Pehansan did betokened the expectation of a long siege, and Will tried to accustom himself to the thought of it.

It was hard to build there on the hill for a long stay, because by day the *Ikcewicaxta* were not visible at all, nor did they make any sound. So far as any physical demonstration was concerned, they might have been a thousand miles away. Twitterings and chirpings came out of the forest, but they were those of real birds; there was a bark, but it was that of a real fox, and a distant snarl was that of a genuine mountain wolf, maybe that of the king wolf himself. All the while the sunshine poured down in wave after wave. The deep green of the surrounding forest had been heightened in a single day, and it seemed to Will that he could almost see the grass growing. All the roaming instincts in him, the desire to look and see, were alive, and it was cruel to toil at a fortification against an invisible foe, when all nature invited.

It was likely that the young Dakota warriors felt the wandering impulse as strongly as Will did, but they, as well as he, did not allow it to show itself. They worked at the barrier until they had used all the fallen wood and loose stones, and, now and then, they went purposely within bowshot of the forest, hoping to tempt the *Ikcewicaxta,* but they never drew an arrow. Nearly all the afternoon they rested within their fort, and now Hoton proved anew his value not only as a warrior but as an entertainer, a highly desirable gift at such a time. He spun wonderful stories of the Dakota nation, he related many incidents showing why Dakota warriors were superior to any other, and the children of the forest, who had no books, but whose craving for romance, natural in all human beings, was supplied by the tale teller, listened with an attention and interest very gratifying to Hoton.

The valiant boaster was still chanting his little historical novels of the Dakota nation when the sun set, and he might have gone on even then had it not been time for supper. Roka did not allow any fire to be lighted, and they contented themselves with cold food, and but little of it. The second night was very much like the first in quality, neither very dark nor very fair, but the *Ikcewicaxta* never stirred. Not a single one of them crept into the open, not an arrow was shot from the circling forest, and, when another dawn came, Will hoped that Roka and Pehansan would give the word to start again, but they merely told the warriors to make themselves as comfortable as they could inside the log circle, although they had the privilege of visiting the spring whenever it was necessary.

Will and Inmu, who went to the brook together, were so exasperated over the silence of the wild people that they lingered purposely, and made a great display, splashing each other with water, but the *Ikcewicaxta* were immune to all such temptations. The forest gave out no sound from them.

"They would not send an arrow unless we went down to the edge of the forest itself," said Inmu.

"Do you feel sure they are still there?" asked Will.

"It is a vain question, Waditaka. They are as surely there as we are here. They intend to make us come from behind our logs, some time or other, and well within the range of their arrows."

"But they can't do it."

"That is for time to tell, Waditaka. You see now very well that it is to be a test of patience."

Two more days and two more nights passed and in all that time the *Ikcewicaxta* gave no sign. Inferior in knowledge and prowess they might be to the Dakota, but they were equal to anybody on earth in patience. The warriors had been in their log ring for five days, when Roka allowed Hoton and Tarinca to

317

venture within arrow shot of the forest. He did it merely that his young warriors, now growing impatient, might have proof of a fact that he himself never doubted. A little risk was worth while if it steeled their patience.

Four arrows were sent at Hoton and Tarinca, none of them coming very near, and the two would gladly have sent their own shafts at random into the covert, but they did not dare disobey the stern command of Roka. Arrows were too valuable to be wasted on chance shots. They retreated quickly, and they and their comrades now prayed to all the spirits of earth and air and water to send the *Ikcewicaxta* against them in fair battle.

But the wild people, knowing their best tactics, clung to them in a way that would have won the admiration of a great general. They stayed day and night in the covert, and waited for the game to drop into their hands. Even Roka did not hesitate to commend their methods.

"If it is our fate to fall," he said, "it will be to foes who are not as much inferior to us as we thought."

It was clear that he found much consolation in the knowledge. Their food, with the most rigid economy, would not last them more than two days longer, and now he and Pehansan talked much together in low tones. Young Waditaka knew that they were seeking a way out, and he trusted those two wise leaders. As for himself, he put most faith in the elements. He recognized now that the *Ikcewicaxta* were willing to wait until the Dakota dropped dead from exhaustion, or, if Roka's men dared to break from their fort and plunge into the forest, they would all surely be cut down, no matter how bravely they fought. But the injunction had been laid by Xingudan upon Roka to bring all the young men back to the village, which had no warriors to spare, and he meant to do so, if it were humanly possible. Will felt sure then that the rush would not be made, unless it was favored by exceptional circumstances, conditions far more favorable to the defense than any that had yet occurred.

Yet young Waditaka never lost courage. He had been saved once by *Peta* and *Mini,* and he believed that as the favor of the good spirits had been showered upon him, so would it be showered upon the band. Why not? He considered himself the least deserving among the besieged warriors, and, as he sat within the log circle, thinking intently about it and gazing up at the sky, it seemed to him that the blue dome suddenly bent down toward him in a friendly and protecting manner, just as the lofty flames of *Peta* had once leaned toward him and towered over him, fending off his enemies. A whisper coming out of the very center of the vault said:

"Trust me and I will save you!"

Will started violently. His companions had taken no notice, and they surely had not heard the words, but he could have sworn that they were registered upon the drum of his ear. It was a voice out of the void. A good spirit was talking and he would have faith. His own Christian religion had taught him to have faith, and faith worked wonders. The creed of the Dakota was not different, and, resolving to believe, he believed.

"I do not know how we shall be saved," he said to Inmu, "but I know who will save us."

"Who, Waditaka?" asked the Lynx with eager curiosity.

"Mahpiya" (Sky).

Inmu never thought of scoffing. He was too devout a Dakota to doubt Waditaka's word.

"Has a voice then been speaking to you?" he asked.

"Yes, Inmu. It came out of the very center of the blue dome. It was but a whisper, but it could be none other than *Mahpiya* speaking."

"What did *Mahpiya* say?" asked Inmu, not without awe.

" 'Trust me and I will save you.' The 'you' meant all of us, and, Inmu, I trust implicitly what *Mahpiya* said."

"So do I, Waditaka, and it is well that we shall have *Mahpiya's* help, because the end of our food is at hand. Our patience has been as great as that of the *Ikcewicaxta,* but when they have food and we have none they can still wait, while we cannot."

It was a fact not at all strange that Will's revelation was accepted with the utmost faith by all the Dakota. They, like all the other Indian nations living from time immemorial in close communion with nature, believed that the spirits now and then revealed to men what they could not know of their own accord. They had been deeply impressed by young Waditaka's story of the manner in which he had been protected by fire and saved by water, and it added faith, if faith were needed, to his prediction that they would be saved from the wild people by *Mahpiya,* the sky.

Roka said but little, though he felt an immense relief. The Badger was a great warrior, and he had the tenacity and fighting spirit of the animal after which he was named, but it would have hurt his pride terribly to think that he was going to fall at the hands of an inferior people, the *Ikcewicaxta,* even though his own hand sent a half dozen of them before him to *Tokata* (Hereafter). Hence he regarded with great favor young Waditaka, because he had been chosen to hear the whisper of *Mahpiya,* and to convey the message to the rest of the band.

So Roka gazed up at the sky and sought to see the beginning of the miracle. He had no idea how *Mahpiya* would send it, but send it he surely would, although there was yet no sign. From the zenith to the circling horizon the heavens were a blazing blue. The far green mountains with their snowy crests were outlined against it in dazzling beauty. It was a majestic and splendid world, and the gallant Dakota warrior suddenly felt, with all the sharpness of a truth not realized before, that he would be loath to leave it in the prime of life. He would die on the battle-field, if he must, because, in his view, that was a noble death, but it was better to live in the royal wilderness. And if he wished to finish out his life, how much more must it be wished by the young warriors around him, mere lads who had just begun to live.

And no leader ever had a finer and braver lot of boys. He looked upon them and, for a moment, his quiet eyes glowed.

"*Mahpiya* does not yet speak," said Hoton, who was also gazing at the sky.

"The spirit of *Mahpiya* is not ready to speak," said the pious Tarinca. "The gods choose their own time for delivering their messages, and they are not affected by the wishes of men. *Mahpiya* has whispered in the ear of Waditaka and that is enough. Having told us that he will act, he will act when the time comes."

Yet the sky remained without a change a long time. The *Ikcewicaxta,* as if feeling that the fruit was ripe and would soon fall into their hands, began for the first time in days to chatter and snarl and growl in the woods, imitating all the animals and birds of the northern wilderness. Roka and his warriors knew well enough that these were sounds of derision, and, although the Indian was peculiarly sensitive to ridicule, they made no reply, but merely shut their teeth the harder.

Roka bade them all to make their packs ready, and to have their weapons in perfect order. He was not absolutely sure that *Mahpiya* would order them to leave the log circle, but, if so, he meant that his people should be ready when the command came. It was well to coöperate with the gods when they intended to favor you. He also sent them down to the spring that everyone might have a good drink and then bathe his head, neck and arms in the refreshing waters. When all had done so they sat once more on the logs and combed their long hair. It was good to bid defiance anew to the *Ikcewicaxta,* and they could not fail to understand the sign. Then the last of their food, a strip of venison apiece, was served, and they ate it, confident that more would soon come from some unknown source, because *Mahpiya* had promised.

Another hour passed in utter silence. Then Roka said to Pehansan:

"Did I feel the touch of *Tateyanpa* (Wind) on my face, or was it only my fancy, Pehansan?"

The Crane moistened his finger, and held it up before he replied.

"It was the faint breath of *Tateyanpa,*" he said, "and I have a thought, Roka, that the miracle which is to save us is beginning."

"It was mine also, Pehansan. How long would you say it is to sunset?"

"About an hour, O Roka."

"Much may happen in an hour. Now I am sure we feel the beginning of the miracle. The wind on my cheek grows stronger, and it comes out of the south."

"And so, a moist wind, O Roka."

The figure of the wise leader suddenly expanded and he stood erect. His eyes glowed and Waditaka saw that this man, usually so quiet, was infused with a great emotion.

"Be ready, O my warriors," he said, in deep, sonorous tones. "*Mahpiya* is about to save us. The miracle is at hand! We do not yet know in what manner it will work, but let us be prepared to do our part when *Mahpiya* calls."

An electric thrill shot through every warrior, and their hearts were uplifted. All felt the south wind, gentle and moist in its touch, blowing on their cheeks, and Waditaka, who had been looking long at the dazzling blue of the sky, asked:

"Don't you think there is a faint tint of gray in the western sky? By comparing it with the center of the heavens I seem to see a new paleness there."

"You see clearly, Waditaka, because what you say is true," replied the chief. "A thin grayness is beginning to overspread the sky in the south, and it is from there that *Tateyanpa* comes."

"And the touch of *Tateyanpa* grows more moist," said Hoton. "I think, O chief, that we shall soon be in the presence of mighty deeds, done by those far greater than we are."

The light mist in the south was spreading, and the wind continued to gain in strength, though it came steadily, never in gusts. Will watched the change with awe. He thought with Roka, and just as devoutly, that the miracle was beginning. He had not been mistaken when he believed that *Mahpiya* had whispered in his ear, and he was too good a Dakota to think for a moment that *Mahpiya* would whisper a promise that he did not mean to keep.

The sun had been so dazzling that he could scarcely glance at it, even between his fingers. It had hung in the west, a gigantic, burnished, brazen ball, larger and more brilliant, it seemed, than ever before in his life. It was apparently impossible that anything could put out *Wi* (The Sun), but he had learned long since that millions of little creatures working together could extinguish anything, no matter how large and strong. The mist was composed of myriads of motes, all making a great veil which slowly, though ever spreading, was dimming the splendor of *Wi* himself. It was another proof to him, and to Roka as well, that the miracle was about to be performed.

"The skies will soon be darkened," said the Dakota leader in a solemn tone, "and they will be darkened by another hand than that of the twilight, which itself is not far away."

A faint sound, almost like a distant groan, came from the south.

"Wakinyanhoton" (Thunder), said Roka.

"Mahpiya speaks first to the ear," said the pious Tarinca, "and then he will speak to the eye. Now we shall soon see *Wakanhdi"* (Lightning).

But *Wakanhdi* did not flash. They heard only the voice of *Wakinyanhoton,* which, although low, spread all around the southern and western horizons and was inexpressibly solemn. It was like the rumbling of a far-away but mighty sea, and the gray mist, the veil that myriads of motes made by ranging themselves together, stole up and up toward the zenith, casting its shadow before it in the west where mighty blazing *Wi* ceased steadily to blaze so much or to be so mighty.

All the Dakota watched with awe, but without fear. The strangest feature of the phenomenon was the entire absence of lightning. They knew that where thunder was lightning was also, but evidently *Wakanhdi* did not wish to reveal himself to them. He must be hiding his flashes on purpose, and, for a reason, behind the distant mountains.

"*Wi* will soon be gone, conquered by *Minibosan*" (Mist), said Roka.

"And will *Minibosan* turn to Marpiya?" (Cloud) asked Pehansan.

"That I know not," replied the wise leader. "*Mahpiya* has whispered to Waditaka that we shall be saved. but he has not told the way, although we surely see the beginning of it. *Wakanhdi* appears not, but *Wakinyanhoton* groans all the time."

The thunder, in truth, was spreading around the whole circle of the heavens, a distant and solemn note like a myriad organs playing together, but still without a sign of lightning. Nor could there be any doubt now that *Wi* had been completely conquered. In spite of his splendor and power, the mists were hanging a heavy gray veil over his face, which would soon hide him, even if the curve of the world did not supervene first.

"In a half hour," said Roka, "night will be here, and I think a great wind will ride on the wings of the dark."

"From what point do you think *Tateyanpa* will come?" asked Pehansan.

"That I know not. Now, Pehansan, the air does not stir. Have you not noticed that the bushes do not move? That they stand straight up?"

"It is true, O wise Roka. There is nothing yet to tell us which way the wind will blow."

"May it not be," said the pious Tarinca, "that the blowing of the wind will be *Mahpiya's* command to us to go the way he sends it? Thunder, lightning and wind all come out of his mouth and they are the voices with which he speaks."

It seemed to them all that Tarinca had divined the intention of *Mahpiya,* and Roka spoke for the others as well as himself when he replied:

"It must be so, Tarinca. That is why *Mahpiya* withholds the real wind so long. When he sends it we will follow it. I know now that *Tateyanpa* will guide us right."

Conviction was supreme in the heart of every one of the ten, and in silence they awaited the call of *Tateyanpa,* while darkness and clouds, thick and heavy, overspread all the heavens.

CHAPTER XIV

TATEYANPA GUIDES

WILL saw *Wi*, the grand, the magnificent, the burning *Wi*, make his last efforts to escape the great gray, and, at last, black net that was thrown about him. Beams bright and then pale shot through the heavy veil, but became fewer and fewer and then there was none, and the heavy, rolling clouds of immeasurable depth covered all the heavens from the zenith to the horizon.

Still there was no wind, while the thunder never ceased to mutter on the whole circle, and Will felt an uncontrollable sense of awe that there should be so much darkness and sound without a single visible flash of lightning, or any movement of air beneath the mists and clouds. He believed as fully as the Dakota that the wind was going to direct them, and his hair lifted a little, as he waited in the intense silence for *Mahpiya* to speak.

All the warriors were taut both of mind and body, ready to go at the first call, and, as they sat close together, they could see one another, despite the deepening dark. They felt that for the present they could do nothing, they were helpless in the hands of the spirits of earth and air, but they waited in supreme confidence. It might be that the wind would blow back toward the point from which they had come, and, if so, they must return at least part of the way, until they had a new sign. But they hoped that *Tateyanpa* would speak with another voice.

It became pitchy black on the hill. Keen as were the eyes of the Dakota, and used as they were to the darkness, they could scarcely see one another now, but such darkness impressed them far less than the uncanny stillness. Will wondered at first if the *Ikcewicaxta* would take advantage of the impenetrable gloom to attack them, but second thought told him they would not. Almost wholly invisible to one another, they could not carry out any plan, and, perhaps while the Dakota were merely awed by the singular night, the *Ikcewicaxta* were terrified.

The passage of time was so slow that Will had no measure of calculation, but after a space that seemed interminable he gave a violent start. An electric thrill shot through his whole body, and yet the cause of it was faint. Something as light as the brush of a feather touched his left cheek which was turned toward the southwest.

"*Tateyanpa!*" he exclaimed.

"Aye," said Roka, in a deep voice, "it is the first breath of the wind. It comes from the southwest and our way lies toward the northeast. *Mahpiya,* speaking through one of his children, *Tateyanpa,* is about to show us the way."

The faint wind that was no more than a breath grew stronger, but it did not blow away the darkness. Instead the night lowered thicker and heavier than ever, but the hearts of the young warriors beat with a great exultation. The whisper of *Mahpiya* to Waditaka had come true. They waited eagerly for Roka to say the word. The leader delayed a quarter of an hour longer, and the wind was then coming with a mighty rush. Off in the forest they heard boughs crackling and snapping beneath its sweep. It would soon be blowing a hurricane, and Roka said in a voice that he was now compelled to raise:

"Come, O sons of the Dakota! *Mahpiya* shows us the way and if we are men we follow it."

They fell into their usual formation, Roka leading and Pehansan bringing up the rear, their packs on their backs, their bows and quivers over their shoulders. But they were in such close order that every man could touch the back of the one in front of him, and there was no danger of any straying from the line. Roka, in front, followed the wind as truly as the needle turns to the pole.

In a minute or two they crossed the opening and entered the forest, no sign coming from the *Ikcewicaxta*. The wind had become a mighty roaring and it was crashing its way through the trees, strewing wreckage as it passed. But Roka was confident they would be spared by *Tateiyumni* (Hurricane). *Mahpiya* would not bring them so far to let them be crushed by the last obstacle. So he led on in the utmost confidence through the impenetrable blackness, and his warriors, in a close rank, followed him.

The thunder, which had been rumbling all about the circle, now crashed directly overhead with such tremendous force that the warriors were often dazed by it a moment or two, though they were not afraid, their confidence in *Mahpiya* not wavering a particle. The lightning came at last, and it blazed with a fiery brilliancy that made Will shut his eyes instinctively.

But through roar and blaze alike Roka led on, stumbling sometimes over the timber that the hurricane scattered about, but never failing to keep his course toward the northeast, exactly as the wind blew. The miracle was still working. Although he heard the crash of falling timber on every side, and the air was full of flying boughs, nothing touched him. Nor did he hear any groan or other complaint from the warriors behind him, and he knew that they, too, were unharmed.

Will, like his leader, felt the working of the miracle. It was a marvel that none of them should be struck by the flying timber. *Mahpiya* had spread his shield about them, and it must be because their hearts were pure. The ten had merely come to find a new home for their village, and they had intended harm to no one.

On they went in the dark, climbing low hills, crossing ravines, pushing their way through bushes, leaping over fallen trees, but always keeping their line. Then, with a suddenness that was startling, the thunder ceased and the lightning flashed no more. The wind died as if *Mahpiya* had willed it to cease at once, and Roka and the whole line with him paused. Then, after a short silence, Will heard another rush, but not that of the wind.

"Magaju!" (The Rain) he exclaimed.

"Yes, it is *Magaju,"* said Roka. "Now we will be wet and cold, but we are delivered."

The rain poured upon them in a deluge all night long, but the warriors were happy. They knew that *Mahpiya,* with his children who were also his servants, the wind, the thunder, the lightning, and the rain, had scattered the *Ikcewicaxta* and had opened a way of safety to them. When dawn came and the rain stopped they were many miles into the northeast.

They had protected their weapons under their thick robes, but all the rest of their clothing was soaked, their bodies dripped with water and their packs were wet, but these were minor ills to such as they. Fearless now of the *Ikcewicaxta,* they coaxed a fire with infinite patience, watched it grow into a great, glowing circle of light and heat, and then stayed a long time beside it until they and their clothing were dried out thoroughly. Then everyone, in his own way and in silence, gave thanks to the good spirits who had saved them. When the tension was released they talked freely.

"I suppose," said Inmu, "that the *Ikcewicaxta* were scattered and perhaps so badly hurt by the hurricane that their only thought was to save themselves; they had neither power nor wish to follow us."

"I fancy," said Hoton, "that they may have caught a glimpse or two of us by the lightning's flash."

"Then, why did they not attack?"

"Because about the middle of our line they saw me, me, Hoton, the great warrior. They knew I was under the protection of *Mahpiya,* and they feared me as well as the wrath of the mighty spirit that watches over us. It was a good thing for you, my friends, that I was chosen a member of this band."

"We know it, Hoton," said the pious Tarinca, "because none can talk so fiercely to the enemy as you, though I will add that you bear yourself as bravely in battle as you talk."

"That is true," said Inmu. "We could not spare Hoton, who both talks and fights."

"And I could not spare any of you," said Roka in his deep voice. "You are gallant lads, all of you, and my heart is full of pride because of you. Never shall we forget the great journey that we have made together through mighty perils."

"A journey that is not yet finished," said Pehansan.

"But which we will finish," said Roka firmly. "Now I think we will shoot game and stay here all day. The *Ikcewicaxta* may pick up our trail and follow, most likely they will, but it will take them a long time to do so, and meanwhile we shall rest ourselves."

Game was not hard to find. Before dusk it was the good fortune of Wanmdi to shoot a deer, and, as they had been without food, they broiled the flesh and ate luxuriously. Then, warm and well fed, they felt equal to any task or danger. But the wise leader gave them a word or two of warning.

"Listen, my warriors," he said. "The good spirits have helped us. Without *Peta* and *Mini,* Waditaka could never have escaped from the great chasm, and without *Mahpiya* and his children, who are also his servants, the *Ikcewicaxta* would have slain us. But we must not rely always upon the good spirits. It may be that, having helped us so much, they will now wish to see what we can do when left to ourselves. So, I bid you, and I give myself the same command, to be more watchful, more enduring and more courageous than ever."

"We will do all you ask," said Inmu, who acted as spokesman, "and we see your wisdom in demanding it of us. We would be lower than the wild people if we asked the gods to do everything for us."

The eyes of Roka kindled as he looked over his young heroes, and he knew that he need say no more. Daring the danger of *Ikcewicaxta* pursuit, he allowed them to remain the whole night by the fire, although a most vigilant watch was kept, and the following morning they proceeded through a wilderness that was warm and dry once more.

Joy reigned in the ranks of the ten. They had triumphed over so much now that they believed they could triumph over whatever was left. They were quite sure that the range of mountains just ahead was the last separating them from the great plains of the far north, where the buffalo grew to the greatest size, and Indian hunters were few. Will understood now, in a few words from Roka, that the desire of Xingudan that they should find these vast, half-mythical regions was due to the old chief's refusal to put him to death in accordance with the command brought by Heraka from Mahpeyalute, the famous Sioux chief, known to the white people as Red Cloud. The hand of Mahpeyalute was heavy, and it might be better for the little village to hide itself in the remote north for a while.

Later on the wrath of Mahpeyalute would pass and the wily Xingudan could return. It might be, too, that Xingudan was not wholly averse to the flight of his own village. He was old, he had seen much, he knew much and his mind projected far. He understood the numbers and might of the white race, and great and valiant as was the Sioux nation, it must lose in the long and bitter war that had begun already. But Xingudan, in the exile that was, in a way, forced upon him, would save his own people.

Will, as he understood, felt more than ever attached to the ten and to the village. Xingudan's wary thought of saving his band from the great war had no place in his own mind. He only saw that this little Dakota group had made a sacrifice to save him from death, and he was full of gratitude. If he could, he would repay in full.

The second day after their escape they were once more high among the hills, where, as usual, everything was on a gigantic scale, vast forests, composed of trees almost incredible in height and girth, clear, rushing streams, and an abundance of game, the moose and bear tremendous in proportions. They were not attacked, however, by any of the bears, and Will was glad to notice the absence of huge timber wolves, which he really dreaded more than any of the other animals.

Pehansan shot a mountain sheep on one of the lower

slopes, and they varied their diet with mutton, which the Dakota knew how to cook in such a manner that it became very juicy. Ripe berries were plentiful, and they ate them in great quantities, making them take the place of bread.

The slight wounds sustained in battle were now healed, and the ten, uplifted by victory, felt more fit than ever for any trial. Yet Roka and Pehansan never relaxed the watch for an instant, and their caution served them well, because on the third night the vanguard of the *Ikcewicaxta,* more persistent than the Dakota had believed, overtook them, and, thinking the Dakota neglectful, attacked. Yet it was they who walked into a trap. The great bows of the Dakota sang and sang again, and their whistling shafts rarely missed. In a quarter of an hour half of the wild people were slain. The rest fled to the main body with word that the game they were hunting was far too dangerous to the hunters, and it would be better to hunt it no more.

Roka divined that they would not be pursued any farther by the wild people, and he and his men, feeling little wrath against the *Ikcewicaxta,* but pitying them for their ignorance, gave decent burial to the fallen. The Dakota themselves had escaped with a few scratches.

"I think we may now go on in peace," said the wise leader; and, for days, they ascended the heights through a wild and magnificent region. When they reached the crest of the range they saw into a vast, dim region beyond, broken nowhere by any line of mountains, nor even hills.

"The plains!" all exclaimed together.

But there was still a long journey down the slopes and the foothills, although they took it at ease. The second morning after they left the crest Will went out to seek game. His course led him through rough country about a mile from the camp, where he found deer sign, evidently not more than an hour old.

He followed the trail swiftly, thinking he would soon overtake his game, which was evidently moving at leisure, browsing here and there.

His attention was wholly on the pursuit, but he noticed presently that the wind, which was scarcely stirring at all when he started, was now blowing swiftly. It seemed an odd circumstance to him, and he stopped and listened. At first he heard only the rush of air, and the rustling of the foliage before it, but gradually something detached itself from the general sound and then, as he believed, he heard the voice of *Tateyanpa:*

"Beware! Beware! Beware!"

It was a note of warning, clear and imperative. He looked all about him, seeing nothing alive but himself, but the voice of the wind never ceased to come, singing: "Beware! Beware! Beware!"

Will would not turn back. Waditaka, the young Dakota, who had not flinched in the presence of immeasurable dangers, could not do such a thing, but when he resumed the trail he watched not alone for the deer, he had a wary eye for every thicket on either side of him. Before he had gone far he was sure he was being stalked, not through anything he saw or heard, but by his consciousness of an imminent presence, something powerful, menacing and deadly. The knowledge seemed to come to him on a wave of air, and his hair lifted a little.

But he would not yet go back. He refused to pause in the presence of an unknown danger, though *Tateyanpa* continually sang, "Beware! Beware! Beware!" and he hurried himself a little on the trail. It led across a gully between two thickets, and, as he stepped down into it, he threw himself with a sudden convulsive impulse upon its very bottom. He had been conscious of a stir in the thicket on his right, and, from the corner of his eye, he had caught a glimpse of a dark form. But he always believed it was more the action of a good spirit than any power of his own mind and body that saved him from the spring of the mighty king wolf.

The huge body passed over him and struck beyond on the narrow floor of the ravine, where the raging brute could not turn instantly. It was well for Will now that he had been trained so thoroughly in agility and promptness. Springing to his feet and no longer depending on his bow, he snatched from his belt the loaded revolver that always hung there, firing bullet after bullet into the body of the wolf.

At the fourth bullet the wolf, although terribly stricken, managed to turn about, and dragged himself forward for a charge. He was in a terrible plight, blood pouring from him, and mad with rage and pain.

Will fired his fifth bullet into the open mouth, directly into the red throat, and then sent the sixth and last crashing into his brain. *Xunktokeca* quivered, fell over on his side and was dead. Will sprang upon the bank and sank down there, too weak and nerveless to move for a little while.

When his strength was restored, he went back to camp, and brought the others to look upon the greatest wolf that any of them had ever seen, or ever would see.

"It was *Tateyanpa* that saved you," said Roka. "If he had not sent the warning *Xunktokeca* would have picked your bones, and he sent it, because your heart is clean and you wish harm to no one, Waditaka. He has followed us, and you in particular, across all the mountains. Only a king wolf could have been capable of so much ferocity and tenacity. But we are freed from him forever."

They descended the last slopes of the mountains, then the foothills, and came upon green plains dappled with flowers stretching away to infinity. Toward the north was a myriad of slowly moving forms, and they cried joyfully together:

"The buffalo! The buffalo!"

Then Roka added, gravely:

"This is the country for us. Here we can hunt forever, safe from the march of the white man."

They camped a few days on the flank of the herd, killing only what they needed for food. But the period was one of wonderful elation. Warriors of the Dakota—and they were the greatest warriors of all—

had never before made such a tremendous journey, one that had been crowned with complete success. The glory of it would be sung by the nation as long as the nation lasted, and the names of all the ten would be honored forever. But in their pride they did not forget the sources of their strength and fortune.

They reverently gave thanks in the Dakota fashion to all the good spirits that had watched over them, and without whose aid they would have fallen long ago by the way. They spoke their gratitude in fervent words to sky, thunder, lightning, wind, fire, water and all the powerful elements that had been on their side.

Then they rejoiced every hour over the limitless plains. For all they knew, the glorious green expanse stretched all the way to the Arctic Ocean, and, where the buffalo ended, the caribou would carry on the tale in countless millions. It was truly a splendid sight for primordial men, and they were content for long periods merely to watch the game drifting in vast quantities over the waving earth in the fresh colors of spring. Here could be no exhaustion.

"The buffalo, like all other animals, is larger here than anywhere else," said Roka.

"But, large as he is, he cannot escape us when we want him," said Hoton. "We have defeated the great bear and the great panther, we have fought off the monstrous birds, and Waditaka with his own hand slew the largest and fiercest wolf that ever lived. There is nothing we cannot overcome, because we have already proved it by overcoming everything."

Then Hoton chanted:

"We are the victorious ten,
  Chosen men of the Dakota.
  The mighty bear we have slain,
  The yellow panther flees from us.

"High mountain and gorge we fear not,
  The cunning wolf hangs on our trail,
  Through storm and dark, fearless we go,
  The wild people lie in the bush.

"Strong are the hearts of Roka's ten.
  The wild men fall before our bows,
  Waditaka killed the king wolf,
  The vast, green plains lie before us."

They felt that Hoton truly expressed their triumph and they joined in his chant with zeal and power. Then they prepared for their return. Roka believed that by curving to the south they could cross the mountains where they were low, and then turn northward to the village of Xingudan. His theory proved to be correct, and, in the early autumn, the ten stood on a hill, overlooking their own village. They saw the smoke curling from the tepees, and they knew that all there was as it should be. Roka, his heart swelling with just pride, turned to his men and called in a clear voice:

"Pehansan!"

"Den!" replied the tall warrior, which in the Dakota language means "Here"!

"Inmu!"

"Den!"

"Waditaka!"

"Den!"

"Hoton!"

"Den!"

"Capa!"

"Den!"

"Tarinca!"

"Den!"

"Tatokadan!"

"Den!"

"Hinyankaga!"

"Den!"

"Wanmdi!"

"Den!"

"All unharmed, and everyone stronger and better than he was when he went away!" said Roka exultantly. "Now we will report to Xingudan."

As they marched down the slope the old chief, his face breaking into a smile of glad welcome through the mask of years, came forward to meet them.